A Perfect Woman

A Perfect Woman

CAROLYN SLAUGHTER

Ticknor & Fields NEW YORK 1985

First American edition 1985

Copyright © 1984 by Carolyn Slaughter

Library of Congress Cataloging in Publication Data

Slaughter, Carolyn.
 A perfect woman.

 I. Title.
PR6069.L37P4 1985   823'.914   84-8838
ISBN 0-89919-342-0

Printed in the United States of America

V   10 9 8 7 6 5 4 3 2 1

For Shelagh Macdonald

Part One

The loveliest thing that has blossomed
on the earth is the binding of man and woman
in one body, one fellowship. – OLIVE SCHREINER

One

A woman stood by her window looking out at the garden with the gaze of someone surveying the sea or a long sweep of hills and fields. Then she smiled – but the smile didn't relax her features, they seemed to clench and her body looked awkward and troubled. It had come back to her; the dream of the night before: a woman's hair on fire – the dark curls, curiously like her own, but longer and more luxurious – leaping into red and violet flames. The sizzling sound and the stench of scorched hair was quite real: it was there on the pillow when she woke. In her dream she had been laughing like a lunatic, quite beside herself.

Her composure returned, but she held to the dream a little longer. Her left hand, with its gold band smoothed and worn by the years, played restlessly with the silky blue drapes of the curtains. The other hand rubbed at the back of her neck, ruffling her hair, making her head rock in a vaguely agitated way.

Now she looked out at the garden itself. It was nearly seven in the evening but the sun stayed up later these days. And there was the apple tree, Humphrey's tree; it was so much a part of their family, had so much a character of its own, that she almost felt she could call it over to her like an animal or a child and touch it a moment. She looked at it with critical but affectionate scrutiny, the way she surveyed her own offspring. She decided it was too perfect. Humphrey stage-managed it, pruning it twice a year to yield a crop of perfect-sized apples. The shape of the tree was wonderful, round and motherly, no long leggy branches, just straight, stout limbs and sparkling leaves. Beyond it, the garden bloomed with lines of early-summer vegetables and banks of flowers.

She turned back to her bedroom. The house reflected her nature, as the garden reflected Humphrey's. Hers was a light touch: off-whites, soft greys and dusky pinks; large porcelain lamps either side of an old brass bed swaddled in an even older patchwork quilt with a faded rose and carnation design stitched on to yellowing cotton.

Indian rugs, supple and soft as cloth, warmed up the long expanse of cream carpet. Flowers in round bowls scented the room: wall-flowers, freesia and the first of Humphrey's yellow roses tossing their petals over the pale pink of the Victorian marble fireplace.

She turned back the quilt neatly and folded the stiff linen sheet in place until its edge was as sharp as an envelope's. She did it as precisely as the maids had once turned down the beds in the Anglo-Irish mansion of her childhood. When it was just so she climbed the stairs, and, in each of her daughters' rooms, performed the same evening ritual. She'd done it since they were babies; to stop doing it was as unthinkable as putting an unironed sheet on a bed. The pleasure she took from it was all her own, but it was tinged now with the knowledge that her daughters would soon be gone; these beds be empty.

A door downstairs clicked, opened then slammed noisily; two bright voices jangled together in the hallway below. She picked up a stray black stocking, curling it carefully on the bed. And ran down the stairs to meet them.

One of her daughters was flung across the kitchen table, her chin cupped in her hand, her eyes closed. The other, a dark, heavy girl, ran up and hugged her mother, who jerked her head at the figure on the table.

'Hullo Cass, what's the matter with her?'

'Knackered, as usual.'

Fran had gone to sleep; it was her most ready facility, she could sleep the instant her eyes closed. Beth looked fondly at her daughter's round, creamy cheek, the fleecy down above her top lip, the black straight brows and the bush of bleached hair. She was a beauty, but Beth despaired of her: she wanted nothing but this frail, fleeting perfection; her vanity consumed what little energy she possessed.

'Cup of tea, Ma?' Beth looked from one daughter to the other, and there it was again – that anxious, needing look that Cass so often turned on her. Cass's thick black hair – tortured into peaks on her crown and shaved down either side of her head as though she were recovering from brain surgery – seemed oddly out of place with the small wistful face.

'Yes, I'd love one.' Beth sat at the table and rested her arms on it. Cass hovered near her and felt happy, her anxiety had left her, as if her mother's presence had in some way absorbed it.

'Um, Ma?' Cass hesitated. 'Will it be all right if Em and Julia spend the night? We're going down the Padded Cell.'

'Hm,' Beth said vaguely and was rewarded by a smile of appreciation. Fran stirred herself and stood up. She was wearing one of her collection of fifties evening dresses bought at a second-hand shop. This was a blue chiffon thing with a low neck and gathered bustline nipped into a tight waist.

'I'm going to have a bath,' she mumbled, 'and before you ask, I did my prep at school. Tell me when it's dinnertime, I'm starved.' Unlike Cass, she took her mother utterly for granted and never had a moment's guilt about her. She trailed her plastic carrier bags behind her as once she'd trailed a gnawed blue blanket.

Beth sat on in the empty kitchen, listened to the music explode in the upstairs bedrooms and watched the light become mottled outside as the clouds darkened. Her dream came back to her, with an odd satisfaction now. Her hand rose and stroked her curly dark hair; it had the feel of something thick and dense like a brocade. She got up and began to cook; something she always did with pleasure.

Her eldest daughter, Abigail, stood at the stove stirring the gravy and talking very fast. Beth found it curious to listen to her at times: she was nearly eighteen and yet her comments and opinions had a well-fingered feel to them, as if she had gathered them in college corridors or a current affairs lesson. She feels herself unreal, her mother thought, and her poses are uncomfortable even to herself.

Em, a friend of Cass's, came in and Beth asked her to make the apple sauce. 'I love this kitchen,' she said, taking the pan to the stove, 'it's so homey, I'm always happy here.' Her pert face with its pink and blonde hair was very pretty. She looked around her at the tall dresser with its thick white plates overlapping one another; the walls covered in photographs and paintings done by small hands, long ago, framed and placed close together with the dates beneath the pictures. A collection of old blue crockery perched on shiny shelves and a row of copper saucepans gleamed against the white walls. There was a long pine table set out for dinner with a bowl of anemones, picked and arranged by Abi, blazing in the centre. The dog, a rather motheaten-looking labrador, lolled in her basket with her eye cocked to the gravy pan.

Em was so at home and familiar with this house and this family that she would quite naturally just put another plate for herself by the stove to warm. Julia, on the other hand, when she entered, was abashed by the warmth and intimacy; unused to welcomes in her own home, she held back, she hesitated, Beth had to draw her in each time. She was round and shy, painfully uncertain of herself; she pulled up her shoulders in the blue cardigan, which, like all her clothes, was worn only to pacify her mother, and whispered breathlessly to Beth, 'Um, is it? Are you sure? I mean, am I in the way? I mean ... about me staying and everything, is it, you know, OK?'

'Don't be daft, Julia,' Beth said, giving her a quick hug. 'I keep telling you, you're always welcome here, you and Em, you're like my own daughters, you ought to know that by now!' She smiled. 'We'd be lonely without you, you know.' Julia's shoulders came down, she relaxed a little and managed a smile.

'Now, sit down,' Beth said firmly. 'No, don't, ring the gong for Cass and let's eat.'

'Oh, how wonderful,' Julia said. 'Chicken and mashed potato.' But she knew that she wouldn't be able to eat more than a spoonful because she felt herself so fat and so revolting that she wasn't entitled to food. As the gong sounded, booming down the corridor and up the long sweep of stairs, Cass, unhappy with her reflection in the glass – that couldn't be her, surely? Where had all that ugliness come from, why did her make-up mock her so? – pushed past it and ran down the stairs to her mother.

At ten o'clock Beth sat in her study, working at her desk. Five girls, all dressed to go out, smelling of strong scent and hairspray, came in shyly, crowding by the door, so that Beth was struck again by their largeness, by the amount of physical space they took up. How hesitant they were, she thought, how uncertain; and yet, how vehement – their faces larded with make-up, thick and matt-white; small mouths like open wounds, aggressively red and shiny, their eyes underscored with the same heavy determination to look tough, to know it all. And Cass, of course, looking most fearsome: purple and grey marks on her cheeks and eyelids, eradicating the soft planes of her features.

Beth had a quick recollection of herself in her first evening dress: white crêpe de chine, a necklace with a single diamond, her first dab of Chanel No. 5, and only the slightest suggestion of lipstick. And now these young women stood there, waiting for her approval, needing her to say, 'Oh, but you're beautiful, how lovely you all look tonight' – her benediction that would bless the night and ensure its happy outcome.

She smiled, she leaned back in her chair and let her hands fall into her lap.

'One at a time,' she said. They nudged one another into line and paraded for her.

'Oh, Julia, that *is* a pretty dress, the blue's so good with your eyes.' Instantly, Julia no longer hated it, and the ever-present echo of her mother's scornful snort ('You're not going out like *that*? My God, girl, don't you know what a sight you look?') fell away from her as she pulled the neckline a little to the right as Beth had suggested. Abi walked with her arms held back, her hair in tiny plaits all around her classical oval face, her clothes boyish and unobtrusive. The passage light cut cruelly through the bunched white gauze that Cass tried to use as camouflage. Oh, if only she didn't wear white, Beth groaned to herself, and, if she must, if only it were *clean*. But she said, 'You're looking very nice tonight, that new lipstick (more black than purple) suits you.' She hesitated. 'But that studded belt?'

Then Cass, as if she'd been stepped on, flailed out and said, sharply, 'I like it.'

Just as quickly, Beth said, 'No, I just meant it looks a bit tight, that's all. Can you breathe?' She laughed lightly; Cass's tears receded, the belt was loosened – a little.

'Yes, now that's perfect.'

And so on she went, to each in turn, stroking, easing their self-conscious fierceness, their terror of looking not-right, until, by the time they were leaving, they all felt reassured and more at peace with the wilfulness of their façades. Cass, before closing the door, said, 'Will you be all right, Ma?' seeing, not for the first time, something lonely in her mother.

'Oh yes, go on now, have a good time.'

Out they went into the soft night. Beth watched them go, her cheek pressed against the window pane. Fran, no longer remotely sleepy, was spinning in her full black skirt, whirling and showing her legs. Abi walked slowly with Em, her head down – never noticing, as Fran never failed to, how the moonlight made each tree in the street starkly beautiful, how it gilded and tempered their tough little faces as they turned the corner, laughing, and were gone.

Beth walked from room to empty room, stepping over mounds of clothes, turning off the lights and the stereo, which blared away, eerily now. She remembered how, when they were babies, she would stand outside their doors at this time of night, listening – and unsatisfied, would have to creep up to each cot to make sure they still breathed. Now, she removed the dirty glasses and a vase of dead flowers, but left their mess – to tidy and take over seemed an intrusion and a liberty.

Walking down to her study again, she remembered how Abi had asked where her father was. She'd replied that he was taking out a prospective client. Then Cass had turned her face away and Fran had looked suspicious, but just for an instant before her sister pulled her arm.

Beth was tired, suddenly. She went to her bedroom and began to undress. She took off her blue dress slowly, then slipped a cotton nightdress over her head. She sat on the edge of the bed, her tapered feet quite still on the carpet. With painful recognition, she felt again as she had as a young woman, the night before she had married. She had sat just so, waiting, on the edge of some enormous experience, knowing it would be the last night of her life when she would be, in that sense, alone. Would her daughters ever know that magnitude of marriage? That trading-in of a solitary life for one which was subject to the demands and needs of one man? Of a child? Of a lifelong ritual of always being second?

She climbed into bed, on his side, and breathed in his unique, dry scent. But at dawn, when she woke, with the splinter of a dream still in her, it seemed to her that the house, or she herself, had cried out in pain. She walked to the window and stood there, folding her arms against her breasts, her face raddled with misery, and banged her head against the window pane again and again.

Two

Humphrey sat at his desk in an elegantly proportioned, sunny room at his offices in Mayfair. A marketing document lay in front of him on the oak desk with its slab of leather embossed in gold. He was reading the document, vaguely, but his mind was more preoccupied by his meeting last night. When he'd managed to settle to the report he was annoyed to see his partner, George Warlock, walk in. George was a hoverer, he never sat down, just drifted back and forth making the place look untidy.

'I just wanted to ask you' – his awkward, poker-faced manner sounded rather worse when he tried to be casual – 'how last night went?'

Finally decided to ask about it, have you? Humphrey thought with amusement. He said shortly, 'Oh, very well, good meeting.'

George, walking over to the window, thought angrily, And that's all he'll condescend to tell me, I suppose.

'Very good if we could could get that deal,' George added, 'quite a coup.'

Somehow, it always irritated Humphrey to hear George use the word 'we' in that way: it implied that they shared something – namely, Humphrey's business.

'Hmm,' he agreed, turning a page.

Then he looked up and studied George's dark-suited back critically. And to think, he thought, that it took a head-hunter six months to find that man and cost me £500 for a psychologist's report. Just look at him – pussy-footing around instead of asking me outright; he's spent the whole morning trying to get round to it and now he can barely open his mouth. Humphrey was buggered if he'd come out with the information himself. He was the one who had to go out in front after all, find the new business, track it down, wine and dine it, make the pitches to those foreign chaps and haughty hotel managers about the saving graces of his gourmet ranges of frozen foods.

When Humphrey had started out, damn all was frozen, and certainly nothing sophisticated; now he could freeze just about anything – cut out all that fiddle-faddle that restaurants still clung to: balloon-whisking sauces, turning out gateaux and profiteroles every second day, plucking and chopping up pheasant and hare, having little boys slicing vegetables day and night – all a thing of the past. Now, this is how to run a restaurant, he'd tell them: get rid of half the galley-slaves, clear the decks of all that expensive equipment from Soho, save yourself hours of preparation and toil, get rid of the pig in the back wolfing down the waste and let's see how we can get this place into the twentieth century. And they listened all right, all over the country they'd listened, in all the grand hotels and restaurants. Where you'd be expecting to have your grouse in red wine fresh from the moors it would arrive on your plate fresh from the freezer and you wouldn't know the difference – and certainly wouldn't expect haute cuisine to pull a fast one like that in a five-star joint. But they did. Humphrey got them to do it. And they liked it, more and more of them.

Now one of the best hotels in London was ready to sign on the dotted line: the manager and chef had really got carried away with the cream soup range and the six classical sole dishes and the salmon in champagne. Humphrey had even succeeded in convincing them that the freezing process improved the flavour – jargon, bullshit, it always worked. Well, the chef wasn't quite ready to go with the meat courses – thought that was a bit of a cheat. Typical Frenchie, with an adjustable morality – it was all right to hoodwink the people with frozen fish, but not frozen meat. Not that Humphrey would have any truck with the idea of deceiving anyone, that made it sound inferior – he always went in on the improvement angle: how carefully the product had been selected, graded, prepared and frozen. Anyway, he'd win them round all right, his products couldn't be excelled – and any quaint little culinary affectations that hotels employed could be specially concocted in ice for a special price. Just a matter of time.

'So it really is a possibility?' George mumbled, turning from the window, where he'd been messing around with the leaves of a weeping fig. He contemplated the long walk from the window to the door, then decided he wasn't going to make it until he'd got what he came for: just a measly bit of involvement on the new-business side.

There is something about George, Humphrey thought, that makes you not want to tell him a thing. But he decided to try: 'Yes, as a matter of fact it's all settled, George. I'll get Miranda to give you a copy of the details as soon as they're typed up.'

George flushed a most unbecoming shade of puce: it was being made clear to him, once again, that Humphrey wasn't about to treat him as a partner, to share his business – all he wanted was someone to do the things that he was no good at: the things that Humphrey considered boring, which were in fact the things that required qualifications and not just plain bullshit. Humphrey decided to throw George a sop, though he doubted it would gruntle him.

'Your report was liked, George,' he smiled, 'very much. Very detailed and thorough, David said.'

Oh, *David*! George, having been reduced to utter childishness by Humphrey, began to fume inwardly: well, Humphrey could worm his way around anyone in five minutes, get them eating out of his hand. He'd checked out that David character himself, not exactly a pushover, in fact a very sharp operator.

'I would prefer,' George announced formally, 'always to be present to deliver my reports myself in future.'

Deliver was the right word all right, Humphrey thought, like a bloody sermon, boring the pants off everyone. What was that Ph.D. George had – what was it in? Wanking or an allied category. Humphrey hated academics of all kinds: wafflers and bunglers the lot of them.

George had a mental picture of Humphrey flicking his perfect report – he'd worked on it for two weeks – across the table like a bit of ash, with a dismissive 'Facts and figures, some of our success stories, profiles and data – something my research and marketing department knocked out to show you we know our stuff ...' God, it made him want to kill.

Humphrey smiled benignly. 'Well, of course, George, of course, it's just that you were in Oxford yesterday so you couldn't come along.'

And who didn't tell me about the meeting until it was too late to change mine? George thought, feeling a strong inclination to smash those sparkling white teeth of Humphrey's down his throat. He was getting so flustered that he had to take deep breaths and tell himself to steady on; it was precisely in such ways that Humphrey undermined him.

Humphrey leaned back in a chair he'd had made specially to accommodate him in twenty different positions. It was beautifully finished in calf leather. He tipped it further back in his relaxed way and gave George the benefit of his wide, generous smile. The large windows behind him let in the sun in thick slices between the dense foliage of his plants. Outside, on the balcony, he'd spent the morning pottering around with his camellias and hydrangeas – the camellias were magnificent right now. He did all his serious thinking out there with his plants. On the balcony above, outside the suite, he was growing prize tomatoes – it was a shame to waste all that sunshine when something could grow in it. The tomatoes were coming along a treat, the smell of the leaves and flowers was one of the best on earth.

'For God's sake, George, sit down if you're staying!' All this wandering around like a tit in a trance, why couldn't the man relax or pull himself together? George sat. He had something to say; they both knew it and it was the reason that things were particularly taut between them this morning.

'I've been wanting to have a talk with you, Humphrey.'

'So I gathered.'

'Did you? How?' George's deep eyes, behind his black-framed glasses, looked quite alarmed.

'Just pick these things up, George,' Humphrey said coolly. Now for Christ's sake get on with it: he had some things to do out on the balcony before lunch.

'It's about my position here, Humphrey.' George took a firm line with his voice and tried to get comfortable in the deep recesses of the maroon Chesterfield that was trying to engulf him. He hated Chesterfields. They were designed for tall, big men, and that's precisely why Humphrey insisted that George sit in his office. He was unnerved to see that Humphrey was leaving his throne and coming to sit on the identical Chesterfield that faced his. Now only the safety of a Persian rug and a mahogany table separated them. Distance: that's what George liked. He was put off by the English-handsome face in front of him – a sort of Sherlock Holmes face, craggy but firm featured, an appealing and assured face. Humphrey crossed his legs and managed to look perfectly at ease on the couch. George was a small man marooned on an expanse of rippling leather. Being small hadn't made him aggressive; as a kid it had made other people aggressive towards him – big people, like Humphrey.

Humphrey was trying to be friendly, trying to get on to a more intimate footing with George. He knew he could be intimidating; he'd learned a lot about himself lately.

'You not happy, George?' Humphrey leaned forward with concern.

It was just like Humphrey, these days, to bring out stupid, emotional words like happy.

'Happiness is nothing to do with it,' he snapped. 'I've been here nearly two years, Humphrey,' he added reproachfully.

'So you have, George,' Humphrey agreed.

'We've got a lot of new business while I've been here. Now, I know that you're the hustler – and extremely good at it, too – but you need all the back-up: the marketing expertise, my research background at Ross has been invaluable with the new range. And there was also that introduction I gave you to Trust House Forte. Fine, I know it came to nothing, but that doesn't mean it won't pay off later. We were just too up-market for them.' He braced himself, encouraged by Humphrey's silence. 'Now, when I came, I was given a directorship, with John. And you, er, promised me certain things as well, Humphrey.'

The only thing that was bothering Humphrey at this stage was whether the bastard had been stirring things up with John, his research man, an easy-going fellow, not a trouble-maker, but the less senior of the two. The last thing he needed was two dissidents; it was difficult enough to keep George in his place.

But George had made an announcement. 'I have no shares in this company, Humphrey.' And there it was – out – it had been sticking in his guts for months.

'Ah, shares.' A little stab of displeasure cut across Humphrey's face. He leaned forward, when George would have preferred him to lean back and away. He grasped his large hands in front of his knees and said, 'As you know, I built this company up from nothing. With Beth. We worked ourselves to death for fifteen years making it what it is now. It wasn't easy, George.'

God, George groaned silently, he's going to tell me again that he was an orphan, that he had to eat coal, that water leaked on to his bed at night – that whole history of deprivation and poverty: spare me, spare me. Humphrey did, he could read people very keenly.

'The point is, Beth has fifty per cent and so do I. So you can see that the question requires considerable thought.' Humphrey leaned back, as if that was the end of that.

'Humphrey' – George was determined to be patient – 'if I'm really to be a partner,' he planted his short legs more resolutely on the rug, 'as was promised – share the risks of the next venture, really break into the big time, as you put it, I have to have some solid security, I have to have some reason for locking myself into this company for the next five years or so of my life. Surely you can see that, Humphrey?'

'So what do you want, George?' Humphrey asked carelessly, but George knew he was irritated by the way his eyebrows twitched. God! Those eyebrows! Why didn't he do something about them? They bristled like an old loo brush, they seemed to be trying to escape his face by flying upwards on great tangled wings.

'I want twenty per cent, Humphrey,' George said calmly, much to his own amazement, forgetting all the months of agonizing trying to reach that figure.

'Twenty per cent!' Humphrey roared. 'Don't be a bloody fool, George, have you completely lost your marbles? For what? For two measly years' work with a fat salary and a fat expense account, a big car and every perk known and unknown to the taxman. And you've not exactly worked yourself to the bone either!'

George had that certain feeling that he was done for. Humphrey in a rage was impossible, well, he was always impossible, but once angry, you'd get nothing out of him. Any minute now and he'd start goose-stepping. And yes, there he was, up off the Chesterfield, charging across the room like a mad bull.

Humphrey was trying to calm down, he marched to his plants and solicited their help. His violent reactions alarmed him greatly, reminding him of his youth, the street fights after his mother and he had left their village in Lancashire for the city. Reminding him of how he had started: those years when he'd pulled every dirty trick a salesman could to get some scrappy deal.

'Sorry, George.' His voice was reorganizing itself with some difficulty. He turned. 'OK. So you want shares. Let's consider it. If you want shares I think you should have shares. If you work for them.' He looked menacing. 'I'm not throwing them away, George. You've been here a couple of years, so you'd like a few shares. OK. We'll talk about it, get something down on paper. But twenty per cent is absolutely out of the question, and you know it.' He wanted to laugh out loud, but he added instead, 'And perhaps you should check out what it'll cost you, George – shares in this company aren't worth peanuts.'

'Yes, I do know that, Humphrey,' George said tightly, 'but I can't think of investing even the next two years of my life in this company without some real promise of shares. You must see that, Humphrey. I'm forty-three years old,' he added with a forlorn bleat, comparing himself yet again with Humphrey – with Humphrey's extraordinary success, his perfect marriage, his easy, triumphant life.

You look it, Humphrey thought. Then said after a silence, 'Now, look here, George, you need a bonus, a little perk now that the deal's clinched. Why not go out and buy yourself a new suit? Stick it on expenses. I'll settle it with Colin.'

George was on the move again, murder in his heart. The con-descension! The utter bloody nerve of the man! And just Hum-phrey's insane way of dealing with things. Gestures like that could make the entire company dishonest, certainly the accountant. All accountants were basically dishonest in George's view. And with the eccentric way Humphrey had of rewarding people it was a wonder the place wasn't bankrupt. It wasn't generosity, it was megalo-mania. Do things Humphrey's way and you'd soon have all the salesmen charging up their underpants and diddling their work-sheets even more than they normally did. Send them to the Bahamas for a holiday, without even the excuse of a sales promotion, as he did, and it was a bloody miracle he was still afloat. Everything Humphrey did was just plain incredible. And now – a suit, buy yourself a suit, he says.

George said primly, 'Well, I won't take up any more of your time. I had just hoped to get something settled about my future.' Though he was livid, he could just as easily have burst into tears.

'Of course, George, of course.' Humphrey's laser smile did its damage before the healing process began. 'Now, look here, we'll discuss this properly tomorrow. It'll be done. Don't worry about it. We'll let you know you're appreciated, George, we'll get something down on paper with Harry very soon. Now look, let's have a drink to celebrate.' He walked over to the drinks cabinet and opened it. 'Things are good, George, and they're going to be even better. You'll see. We're on an upswing here and everyone will benefit from it.' He smiled again. 'Things are going to be wonderful, George.'

To his complete disgust, George found that he began to feel

relaxed and reassured. He had that feeling of being in good hands, that all was really going to be fine – even though he'd achieved precisely nothing. It was Humphrey, bloody Humphrey, he had such a way with people, he was such a performer. It was like at those meetings when Humphrey was out to impress; you couldn't but watch him, spellbound by his charm, by what he could get away with. He had such brilliance, such perfect timing. He leaned forward and grabbed the client by the arm, he would bully them with his enthusiasm, chuck out all their objections, lie his way through any dodgy areas. They would end up feeling he could do anything – would end all their problems of distribution and stock, would make their operations more efficient and – most of all – give them quality: his favourite word. He would get the salesmen knocking on the doors of the Palace if he asked them to. Yes, Humphrey was eccentric and wild and his methods were peculiar all right, but you couldn't help admiring and respecting him. He was impossible to resist if he was charming you. He was a first-rate manipulator, the best.

Now he was lifting his glass in George's direction and saying warmly, 'To you, George.' And then adding, 'And do get that new suit, old man . . .' Smile, smile, and looking at George's faithful pin-stripe in such a way that George wanted to burn it immediately.

'To us, George,' he added gently, raising his glass.

Three

Beth heard Humphrey's slam of the door downstairs; she could generally tell his humour by the pitch and pressure of the slam; this evening both she and the door detected some displeasure. She ran down the stairs to meet him, catching the warmth of his smile. He noticed that she was wearing lipstick, which she hardly ever used to do. It saddened him a little, its implications, like the way she'd cut a fringe after all those years of pulling her thick hair away from her face. She was restless with her appearance now. That olive skin of hers was so lovely, so lush, it was terrible to hide even an inch of it. He wanted to say, 'Don't change, Beth, that's the last thing I could bear from you.' But he didn't, he swung her around and against him instead and kissed her firmly on the mouth.

'I've missed you,' he said.

'I missed you last night,' she said quietly. But never a word of reproach, not Beth.

He walked with her into the hall, dipping an arm through the crook of hers. He sniffed, 'Garlic?'

'Of course.'

'I didn't have lunch, had some nonsense instead with George. He was pulling his martyred bit. But there's something about him that always makes me think he's an evil bastard, secretly plotting against me.'

'You can't get paranoid about George,' she said scornfully. 'You've battered him into the ground and you know it.' She took his briefcase, which was actually a music-case, from him and put it in the corner.

'The little wimp wants shares now, if you don't mind.'

She looked at him with a touch of disbelief. 'But of course he does. You would too, if you were him.' It was odd, she thought mildly, how completely Humphrey's insight left him when confronted by self-interest.

'Well, he can earn them, like I did, like you did.'

'You don't share easily,' she said, giving him a look, but the ringing of the phone nipped the moment in the bud. Humphrey strode over to the table with the leaded stained-glass window above it. Before he picked up the receiver he put on his glasses: he couldn't answer the phone without wearing his glasses any more than he could listen to music without them; no amount of teasing could break the habit. All his senses had to be activated, fully functioning, for him to participate in anything acoustic.

Of course the call was for one of his daughters.

'It's for one of you,' he bellowed up the stairs.

'Which one?' came three voices in dreadful suspense.

'Wasn't listening,' he said vaguely.

'*Must* you be so useless?' Abi snarled, yanking the phone out of his hand.

He went to his bedroom and changed into an old pair of jeans, put his suit away and wandered downstairs. It was the best part of the day. They all felt it, coming home to this house, it seemed to just ease away any misery or weariness. He noticed his roses in her jugs in the corridors, the way the furniture gleamed and the pale walls and drapes radiated her warmth and serenity. He wandered happily through his home, and walked through the drawing-room into a large adjoining conservatory that led into the garden. Surrounded by a jungle of exotic plants and flowers was a white grand piano. He sat down and played a fragment of 'Who could ask for anything more'. He played extremely well. But not well enough, he'd decided years ago, to be brilliant. It would have been easier, he often thought, if he'd had no talent at all, then he wouldn't have been tempted by dreams he couldn't bring to pass. But the pleasure made up for it, almost. As he played, he could see, through the sparkling glass, his tree. He was drawn to it, and to his garden, but they would have to wait. Tonight he wanted to be with Beth. To talk to her, he had to, but it seemed so unfair. But who could he talk to, if not her? And how could she bear to listen? She would listen though.

He went to her. And seeing her, her head bent, her curls around her face as she peered into a deep casserole pot, it frightened him to realize that he simply couldn't live without this return to Beth, to the centre of his life. He knew men who were miserable at home, whose kitchens and bedrooms were battlefields. How could they bear it? What had he done to make him so lucky?

He had met her at a party; walked up to her and said, 'I claim you.' Even now it didn't seem absurd.

'Claim me?'

'Yes, you're mine. For the rest of this evening, or for the rest of your life, if you agree.' She laughed, and then stopped, then laughed again. He would have written out a marriage certificate, then and there, no question about it. She was, quite simply, the most beautiful woman he had ever seen. Classy-cool, her eyes honey coloured and full of some wonderful wisdom and promise.

'But of course I'm married,' he'd laughed.

'Of course,' she said serenely, turning away.

That night he walked out on his wife, left her at midnight and went to a hotel. Without Beth. He'd never looked back. He was twenty-two then. 'Trigger-happy,' Beth said.

He came and wound an arm around her waist and pressed his chin into her shoulder. Inside the pot something thick and fragrant gurgled and exploded: beef, almost syrupy with oil, spices and long stirring. A rich smell of ragoût filled the room, her hair, even her skin. He kissed the back of her neck. 'Want me to peel the potatoes?' he asked, partly to distract himself from his lust and partly because he'd always been that kind of man.

'No, we're having rice – oh, what am I talking about?' Her hand fluttered in annoyance and swiped back her hair. 'Yes, please, darling.'

The doorbell rang and was followed by a landslide on the stairs.

'I suppose we're going to have all the strays around tonight!' Humphrey said accusingly, glaring at a large pile of crockery and cutlery. Then added, spikily, to hide his disappointment, 'There's enough food here for a refugee camp. And God, Beth, all these flowers, has somebody died?' His humour was a wilful thing, combining elements of cruelty and sadness.

'Oh, that's Abi,' Beth said. 'She suddenly decided to ravish the garden.'

Humphrey nodded and bit into a stick of celery. If Abi had plundered his garden, that was all right. He was more tolerant of his oldest daughter: she was more boyish than the rest; she even wore jeans occasionally. He wasn't really sure about his daughters; they gave him the willies most of the time; they were creepy, bloody creepy. One looked as though she ought to take up a career in haunting; the other was trying to be a re-make of a dead sex-pot with hair that had been bleached and brutalized beyond recognition. He would swat at his children if they got too close to him, particularly as a group. He could almost manage them one at a time, preferably in the morning.

'Beth,' he said, counting the glasses, 'there really are an awful lot of people coming to dinner.'

She turned to him affectionately. 'It's all right, don't go and hide, it's just their friends.'

'Is that supposed to reassure me?'

'Oh, darling, don't make a fuss. They're OK. You should feel sorry for them, they have no home life.'

'Some parents have the sense to kick their kids out of the house at a certain age.'

'Listen, Humphrey,' she said, chopping some celery and giving him a large bag of potatoes, 'they're all broke, out of work, they hardly eat and live from one dole cheque to the next.'

'Is that my problem, Beth?' My God, she had some mushy ideas about saving the world. He thumped the potatoes out on to the table and noticed with annoyance that one never got mud with one's potatoes these days.

'You can be a bit of a shit,' she said.

'Can't have everyone sucking the tit of the state for ever. Start 'em off this early and they'll never be weaned.'

'It's not entirely their fault,' she said.

'When I was sixteen,' he began, but she held up her hand and said, 'Stop, I know: you'd turned down a scholarship to Cambridge, you'd got your first job ... you, Humphrey,' she glared at him fiercely, 'have a lot of natural advantages that this lot does not. You've always had all the accoutrements of success, in spite of your background.' She passed him the peeler. 'Anyway, peel those potatoes and try to be decent for once tonight. They'll eat and run.'

'Then can we be alone?'

'Yes.' She came over and hugged him tenderly, putting her arms around his waist and resting her cheek against his back. 'Of course, Humphrey, then we can be alone.' And how much she needed that, to be alone with Humphrey, after a long lonely week.

He kissed her as people don't often kiss after nearly nineteen years of marriage.

Four

Entering the dining-room that evening Humphrey was peculiarly disaffected. Why did Beth fill up his house with these people? Where was all that peace and quiet that he used to escape home to? That orderly calm, that woman with long hair pulled back from her forehead? Did *all* these people need his wife? Did she have to mother the world, in their house, at eight-thirty on a Friday night?

He placed himself, gingerly, at the head of a table filled with, surely, the most revolting specimens of humanity. He'd known what to expect when he'd found the dog hiding in the lavatory and the cat vanished: the punks had arrived. The animals got the scent all right. And those bloody nancy-boys had to be here too, mouths clogged with blood-red lipstick, their chins and cheeks ghost-like with thick make-up through which the stubble gleamed, eyes done out in a nice shade of lilac or frosted pink. In his kinder moments he warned his daughters: you live with one of those half-hearted faggots and you'll never get to the mirror in the morning, you'll have to share your clothes, have your hairspray swiped, your lipstick all used up and a state of confusion in the bedroom.

'But ah,' said Fran, 'at least I'd get my hair done every day.'

Now, as Humphrey surveyed his dinner companions, he was appalled. Why did they try so hard to be so repulsive – because this nastiness was quite deliberate. They spent their entire day at it. That one over there with his massacred T-shirt: the arms torn out by the roots, DISCHARGE written in large yellow letters across his front. Well, he was quiet enough, even ate with a knife and fork, his albinoïd features chewing happily, his hair dyed green and cut to frighten lice. And his friend, the skinny yob with the shaved head and one long thin plait hanging from the back of his cratered neck. The only thing that kept his emaciated body on the ground must be the weight of his granny-bashers. And his daughters talking happily to them; his wife feeding them with the same pleasure that she took in feeding anyone. There was no question about it: their heads ought to be pinched off, should have been done at birth.

Beth, diving into her deep yellow pot, placing the meat carefully on each porcelain plate, arranging the piped potato around the rich sauce, smiled around the table and drew them all towards her, making each one her own, her child; ladling out safety, love, home; watching with pleasure as they loaded their forks and bent their heads to her cooking. Humphrey watched her in amazement: how could the woman do it? She had that wonderful air of being laden; she was a ripe, enveloping presence, making them all turn to her, seeking something which she seemed certain to provide. She encouraged Berni to talk about the art course he was about to start. Antonio enthused about his trip to Italy as a courier. Another moaned about the hopelessness of finding work. Oh, she knew all their histories, had cups of tea with them and shared their Camels. The Italian had brought her a bunch of red carnations, said he felt a right tit walking down the King's Road with them – but did it. They adored her, it was infuriatingly clear to Humphrey that they adored her.

He drank even more Côtes du Rhône: He watched with dismay as a monster dunked a hand into the exquisite salad bowl and plucked out a radish. Then passed the salad on to Humphrey, who had to stop himself from shuddering. The mouth with its crusted sore (Herpes I, II or III?) began to chomp through the radish. Humphrey's stomach had acquired a sea motion, his mouth watered with nausea: he began to imagine himself going through the final stages of syphilis. Then the monster smiled at him and went for another radish.

Beth poured more wine for everyone and filled up their plates. Then she turned to a pretty thing in a black T-shirt and cling-film leather trousers and asked him the colour of his lipstick. 'It's a really nice red,' she said with amusement, 'I must get some.'

'Oh,' he said, 'glad you like it, it's Mary Quant, Bloody Mary. You can borrow mine if you like,' he added chattily.

It occurred to Humphrey that perhaps he should have sent his daughters to boarding school: maybe the appeal of this asexual group was the chummy girly support it offered, the exchange of information and beauty tips?

'Having a good time?' Wilf seemed to yell at Humphrey from just beside him, bashing his elbow in so friendly a fashion that the fork in Humphrey's hand took off and landed on the white cuff of his shirt. He watched as the dark sauce made itself thoroughly at home on the cotton. He felt distinctly queasy and surrendered his appetite along with his knife and fork. Perhaps it was already too late, perhaps he was infected even now?

As Julia and Em kept their heads together and laughed, as the punks and pretty boys rose, hesitantly, to remove the plates (oh, she has them trained even!), Humphrey began to feel uncomfortable, and yes, unnecessary. They didn't give a damn whether he was there or not. He looked towards Beth, but her lovely face was bent towards her favourite, Antonio, as if her life depended on what he would utter next in that cracked accent of his.

Then he saw, to his fury, that his youngest child, Fran, was noshing away at some disgusting mixture in a bowl. She was actually eating a mound of pasta mixed up with baked beans and something else too squashed to be recognizable.

'What are you eating, Fran?' he roared, suddenly feeling a little restored. She showed him.

Julia, because of the deep authoritative tone of Humphrey's voice, looked distressed. Only the five girls were still at the table – clearing was done on a sexist basis. Beth was in the kitchen. They watched Humphrey with wary, scornful faces.

'Why aren't you eating what everyone else ate? Making extra work for your mother?'

Fran declined to answer, her delight in her food all spoiled.

'She made it herself,' Cass said, 'she doesn't like posh food.' God, where did he *live*, she wondered, that he didn't know that Fran was only at home with baked beans and sausages? that her mother's cooking meant nothing to her? And why must he bully so? Always push himself forward so roughly?

He knew that he'd ruined the happy atmosphere, and he regretted it. A silence, of a kind unpleasantly recognizable to Julia in her own home, settled. Em broke it up by suggesting they go into the kitchen and help. Fran followed with her bowl, sulking but mumbling, 'Fuck him', under her breath. Humphrey just couldn't understand Beth; she'd always been like this: letting people be, letting them do and grow in their own way. When Fran was tiny and fell asleep over her toys, Beth would cover her and place a cushion under her head; she never woke her or disturbed her by carrying her to bed. She let her be. She let them all be. He drank more wine and felt its effect, numbing and stilling his stomach.

When everyone returned, carrying delicate blue bowls and a cut-glass bowl of fruit salad (Antonio was still in the kitchen finishing the zabaglione), Humphrey made one of his enormous efforts. He spoke to the boy on the other side of him, who, even in the warm room, refused to be separated from his black leather jacket, punched all over with studs and slashed with long zips; a close relative of the lavatory chain dangling down the back. He had a tattooed scorpion crawling across his cheek.

'Where do you live?' Humphrey asked, with an amazed and exhausted tone to his voice.

'Um, er, down in Islington, with the French punks – we live in a squat, right? Ten of us, yeh, ten ...' he nodded his head in a dazed way.

'Running water?' Humphrey inquired hopefully, as if checking out a holiday camp in Bolivia.

'Nah, we don't have that.' He shook his head and Humphrey could have sworn that the scorpion lifted its tail.

'How d'you bath, or wash your clothes?' Neither appeared to have been done for some considerable time.

'Yeh, well,' he slurped up the fruit salad, 'I've only got the one pair of trousers, see, so it's not a problem. Right?'

'Right,' Humphrey agreed.

He caught Beth's eye; her face was trembling with amusement and tenderness. And yes, that's why he loved her so. The way she would look up and smile at him, reassure him when he'd been an ass, return his confidence with her adoration. Even when he was being an egotistical child, she would restore his manliness. Her grace and poise would carry him to safety, would protect him from any sense of failure. Yes, she was a perfect woman. He worshipped her. And taking her love, tucking it safely under his arm, he could relinquish her, almost gracefully, to the horde around his table.

He quaffed down the last of his wine and said, 'Well, you'll have to excuse me, it's Friday and I've got to put the laundry on. Anything not in the basket' – he looked sternly at his daughters – 'will not get done. Right?' He looked at the rest of the table and said, 'I'm sorry, gentlemen,' he beamed, 'I'd love to do yours – but if you've only got the one pair ...'

'Not a bad geezer,' Wilf said, after he'd gone.

The atmosphere around the table grew animated and relaxed. Beth asked Cass to light the candles and in the soft light she felt she cradled them all in her protection. They were so young, so frail, it was a little painful. And now they all seemed to catch fire, to laugh, to almost shout at one another in their enthusiasm; happiness licking from one bright face to the other. Antonio found the last strawberry and placed it, like a flower, on Beth's plate. The pretty boy seemed less camp now he was less threatened and he told a lewd story. Fran's face opened as she bent forward to listen. Beth sat in the midst of it, glowing, radiant, feeling a sense of achievement, and yes, even a great power over them all.

Five

Humphrey stood in his garden. It was blowsy and heavy scented. He rested his back against the trunk of the apple tree, heard the laughter wafting to him from the dining-room, and felt distinctly old. He often felt old these days and found he couldn't bear to look at the slack faces of men of over fifty; those cheeks that had begun to slop down under their chins; that dead hair, those vile freckles on their hands. Talk about the young needing their heads pinched off. Well, he was in mint condition, only forty-four, dammit, his body beautiful from running. But it had been such a shock for him to realize that he was, like everyone else, growing old. That lines *had* winkled in among the fine skin around his eyes; that he got tired – extraordinary that – he even got tired, and that some nights he was in bed by two o'clock. Though all his life he'd been nocturnal, his best hours, thoughts and plans came after midnight. And the horror of that discovery, a few years back, when it had seemed a distinct possibility that he might actually die one day.

And worse, this daunting self-knowledge as well, when he'd been so much happier without it. He was actually beginning to investigate himself, after years of self-contentment and ignorance. Now, of course, he could see what a pain he'd been tonight, when once he'd never have given it another thought, never considered that there might be any other way to behave than the way he did. Now he saw himself from the outside; it was as if someone had handed him a mirror and said, 'Here, have a good look; not a pretty sight, is it?'

But surely, also, he had a right to feel infuriated by nights like these? All those people come to roost in his life – his life which was running out. Where would they go when they left the tranquillity of his home? Where would they take his daughters? His little girls, they'd been so pretty once, when you could still see their faces. They'd planted carrots and beans in their own little patches, shown him with such pride the stars in their school-books. He didn't know them any more, he didn't know the shape of their lives, he had no idea of what they were capable.

It was too bloody depressing. Beth thought that Abi had already squandered her virginity. Well, he wasn't going to give in. Some standards would be maintained. Beth had her own way with them, it seemed to work for her. He preferred the traditional approach, but only in this area of his life. If they thought him an arsehole, well, that was their problem. Maybe he was an arsehole.

Then he looked up into the leafy branches of his apple tree. What a crop there'd be this year. Big beautiful apples. And the pleasure of picking them, rubbing them against his sleeve, putting his nose to the sharp tangy scent of their ripeness. That's what he really liked: watching things grow, making them bloom for him. Why didn't he pack it all in – chuck up the business and get a market garden? He was sick of the business, sick of being propelled all these years by not much more than achievement. It was a disease. Like animals, when people like that were really hungry, they ate each other. He'd done it. To remember how he'd feasted on other men's disasters, organized them himself sometimes – it sickened him.

His life was becoming frighteningly clear to him again, as it had when he'd first fallen in love with Beth. It was a little like an epiphany. Love did that to you. Now he felt it again. He must change. Tonight, this minute. It was his philosophy, after all, never to hesitate or consider: trust your gut instinct, when it was hot in you, grab it. It was up in him again, an urge for life, for change. Perhaps he could escape middle age, after all?

Six

'I really hate the old fart,' Fran said furiously, slamming her hair under a black fascinator with a dotted veil. 'What's he want to go on about the food I eat? He doesn't cook it; Ma doesn't mind. "What are you eating, Fran?"' she boomed in a voice cleverly akin to his. 'Bloody pain.' She drew the curtains violently and nearly knocked over all the pots and bottles of make-up arranged on a long pine table with three mirrors, three stools.

'And why,' she spat, 'does he treat everyone we bring home as if they were – God – *violent* or something? As if they were going to crap on the carpet or do something really scary? The most scary thing they've ever done is enter this house.'

Julia, who, after plaiting Abi's hair into Afro tendrils, was now sewing up the ends, said hesitantly, 'You don't know how lucky you are ... um, I mean, dinner at home is silent, we never talk about *anything* ... not even what I'm going to do with my life. They've just sent off the forms for me to go to finishing school ... they didn't even ask me. I mean, here, well, you talk about everything with your mother, what you're going to do when you leave school, sex, the pill, even your problems and stuff, even sometimes when your father's there. I'd rather DIE than try that at home.'

Em, stepping gracefully out of the white pools of her petticoats, murmured in her soft serious way, 'Your dad can be a pain, Fran, but he's OK really. Imagine my old man coming home in his bowler hat to that lot downstairs? He'd throw up. And Valencia wouldn't even let them in the house. As for my real mother, she'd make Daddy send me to boarding school, and' – she grimaced at Julia – 'finishing school after that. All they're doing really is trying to keep me out of the way. Here, it's' – she fluffed up her pink and blonde hair – 'oh, it's so – so family-like, so *real*. I mean, you lot are a proper family, not all bits and pieces and step-brothers and things. It's proper.'

'Yeh,' Fran said, bored, looking at herself in the full-length mirror she'd been given for her fifteenth birthday and wishing with all her heart that she could be perfect. Her legs weren't long enough, her face was too round and there was that revolting thing, that mole that she sawed off in her dreams, still perching there on the bridge of her nose. Why wouldn't it just go, walk off or something? She wasn't brilliant so she must be beautiful, perfectly so, like Marilyn Monroe, someone the world would never forget: oh Marilyn, my idol, my sister, poor Marilyn, perfect Marilyn. Dead Marilyn. Oh, she wanted to be blonde and beautiful and famous. And famous and famous and famous. Her sulky full mouth with its slightly pouting teeth moved into lassitude and displeasure. She was certain everyone was disappointed in her, and was determined not to let them know she knew. Perhaps I'll never be famous, perhaps I'm just no good at anything, her face whispered heartbroken to her reflection, which threw back, like a golden ball, a girl in a full black dress, lace over her shoulders, skin the colour of Cornish cream and quite flawless; a lovely face with black brows under which blue eyes smouldered. But tonight, like a mirage, all she saw was the mole on the bridge of her nose.

'Want to borrow my black shoes?' Cass said, smiling with jealousy at her sister's beauty – not hateful, not wanting to crumple it up or break it to pieces, just sad.

'Yeh, thanks, what'll you wear?'

'Oh, I don't care.' She wondered if it would be another night when she'd find herself comforting all Fran's rejects? Was that all she was ever going to be to boys – an understanding friend, a sister? That one boy, oh, it seemed so long ago now, six months or more, he'd said he loved her. She saw him again the other day and he walked straight past her, turning his face away, with another girl. Why were they so careless? Why did they just disappear while you waited for the phone to ring? Suddenly she wanted to be annoyed with Fran, and partly because she couldn't stop herself and partly because it was her role to be nanny of the household, she said quietly, 'Why did you have to go on about Dad like that?'

Fran flushed and lashed back with her scalding tongue, 'Why shouldn't I? What's so bloody perfect about him that I can't criticize him? Who's he think he is? Look at him: he's old, he's past it, he should be put down. He goes on about discipline and rules and self-control. What the hell does he know about it? One of these days I'm going to come straight out with it, instead of us all pretending to be so civilized.' Her whole face quivered at the last word.

A hush had overtaken the room; brushes were held poised above cheeks; Abi's hand slipped in the middle of a lipstick stroke; Cass's face had gone white and stretched and Julia was teetering on the edge of tears. Em, feeling her idyll of the perfectly happy family begin to rock precariously, leaving her homeless again, left the room hurriedly.

'Oh, *leave* it,' Cass yelled in an odd, constricted way.

'No, I *won't*,' Fran screamed. 'We just go on ignoring it, not talking about it even among ourselves. He's vile. How can Ma put up with it? It's immoral, it's sick, it's disgusting.'

'It's their business,' Abi said quietly. 'No one tried to hide it from us, we all know. It's their business, not ours.'

'Oh yes, it is, it is ours.' Fran would have cried but for the devastation that would cause to her mascara. 'It's our business because it's Ma's,' she insisted stubbornly. 'I don't believe she doesn't mind, I just don't. She hates it, I know she does. How can he do it to her? How can he go around fucking someone else?'

The word 'fucking', applied to their father, utterly appalled them, they recoiled as if an icon had fallen shattered to the floor. They watched, horrified, spellbound, as Fran exposed, with fascinating cruelty, their own secret and unspoken thoughts. Would anything return to normal again? Would this tranquil room, once the nursery, then the toy-room, now converted with loving care by Beth into their dressing-room, with its hall of mirrors and make-up deck, would it survive the blast of Fran's truth? Would it not just collapse, taking with it those happy childhood days of toast and honey, nursery puddings with fat sultanas, cherry pips you lined up around your plate, asking, Whom will I marry? How many babies will I have? And in pain, running to the haven of Beth's arms: Mummy, make it go away, make the hurting stop. Make it stop.

Seven

Beth came out of the adjoining bathroom in a vapour of Chanel No. 5. Humphrey was pacing up and down their bedroom with a lowered head; he was clicking his fingers, which she always found unbearable. She was surprised in a way that he wasn't in the garden; you would find him there at three in the morning if he was worried or unhappy.

But then he looked up, bright as you please, her presence pulling him away from whatever troubled him, like the transformation you see in a child's face when its mother returns. He said – though it was the least pressing thing on his mind – 'I sold my car today.'

'Did you?' She was startled. 'I thought you loved that car ... it was such a lovely car.' She was preoccupied, moving towards her bureau and picking up her hairbrush, then tugging out long strands of hair and rolling them into a ball.

Watching her, it occurred to Humphrey that he'd probably only wanted the car because it had looked so well-bred and superior parked beside George's BMW.

'God, how petty men can be,' he scoffed.

Beth frowned a little; there was a tendency lately in Humphrey to denigrate his own sex, even himself.

She sat on the bed, leaning back against the brass bars with a welter of silky cushions around her. Her hair was scraped up into a top-knot, her dark skin was shiny and clean; her eyes were wary and if he looked directly at her they would take up a pretence of being interested in something at the other side of the room.

'What will you get instead?' She asked it carefully; it wasn't important, but approaching Humphrey the right way tonight was. He was in a strange mood, restless, peculiar, all evening. He was such a volatile person that she had trained herself to walk quietly beside his moods, keeping up with them, even anticipating or overtaking them.

'Well, I've got what I wanted,' he grinned like a boy, 'it's really marvellous.' He stopped his pacing. 'It's a bright green bicycle.'

She laughed – a deep, infectious sound. Oh, what a joy he was; there was no one like him. A green bicycle! He'd traded in his blue Bentley for a green bicycle. Lovely, quite perfect. She adored his eccentricity as she'd loved her brother, Hugh, for his loony ways. Hugh had declined his father's Royal Navy for a job as a magician in the circus. He was so brilliant he could have been world-famous. Off he'd gone, leaving a note on the table: 'Gone to join the world'. Hugh was like that. Hugh hated Ireland: said the Irish were in love with their sickness, said the Irish would never get better.

'I was a lousy driver anyway,' Humphrey was saying. 'I saw a bloke knocked down today, gave me the willies, couldn't stop thinking about it all day.' He added morbidly, 'Always thought I'd do myself in in a car. Anyway, I took it back and I feel much better without it.' He came and sat on the end of the bed, placing his hand on the cover above Beth's leg and rubbing it gently back and forth.

'We have too much of everything, Beth,' he said with a melancholy smile.

She watched his face as it darkened. Then she looked around her at the room she'd created: the Victorian ceiling with its cornice and ornamental centre rose; the cloud-scattered wall-paper, dumpy blue chairs with white brocade cushions, the sash windows with their soft blue drapes, the pale marble fireplace with its jug of roses.

'Rubbish,' she said. Money didn't bother her. She'd grown up with it – it was something you were generous with because you had it and other people didn't. Her family's money had gone, long ago. Taxes on a vast estate had hacked into it, feeding the animals became too expensive and they were all sold, then the land, finally her father's hunter had gone too. Cancer had eaten into the rest: both of her parents had died slowly of it, one part of their anatomy after the other going under the knife. Now, only her mother's house by the sea remained. She loved that. But Hugh was right about the Irish. Perhaps they were the last true Romantics: if I can't have my dream, I will die. And kill. The poor Irish, she thought and brought herself back to Humphrey.

What was the matter with him these days? He was becoming more and more uncomfortable with his wealth and success. And yet he had shrugged off the deprivations of his childhood with dazzling ease: inventing a new life for himself and a past to fit his present;

he never gave a thought to how much money he had. He splashed it around like water. Once, on April Fools' Day, he'd sent £100 notes to all the secretaries in his office.

'I never needed all this' – he waved his hand around – 'property in Chelsea, all the rest of it.' And it had been so easy, he laughed to think of it, a mere decade of hard work and now he was rolling in it. It had started with Beth. From the minute he'd met her his life seemed one long windfall. 'I was a yob when I met you,' he remembered with pleasure, 'a real yobbo, bad as that lot downstairs, almost. God, how you swept me off my feet, turned me into something! Just touching you gave me a sense of security, kissing you was like robbing a bank. Suddenly, I could do no wrong. Do you remember, Beth, do you, how wonderful it all was?'

He wanted it all back, the uncertainty, the delicious headiness of those days. He wanted her back, the way she'd been then, the way their feelings had been then, at the beginning. If it could be like that again, just once – with the landlady snooping around outside the door of his crummy room – and that marvellous night when he'd just climbed up the drainpipe into her bedroom and crept into bed beside her; the joy on her face when he woke her; the exquisite pleasure of her body.

Without him even noticing it, she'd changed him from the rushing, grabbing little slob he'd been. She transformed him without asking him for a damn thing. She needed nothing from him but she made him feel he was capable of anything. He found himself giving up his old habits of paying cash for everything, of buying everything below the retail price. She stopped him being crooked – that was the right word for it – no point in ducking it, that's what he'd been, though she never knew it. What he needed, her own sense of straightness seemed to imply, was moral refinement. He learned it so quickly from her that only his sharp salesmen friends noticed the difference. But she never told him anything, never once humiliated him even by her example. She let him be. It was he who changed. She let him go on wearing those crass suits and that one spotted tie without saying a word. She walked proudly beside him when he did; she never apologized in any way for his lack of breeding among her circle of grand and disapproving friends.

She was just too upper-class to make anyone feel it. She'd been trained for attentiveness: she humoured him out of rages, let him sulk if he wanted to, circumvented his silences and dissatisfactions with himself. Her capacity for devotion humbled him and made him grow up. Thinking about it now, he realized that she may not even have realized what a lout she was taking on: she saw only the best part of him, she homed in on that and polished it up till it shone like vintage silver. She didn't place herself before him like a rare beauty that he must work himself to death to win; she gave herself to him, as he saw it – for nothing.

'What is it, darling?' She reached out her arm and took his hand. It was Friday, bad days, days of dislocation for both of them. She could feel it edging up as the week drew to an end, but Fridays were the days she longed for all week. And they were never easy. She moved up and curled herself against his body. Why was it, he wondered, in this house as in his heart – she brought things together, she gave them coherence and depth – and when he entered, everything was punctured. He felt destructive, full of conflict and pain. She tried to right him. 'Tell me,' she said, 'it's all right, I won't mind.' She said it softly, still holding his hand. To her – though he never knew it – his vulnerability was his most appealing quality. Having asked for the truth, she didn't want to hear it. It was like baring your back to the rod because it was inevitable, wanting to get it over as fast as possible, while drawing back with all one's soul.

He threw himself off her and lay back, cuffed the cushions impatiently, then crossed his arms beneath his head.

'When I'm with you,' he said, 'I want to be with you.' His voice took an angry plunge. 'But when I get back to this mob, I just want to be somewhere else.'

'We could go away somewhere,' she said.

'I'm too busy at the moment.' Immediately he reached out and grabbed her hand. 'I'm sorry, I didn't mean to sound ...'

'It's all right,' she smiled, all her pleasure emptying.

'And it's so difficult.' He watched the moon nose up to the corner of the window. 'The weekends are so difficult, I mean. Beth, for God's sake – look – I don't want to go into this, it isn't fair, it's almost criminal ...'

'No it isn't,' she said calmly. 'Tell me.'

'The weekends are a strain,' he said reluctantly, 'because they begin badly: God, every Friday I end up having a row, with her, as if, well, as if then I've got a good reason to leave her.'

Beth seemed to be watching the moon over his shoulder, it was so steady, solid as gold.

40

'And then you feel unhappy thinking about it all weekend,' she said, quickly, wanting the conversation to end, but equally, wanting him to say that he wasn't unhappy all weekend.

He sat up restlessly, pulling up his knees with a quick, athletic jerk, 'You see, she's not as competent as you are (Beth flinched, and as though he knew it, he didn't look at her). She seems damned tough, but she's insecure really, very dependent on me in a way, though she'd never admit it.'

Beth ground her nails into her palms. How dare he! Was she expected to have sympathy for her as well as for Humphrey? He asked so much, he needed so much, so much sympathy, so much reassurance. And she had to give it and give and give, only to feel in the end it wasn't enough, he needed someone else's sympathy as well. Suddenly her pliancy to all his needs seemed to rise up and choke her.

She managed to say, 'She does have most of the week,' her voice taking that clear ring of deeply cut crystal.

She, he thought, always she; neither used her name; she remained less of a person to Beth that way and Humphrey felt he protected her that way. He remembered now an old mate of his, whose wife had referred to her rival as 'The Bit'. Beth would never stoop to jealous euphemisms like that. Beth understood too deeply to be jealous; her tolerance came from a total acceptance of him and his needs. He had never lied to her or deceived her in any way. He simply needed both women. It had happened suddenly, he hadn't plotted it or pursued Sylvie. She'd just turned up at his office. Like another windfall. He couldn't resist her. He couldn't not have her. And now she was as vital to his life as Beth was. He couldn't give one up, or the other. Beth was far too well loved to be insecure.

Sylvie, on the other hand, did not understand. But in time she would. What Sylvie needed from him was time, the length of time that Beth had had. All she'd had was one meagre year to put her faith in, and a difficult year, when they'd both had to make so many adjustments to and for the other.

'You should go,' Beth said softly, smoothing the dun patch of the quilt, feeling the raised edge of the appliqué, letting her fingers trail around its edges – how old and worn it was, how long it had been with her. 'Go and see her now, Humphrey,' she said, her head still bent, her face quiet with some maturity and strength that astonished him, 'or you'll only be unhappy.' She flung her head up;

41

she was so queenly when she did that, he thought, she was quite noble.

And he knew he would go; she was quite right, it was the only answer on this occasion: it was as if she'd divined how unhappy Sylvie had been when he left her. She swung her long legs off the bed and pulled out the elastic band from her hair, so that it fell about, dishevelled and heavy. He came to her and took her tenderly into his arms. 'You're sure you don't mind?' His face, strong, humourless and uncertain now, bent towards hers for reassurance, for sympathy – and reaching her hand up to his cheek, she wanted to claw her nails through his skin to see if the blood would run.

'I'm sure.' She turned and walked out of the room.

Eight

Beth walked slowly into Fran's room; the lights were all on, the radio kept up a lonely serenade, the child lay sleeping in her black evening gown, her little bit of a satin hat tossed on the floor; one stiletto on the bed, the other pointing sharply to the door. Beth doused the din, and all the lights bar the night light, a left-over from Fran's anxious childhood: a china doll with a bonnet of cherries on her head making a small halo of light. All Beth could see of her daughter was the tousled blonde hair, dark roots making stains across her scalp. She touched the ruined hair softly. Then sat on the bed and looked up at the cupboard where a treasured doll in a taffeta dress lolled tirelessly against a middle-aged teddy and a rabbit with one ear. How little of childhood remained, and yet, how fiercely that little was held to.

She remembered her daughters before puberty, naked in streams, cavorting and splashing, those straight, bullet-smooth bodies innocent and quite fearless. It was odd how breasts and hips, making you older, only seemed to make you softer, more vulnerable. She remembered them long before that, with round legs and fat bellies, the sweet smell of their breath and the dampness at the back of their necks when they slept on hot summer nights. How she missed them. Fran used to piss just like a boy, standing, leaning backwards a little, taking aim and firing. No one else could do it. Beth laughed quietly, thinking of it.

Fran turned quickly and surfaced.

'Shamming, were you?' Beth pushed her hair back from her face with a practised movement.

A grumpy face looked away from her and at the wall.

'Why didn't you go, Fran?' Beth moved closer, pushing up the arms of her nightie, and pulling her knees up on to the bed.

'Don't know, don't like those punks much. Bunch of losers. Why don't they *do* something with their lives? They'll be dead soon, I'll be dead soon. We'll all be dead soon.'

Beth laughed and Fran looked at her mother sharply. 'I thought you'd gone to bed. Still here, is he?' She meant her father, Beth knew it by the tone of voice.

'No, he had to go out.' She looked away from her hostile child to the windows; she thought the curtains could do with a wash.

'Where to?'

'Oh, I don't know . . .' Beth was a most unconvincing liar.

'Ma?' the blue eyes flashed menacingly, 'he's gone to see *her*, hasn't he?'

'I said that he should,' Beth interjected with the swift protection she always gave him under any attack: she would not allow them to criticize or laugh at him behind his back. Fran's face came clean and broke into the misery she'd felt all evening and tried to escape from in sleep. It was the sex, that's what bothered her most. You couldn't get away from it, it was all over the place, everywhere, like a rash, it was pushed in your face all the time. Here, even at home, where it had least right to be. Her parents. Her father. It was disgusting. They said she was a puritan at school. But it was just . . . oh, she didn't know. It scared her. She didn't want it. It was too soon. She didn't want it.

'You must understand,' Beth said kindly, taking Fran's hand, 'that you *don't* understand. And you mustn't judge. Or take sides. You must also understand that I'm all right and that I do understand.' She pushed back her hair. 'Fran, I can't explain marriage to you, or even to myself.' She looked shy for a moment. 'It's too private, but it's strong enough, this marriage is, to survive. Don't let it make you unhappy' – she saw the tears quivering – 'your life is out there and you're at an age when you're, well, still very conservative, you feel safer with things normal, as they always were – simple, child-like, so you didn't have to question and judge. Later, it'll seem different to you. We're not unhappy, either of us. So you mustn't be.' She looked stern. 'You're not the family conscience, Fran, don't frown at me like that, you're not my mother. I think sometimes you'd like to tell me how I should be behaving!'

There was a silence, while both listened to the red clock ticking, while a car slowed to turn a corner and the dog could be heard plodding heavily up the stairs. Then Fran moved quickly, flinging her legs off the bed. 'I'm ever so hungry,' she said, stretching her white arms.

'I'll get you some toast and honey, shall I?'

'No, I can do it.' A sudden intimation of her mother's tiredness came to her. She felt a painful, tender resurgence of love for Beth, she wanted to look after her for once. She was still young enough to feel that awed and intense adoration of her mother, of her beauty, her serenity; her life that seemed settled, even over – when Fran's was full of uncertainty and fear.

'We'll do it together,' Beth said, standing up. 'I'll make the tea if you make the toast. But why not take that off and get into your nightie first?'

Fran, seeing her mother's straight, tall figure walk slowly to the door, and turn and smile, felt she would begin to cry all over again. She was so full of emotion. She didn't know what to do with it.

'Oh, how left-out she must feel,' Fran wailed for her mother, 'how left-out.'

Nine

Imagine, Humphrey thought, entirely happy now, running in a smooth, animal-lope down the road, that people are actually going to bed now – when all this is out here: these lungfuls of sharp air, that moon to be kicked straight into the goal of the sky. He hated sleep, couldn't bear oblivion. Every time you slept you were missing something, wasting time, letting someone get one over on you, preparing for death. He ran. His dark head thrown back, his arms pummelling the air, his breath coming regularly through his bared teeth. He wasn't jogging: jogging was for idiots, for clapped-out men trying to find muscles that had gone to fat years ago. He was a *runner*. He'd run from the moment he could walk. Midnight or later was his running hour. You'd never see a jogger at midnight: they did it to be seen, at six o'clock, and God, what a sight! No one looking at those beetroot faces, flaring eyes and death-rattle exhalations could possibly imagine they were doing themselves any good, or having a good time. Not like a man who ran, especially at midnight, when you could soar over the cusp into another new day, be there first. He felt good, amazingly so.

Now, leaving behind him the leafy streets of his homeground, he sprinted along the Embankment and then on to the pathway along the river. He ran with his head forward, a slight stoop to his shoulders, making him look a bit like a pugilist about to attack. He got the full stink of the river: mud, dead fish and debris, the effluence of house-boats, a trolley from Sainsbury's, a drunk vomiting quietly into the water. But God, he felt quite wonderful tonight, he felt like the young man he'd been – crashing out music all night in that club in the East End, gulping down the smoke, the dope – relentless hours of pure pulsing pleasure and noise. He felt the same exuberance as he'd felt then. So he was the same man after all.

If he could change his life, if he could start again in some way – it'd give him the greatest feeling of power, of real freedom. If he could break the rituals: the rising, the working, bullying the hours to yield up the maximum turnover; returning to the same door and another set of certainties. He needed more than this, everyone did, or they were no longer fully alive. A man should change his work a number of times in his life, or he'd grow sloppy and worn. Uncertainty: it was delicious and heady, it made him alive and aware; he was on the brink of a mighty change and nothing would stop him from taking the opportunities that this would bring him.

He ran on, with a steady rhythm, over the pearly Albert Bridge to Battersea, to Sylvie. Sylvie that day: driving him to some lousy outpost of Balham and announcing, 'See those houses? my grandfather built those, three identical, adjoining semi-detached villas for his two sons and one daughter. He gave each of them one when they married; they were locked together for the rest of their lives, never moved, never changed. Wonderful.' Her eyes were almost bristly with pleasure. 'I love it, Humphrey, I really love it, don't you?' It gave him the willies. But she was wonderful all right. She had not a shred of shame about her past, not like him. She handed it to you proudly, on a plate, cracked and ugly as it was, as those houses were, one of which had produced the miracle that was Sylvie.

He stopped to cross a road, and for a moment reeled and almost fell. His heart seemed to be trying to batter its way out of his body, those lungs he'd stopped persecuting with smoking seemed to be actually turning on him. Then it passed. He took ten deep breaths, then kicked off again, just as fast, just as steady as before. Thinking of Sylvie would give anyone a heart attack.

A little way ahead of him, when he was nearly there, he could distinctly feel her beckoning him; he felt he knew exactly what she was doing and feeling at that moment. He wanted great things from Sylvie, as he'd had great things from Beth. He liked to really *have* a woman, to explore and adore her, to penetrate and share the most intimate life within her. Some men wanted tarts, others the odd lay, others a traditional wife/mother. What he really wanted was wives. In his experience, if you'd found something wonderful that worked, you could do it again; if you were honest and straight you could repeat any success.

He leapt up the steps two at a time, ran his hand across his brow and clicked his key into the front door. A woman, watching from a window above his head, saw him and began softly to laugh. And once she'd started she couldn't stop, her happiness was unstoppable.

Ten

Fran, standing next to Cass, looked out of the window at her father riding his bicycle round and round on the grass, and said, with excruciating boredom, 'When *is* he going to grow up?' She watched his blue-jeaned legs as they whirled the pedals, making the bike wobble a little, and added dismally, 'In a year or two he could be quite embarrassing, you know. But of course we could put him into care.'

Cass laughed, then grabbed Fran's arm and said, 'Hey, remember our lovely bikes, long ago? At the old house? Come on, let's get that off him.' They ran out of the house, eyes flinching at the bright sunlight, hoicking up soft rolls of long nightdress as they ran. Humphrey waved like royalty and nearly fell off. The labrador watched him patiently, resting his chin on his paws with his hind-quarters raised and his tail up, in that sinister way that preceded a fart.

'Come on, get off, give us a go,' Cass yelled, chasing after him, snapping at his heels as he pedalled furiously to escape her. Fran stood back in disdain, not begging for anything, not her. Then, when he'd had enough, Humphrey got off and handed it over to Cass with a casual, 'Nothing fancy, you know, not a ten-gear racer, much too boring for you, Cass.' He pushed his hair back, boy-like, then retreated in alarm as Cass seized the handlebars. 'No, hang on, if you're going to swing your leg over in that nightie, I'll look the other way – don't want to see your breakfast.'

'So *crude*,' Fran's lip sneered, her nose quivered. But seeing her sister soaring away towards the roses, she ran after her, the nightie, almost transparent with washing, tied into a knot above her knees. She was remembering the pleasure of those long bike-rides on her grandparents' estate in Ireland, with her mother's picnics strapped to the back in plastic ice-cream containers. She couldn't imagine herself being so *young*, ever.

Cass bored easily, she handed over the bike without fuss and watched Fran trying to get her legs to reach the pedals. Round and round she went, and, as the wind pinned back her hair and made her breasts stand out like plums in cellophane, she could feel the arc lights on her, the movie cameras homing in for a close-up, the zoom lenses catching the full morning of her beauty. She tipped her smile heavenward and basked in the adoration of her fans.

'You're making lines on the bloody grass,' Humphrey snarled. She looked at him, stunned. And came down from the bike with a feeling of having fallen, of having been roughly pushed: how could he be so ... clumsy, so shitty ... how could he not see her as she really was?

He walked away towards the house, thinking that the Bentley hadn't been fun like this, hadn't really been fun at all – even an embarrassment to the kids when the yobs came round. He walked into the conservatory and sat down for a little strum on the piano. Somehow 'Who could ask for anything more?' didn't sound quite up to scratch today.

In the kitchen, his first, hardest and often most brittle child came in. Like a mole hatched uncomfortably from sleep, she groped her way over to the kettle.

'God, you look horrible,' he said, looking at her face, which was like a lump of pastry with an elastic band where her eyes should be.

'Thanks, Dad.' Her voice moved through gravel. 'Living with you has really given me confidence, and a sense of my feminine attractiveness.'

'Just make sure you're actually married before you make a morning appearance, OK? I don't want you on my hands for the rest of your life.'

'OK, Dad.' She fumbled for a tea-bag thankfully, remembering a time when her mother wouldn't tolerate bagged tea or fingered fish. 'No garbage,' she'd say sternly, 'no fruit out of tins, no cake mixes.' Things had gone downhill since then, thank heavens; you could even tease her about it.

'You're wearing my dressing-gown,' Humphrey accused in a petulant voice, pouring the coffee Beth had left at the back of the stove for him.

'I didn't think you'd need it, not last night anyway.' She gave him a look. 'You didn't seem to be here when we got back.'

'Sarky this morning, aren't we? Having a go?' He glowered at her. A splat of boiling coffee attacked his hand and he yelped in pain.

Abi sipped her tea. 'Have a good time last night?' she asked innocently. Humphrey stiffened. Abi sat down at the long table and bent her eyes to the steam from the tea; they began to open slowly like those Chinese paper flowers you put in water. Refreshed, she now asked, knowing only she of his three children might get away with it, 'What's she got then, this fancy woman of yours? What gives her top marks over Ma?' Now that the taboo was broken, now that Fran had opened the subject, she wanted to know.

He was too shocked to be angry. Then he found himself defending himself and that did make him angry. 'It's not a question of that: it's not a competition.'

Abi's eyes turned on him with interest, which made him feel he had to go on, making more of a fool of himself.

'Sylvie hasn't *got* anything over your mother. I care for them both differently, that's all.' Oh, for God's sake, he thought, what *is* this?

'Well, why then?' She drank placidly.

'Why then what?'

'Why bother?'

It was intolerable; one's own flesh and blood! And speaking to him like an equal, like a mate across a bar. And not a shred of bloody respect, of . . . of . . . well, daughterly subservience.

'Your mother tells me you're on the pill,' Humphrey announced with his neat gift for deflection. He was looking at the collection of photographs that Beth had pinned up next to the dresser – and who *were* those little girls in party dresses holding balloons?

'Oh, we're swopping from your sex-life to mine, are we?' Abi said.

'I don't have to discuss my life with you,' he roared. 'I don't have to listen to this shit. Just remember who you are, who you're talking to.'

'I'm not *just* your daughter,' she said, coming to life at last.

'And I'm not *just* your bloody father either,' he yelled back. 'I've got a life of my own too. And I don't splatter it all over this house either, not like you lot.'

'Oh yeh?'

'Oh YEH.'

She knew she had to stop; if she pushed him further he'd get vicious; he was so much better at it than she was. She withdrew. Didn't really care anyway, just felt like a bit of a row this morning.

'Where's Ma anyway?' she asked, after giving him a few minutes to simmer down.

Humphrey was looking out into the garden where Cass and Fran were sprawled on the grass like sheets fallen off a line. He was suddenly quite intimidated by them all – in their egocentric universe that was so happy and hopeless, so innocent and so wise.

'Oh, she's with Mary,' he replied vaguely, 'giving her a bit of moral support with that case of hers.'

'The kid? That battered one?'

'Mn. Mary doesn't like doing her social worker's number alone in the O'Reilly household: she could lose her kneecaps.'

'Ma should go back to nursing,' Abi said, boiling the kettle again.

'Yes, perhaps ...' Humphrey leant against the door. He knew Beth was restless, she might well go back to nursing. Perhaps it hadn't been such a good idea to invest all those years of hers in their business. She was such a good nurse, the Westminster had been very reluctant to let her go. But perhaps so many things.

'I don't remember her when I was little,' Abi said quietly, pouring the water.

'That's because she was always at the hospital,' he said – unfairly, he thought, after he'd said it.

'But she gave it up – nursing I mean – to work with you,' Abi said, injury rising in her voice.

Humphrey gave her one of his small corrosive smiles. Jealousy: it was Abi's worst affliction, she was jealous of anyone who'd stolen her mother from her. Abi walked back to the table, the far end, as far away from him as possible; she seemed to slump down on it.

She thought, I remember that afternoon. I was doing my home-work and she came in. She looked so exhausted. My books and toys were all over the place: she started hurling them about the room and shrieking at me that she hated me, she hated all of us, was sick of everything: the mess, the mess, everywhere. And us, all of us, never leaving her alone for a minute. She picked me off my chair and threw me at the wall. I've never been so terrified in my life than by that serene woman gone mad. I wanted never to say another word, I wanted to dissolve in the wall and never return. I tiptoed for days, I barely left my room, I picked specks off the carpet ...

'Why do you mind that she came to work with me?' Humphrey said, moving towards her in pity. 'Would you have preferred her to stay at the hospital?' He was a little confused. 'When we worked together, at least we could share things out between us, and she could be at home more often – she did a lot of work from home,' he insisted.

'I mind,' Abi said with an exhausted gasp, 'because she was giving up what she wanted for herself. She gave it up – for you. She gave us up too, for you.'

'Rubbish. It was her idea. She was worn out by nursing, pulled all over the place, terrible hours, every second weekend. No time, no rest. Never at home, it was much better after she stopped.'

'It was the only way she could spend time with *you*,' Abi snarled. 'You were like a machine then, she never saw you, we never saw you, *you* were never at home. You worked all the time; we had no family.'

'Oh crap.'

'We never saw you!' she wailed. 'We didn't have parents, we only had her. Only her. And she was getting so tired, doing your bit too – so she stopped nursing. She had no choice. You weren't going to change anything.' She got up and pulled the dressing-gown closer; Humphrey was shocked and silent, watching her. 'She decided, you see,' Abi said spitefully, 'it was a choice between you and us. We lost. You won. You always do. You had her.' She looked at the long tails of her mother's onions and garlic hanging in the corner, the neat jars of jam and chutney, the orderly rows of spices. The mess, the mess, her memory yelled, scaring her all over again.

Humphrey came and put his arm around her. 'Yes, you're right,' he admitted quietly, 'it was like that, sometimes.' He said tenderly, 'But she was a good mother, Abi, a near-perfect mother, don't just remember the bad bits. If you must blame someone – blame me, not her. I didn't help her. You're right: I was absent, quite selfishly doing my own thing, working out my absurd ambitions and pretending it was for you. It was for me, I know that now, then I didn't know any better: work was all that really mattered to me, you and your mother were just a back-up service. But she was a good mother, a fine mother, you must remember that.'

'Oh yes,' Abi squashed the heels of her hands into her eyes, 'she was a good mother, to you, to them, she was a good mother – to everyone but me.'

'Oh Abi.'

He wondered if you could learn, when your children were about to leave home, how to actually be a parent and a father?

Abi's face, desperate, but forgiving, seemed to assure him that he could, that all she wanted was just for him to try.

'Abi,' he said, 'since you've brought it up, and since you're old enough, I'd like to explain to you, or try to, about Sylvie. But please don't ever refer to her as my fancy woman again, and please don't think that I love your mother less because of her – if anything, I love her more. Do you understand that?'

'No.'

'Well then, I'll try and help you.'

Eleven

Humphrey lay full-length with his face pressed into the cut grass and breathed deeply, stretching his arms out. It was good to have the garden back. He felt sorry for it in the winter; it waited and endured through the biting rains of November and the snows of January. No one visited it except him. When early spring came it leapt into life. As soon as his fingers pressed against its roots the slippery buds began to fill; it was as if a magic connection pulsed between him and his garden which brought it to blossom.

He turned over to feel the sun on his face. Even more than in Beth's atmosphere, in his home, even more than that, he was at peace in his garden. The brick walls, secluding on either side, were draped with ivy and clematis. Hollyhocks, with their soft crêpy faces, pushed above the daisies and lilies; hydrangeas and magnolia sprawled among great bushes of rosemary. It looked like a rather wild country garden, with plants that had been allowed simply to ramble, but in fact everything had been carefully trained and pruned to give this feeling of lush, overgrown exuberance.

Beyond the roses at the bottom of the garden, behind a long line of raspberries, lay his real garden, the vegetable garden. He would stand there for hours, marvelling at the life pulsing beneath the soil, roots sucking and swelling, the beans hissing, winding into small green horns, the lettuces putting out soft floppy leaves. Nothing gave him so much pleasure as watching them grow, spraying and trapping intruders, watering the lines late in the evening.

He remembered, as a small boy, the pleasure of lying on top of a greenhouse in the next-door garden, pushing his fingers into the streaks of dark putty, staring down at the carnations and cyclamen, the toppled pots, the bulbs with roots waving in the air. It was like a jungle down there as the tomato plants writhed among the lilies and the sun blasted on to his back. The pure joy of watching all that growth. And then the furious shout from his mother's face over the fence – 'Get off there, you little devil.' Crashing down to earth with its slug's view, the wind quite gone from his wings. That was how childhood came back to him – piercingly clear, but defeating.

Now, the closest he got to that heaven on top of the glasshouse was when he climbed his apple tree and lay along a straight branch that gave an entire view of the garden. He felt safe there; all his toughest problems became solvable up that tree. As a boy he'd hidden from trouble up trees, and it was doing that, at twelve, that had made him discover the unique pleasure of being up a tree: swaying to its gentle rhythms, hooking your thighs around its curves and lying back with the leaves pushed into your face, pouring shade all over you. Hiding from the world until you chose to enter it again. He still did it. And this tree was a particular shelter for him; when he was in it no one bothered him: it was a sacred place they all respected.

When he sat up, he saw Beth walk out of the house and across the grass towards him, the bright scarlet of her skirt reminding him of the wonderful gypsy skirts she used to wear. She was a dramatic woman to look at: very tall, shapely, her head always held still, her expression serene. He called that particular look her smile of the Lady of the Big House; she must have learned it from her mother. He loved that smile, he wanted to doff his cap and bow to her.

But there was something a little sad about her now. Watching her from a distance, he saw it quite clearly. It was since her mother's death some months ago; her perfect balance was lost, she looked at herself from another angle and was a little frightened. As now, walking towards him, he saw her face tremble with some hesitance. He ran up to her and hugged her hard; but all he could feel in his heart was the emotion he had felt wrestling with Sylvie in the long grass by the river. It had felt like the most erotic moment of his life.

He walked with Beth towards the vegetable garden, the sides of their bodies very close. Later, he would begin to transplant the lettuces with those long, expert fingers of his, one quick movement, then the plant plunged into the peat and pressed firmly there. Everything bloomed for Humphrey. There was in this garden, as in himself, no soft spot, no edge of decay waiting to spread. All was prime, healthy and fertile; no chance for death to get a foothold here.

Abi watched from the window as Humphrey took Beth's hand and raised it to his lips. Seeing them together, their heads close, canted to catch one another's words, she had a wish to shatter their perfect poise, to topple her mother's power over her father as he looked towards her and laughed, with that idiotic overflow of love that she herself could never feel, for anything, for anyone.

Twelve

Back in his office on a sunny morning, Humphrey swivelled his chair round to position ten, leaned back and surveyed the beautiful white expanse of his ceiling. And was reminded immediately of Sylvie. He'd missed her – two days without her was quite unbearable. He reached for the phone and got her number, but she was out. Working. Sylvie was always working; she was worse than he'd ever been, but when he tried to give her the benefit of his experience, she looked at him in that patient, bored way and he stopped. She'd find out.

Sylvie was a builder. He'd met her when his office ceiling had collapsed. He'd felt, with that tendency of his to overreaction, that no one could put it together again. It was such a beautiful ceiling, with a delicate cornice running around the edges – and then, one afternoon, down it came. Could have killed him if he'd been sitting at his desk.

'It's all those stupid plants on the balcony above,' she said, 'that mud and water seeping through for years. What do you expect from a Victorian building – that it'd never get dry rot?' Why hadn't he got someone in to look at it years ago? Yes, she imagined there had been leaks, and cracks. 'Get that lot off, all of them,' she ordered, 'clear the entire balcony.'

'I can't live without my plants,' he said, hating anyone to tell him what to do, most of all a scrappy little woman in overalls. He was in his pyjamas at the time, having spent the night at the office (not something he did often these days, of course, just some work that had to be finished, and no point going home at five a.m.). It was just as well that he was there very early on this occasion because builders did turn up at ungodly hours. Before a chap had time to get his clothes on. And she wouldn't have hung around for anyone, that one.

'Get them off,' she repeated, 'then we can open it up and look at the damage.' It made him feel rather queasy.

'Going to cost you quite a bit,' she added brightly, hands in pockets, head tilted upwards. He'd felt like an anxious patient in the presence of a ruthless surgeon.

She'd really taken the place apart – crawling with dry rot – look, see how the wood crumbled in your fingers; how could he have let it get so bad? She was quite indignant.

It had broken his heart to see it hacked off, the ceiling like an amputated body with half its torso missing. But Sylvie had put it together again with great expertise. She'd taken a mould of the intricate cornice, come back and matched it all up with her own hands. It was beautifully done, a perfect job; and he'd never seen such efficient, well-trained labourers: no slopped tea, no radios blaring, no cigarette butts. Immaculate. Everything restored the way it was before, with the exception of the carpet which had to be replaced.

God, she was marvellous. And she smelt so wonderful: of plaster and putty, cement and emulsion. She was so offhand with him, and yet, at the same time, seemed so raunchy. The first day she'd been in his office his entire body had been on edge with horny adolescent tension.

Humphrey saw George strutting down the corridor, swivelled round and yelled at him to come in. George came and sat where he was gestured to sit. Humphrey, high in that absurd chair, George thought, looked so healthy it made you sick: there he was, bronzed and happy, always so irritatingly happy. On a Monday morning too. When he, George, had spent the entire weekend listening to the exhortations of his wife, Marcia: George, why don't you assert yourself? Why do you let him manipulate you all the time? George, we can't go on like this! What did he *agree*, George? Oh, I see – nothing. Well, that's terrific. Why can't you ever insist on anything? Why must you always be such a milk sop? He should be grateful, George, for the work you've done, he should demonstrate it. Oh, stop moving *about*, George.

'George, old fellow,' Humphrey murmured benignly, 'couple of things I'd like to talk to you about. Have a good weekend, by the way? How's Marcia?'

'Fine.'

'Good. Now, I thought we could go through the budgets today. Do the housekeeping. OK with you?'

'Harry's not in today.'

'Harry never comes in on Mondays. No, it's all right, Colin can handle this. I just want a run-through with the figures.'

'We've just had a board meeting about budgets.' What was the sly bastard up to now; he had that smirky look on his face again.

'Yes, I know we have, George.' Humphrey moved his hands impatiently. 'There's no problem, I just need to look at the figures. I had a thought over the weekend.'

George looked cautious, then downright nervous. He'd spent the weekend hatching a plan of his own. A brilliant plan: a whole new base for development, something they'd thought of and discarded as being too ambitious, but which he, George, had worked out. It could work all right, he'd solved all the problems: an expansion into the consumer market without damaging their exclusive image with the caterers. Need to try it out in a test area first, of course, but there was no reason why it should fail in selected outlets, carefully handled. Nothing downmarket, just a few key outlets and a carefully selected range. The money was there, all that was needed was a complete market breakdown, research, a clever advertising campaign. It was something he'd been waiting for, an opportunity that he could handle, one that needed his kind of experience.

But Humphrey was saying, 'I thought we could invest some of the profit from last year.'

'In what?' He tried not to sound snappy; he hoped Humphrey hadn't got there before him.

'In woodland,' Humphrey said with a smile, 'buy up some forests in Gloucestershire – idea appeals to me.'

'*Woodland?*' George's face was a spluttering mixture of horror and astonishment.

'George.' Humphrey leaned forward with that patient look he reserved for morons. 'There are ways of losing one's profits cunningly, of using one's capital to advantage. Five hundred acres of beech, say, mature beech, can be harvested for a huge profit in a few years, meanwhile our ...'

'Humphrey, look, I mean, I know you're keen on that sort of thing, but really, it's hardly the sort of thing' – he readjusted his glasses – 'I mean, it seems a bit crackers to me. The money should go straight back into broadening our base, as it always has. Right now we've got more to spend than ever before. The time's right. We've talked about this, Humphrey, you did agree ...'

Jesus, Humphrey thought, old George was actually getting

excited, was waving his short arms around, was fighting back; little bugger must be up to something, got some scheme up his sleeve, wants to carve out a niche for himself somewhere, break into the consumer market I shouldn't wonder.

'You think we should expand, do you, enlarge our high-class image by breaking into Tesco?'

'Oh for God's sake, you know that's not what I mean!'

'But,' Humphrey continued calmly, 'do we really want to do that?'

'Want to? What do you mean *want* to?' George was on the edge of the Chesterfield, he had rumpled up the rug at his feet in his perplexity and now tried to straighten it, his head down, pulling with his hands.

Men with those sorts of head, Humphrey thought, always go bald quickly. He looked down in amusement, and I bet he'll be one of those who parts his hair by his ear and spreads the last three hairs over his dome, one by one.

'I mean,' Humphrey said, with that slow drawl of his, once George had surfaced again, 'do we really want to shove even more of our ghastly frozen fodder down people's throats? They'll eat anything, you know, anything that requires no effort, anything you tell them they ought to eat. You should look round a New York supermarket sometime. One of these days we'll be freezing a boiled egg. We'll take every ounce of ingenuity and effort out of people's cooking habits. They'll be peeling off slices of smoked salmon, chiselling out Boeuf en daube, hacking off lumps of stew and mashed potato.' He got more carried away with his eloquence, it was irresistible to him: 'For God's sake, think of Pancake Day – instead of all that marvellous flipping of pancakes, we'll be having them thawing in puddles all over the kitchen. The world's going to hell, George, and we're helping it. It's almost immoral to encourage such idleness, to destroy, little by little, the art of cooking as we've been doing with such success in hotels and restaurants up and down the country.'

'But, Humphrey ...'

'Wait, George, I haven't finished. Look how well we've done, that's what bothers me. Those idiots paying thirty pounds a head for some meal that's been in cold storage for months, that's been churned out in some factory – never seen a wooden spoon or an individual stir.'

'But this is our *business*, Humphrey, this is what you and Beth have worked yourselves to death for ...'

'Yes, and it makes me sick. It's a con-trick.' His head butted forward aggressively. 'I'm sick of it, George. I want to do something else. Surely a man's entitled to change his mind, to begin something else?' He leaned back.

'That's all right for you, Humphrey,' George spat, a little pellet of saliva flying in Humphrey's direction. 'You've made it, you can afford to be bored and have these daft ideas about buying up half of Gloucestershire. But ...' and he looked very determined and spoke like a man defending his last piece of bread, 'there's much more mileage in this business, you've just admitted as much – vast opportunities for expansion. We can't stop just because you've discovered you have some scruples about selling frozen food.'

'Oh yes,' Humphrey agreed sagely, 'I've no doubt that we can put butchers out of business, and I expect by the year 2000 nobody will know what an oven looked like, we'll just have heating-up machines, warm-overs, and no one will recognize an uncooked piece of fish or an undiced vegetable.'

'Humphrey, for heaven's sake, let's not go over the top ...' What had got into the man these days? Disillusion was downright dangerous in a cynic like Humphrey. He shifted his ground. 'Humphrey, I really don't know what Harry's going to make of all this forest business.'

'Fuck Harry, he's only a consultant.'

'He's only the best financial head in the business, Humphrey,' George said with a warning note.

'He's past it.' But Humphrey stopped to consider something; this was a new tack from old George, pally-pally with Harry, whom he'd always felt intimidated by. Come to think of it, they'd had lunch the other day. Better get Beth to check it out.

'And what about Colin?' George went on relentlessly. 'This is not a day to put something like that to Colin.'

'It's *never* the right day to put anything to Colin. What's different about today? Has he murdered his wife?'

George frowned with disapproval and Humphrey snarled at him: 'Look, I am not going to be sympathetic about Colin. His life's one long catastrophe. Listening to him's like reading reports from a disaster area.'

'Well, he's not in today till later anyway. His kid's sick.'

'Of course his kid's sick,' Humphrey said tenderly. 'One kid's always sick and the other's always autistic. His wife has back failure and can't look after anyone and he's about to have his third operation for piles. He's developing arthritis so that it can take him more than a month to do the bloody expenses and now you tell me that today's not the day to put something to him. I mean, how much more bloody can life get for a man? I daren't ask him how he is any more. I think he'd die if something good happened to him.'

'You have to feel sorry for people like Colin,' George said piously.

'I *do* feel sorry for Colin, so sorry that I think it'd be a kindness to put him out of his misery. We'd all appreciate it. Even old Col would appreciate it.'

Humphrey's private phone rang. Humphrey looked at George, but George didn't budge. Humphrey picked up the phone and said hullo.

A voice on the other end of the line said brightly, 'Hey, when're you coming over for a hand-job?'

'Um ... well, let me think now ...'

'A gobble maybe? What can I tempt you with? I'm not working, Humphrey, my little darling, I'm a free woman,' Sylvie crooned lovingly.

'Well, it's er, just a bit difficult right now. George ... ?'

George didn't appear to have heard, so engrossed was he in a trade magazine on Humphrey's table.

'Oh *George* is there, is he? How about a threesome with George then?'

'I'll ring you back in a minute shall I?'

'You can't, I'm at the hotel – just pulled off a marvellous deal, got my estimate accepted just now.'

'Oh, that's wonderful. Congratulations.' He beamed down the phone, then turned back to the implacable George.

'George?' Humphrey ground through his teeth.

No response.

'George,' he bellowed, 'can you fuck off for a minute? I'm trying to take a personal call here, George. Personal, George. O K?'

'Oh, of course.' A most hideous suggestive smile crept across George's less-than-average features. Such were the small pleasures of revenge.

'Give Beth my love, won't you?' he sneered.

'Fuck off, George, all right?' Humphrey's face, crouched above the phone, took a decidedly nasty turn.

'Just fucking off, Humphrey,' George sang, breezing out of the office, feeling a lot happier than when he'd come in.

Humphrey turned back to the phone. 'Now, my little petal, what was it you were offering me?'

Thirteen

Humphrey was in Sylvie's kitchen, cooking, waiting for her to come home; waiting impatiently because she was, as usual, late. The kitchen, like the rest of Sylvie's flat, was extremely bare. Her flat was like a warehouse. She'd pulled down most of the partition walls and returned the few that remained to their original, unpainted brickwork. There were no pictures and only a few books. The floorboards were shiny; at the windows were red blinds, and, close together, two red Conran sofas. Humphrey had bought her a stereo, but she didn't play it much. The only exception to this spartan habitat was the bathroom, which, with its hanging plants and ferns, resembled a small corner of stolen jungle. Soon the jungle would overtake the bathroom; already the creeper at the window had blocked out the light so that it felt like a green cave, and the ferns and bamboo plants were clambering all over each other in their quest for some brightness. When it looked really overgrown and out of hand he'd be happy with it.

As he chopped onions, a knife clenched between his teeth to stop him crying, he wished Sylvie didn't work so hard. He was jealous of her work, it took up so much of her time and interest. He'd never have believed he could love a woman who couldn't cook; Sylvie not only couldn't cook, she didn't have anything to cook with. She liked fish and chips and Chinese takeaways, huge Greek meals washed down with strong ouzo, litres of rough Italian wine accompanied by big bowls of pasta. She drank as much as he did.

As he stood by her kitchen window, looking out over the road, he felt almost anxious about her. She spent her day with those rough working men; she ruled over them like a tyrant, though they seemed to love it. She was not large as women went, but she seemed to inspire a lot of respect because of her dedication and sheer hard work. With her everything had to be one hundred per cent: she remembered too well the people who said she wouldn't make it as a builder. She felt she could never afford to fail, and if anyone around her did, they paid heavily for it.

She'd not learned it from her dad, this striving. He had been a carpenter, who, after her mother died, dragged her around with him on all his jobs. While other children were on holiday, Sylvie had spent her days in freezing houses, banging her legs together, stuffing her hands into her armpits, pacing up and down, watching him work, talking to the other men and fuming silently that life could be so shabby, so empty, so *cold*. She developed chilblains, a constant cold, an ability to be totally at ease with working men and a furious ambition to achieve whatever she set her mind to. She was going to have a life completely her own: she was going to make it, force it if need be out of bricks and mortar and hard work. She would grab it from anyone who threatened to take it from her. And she wanted no one to defer to her because she was a woman: she started from the bottom, loading the vans, humping timber about, learning how to lay bricks and taking all the taunts and sneers in her stride.

Thinking of her, Humphrey was filled with a sense of recognition; he and Sylvie were very much alike. She was dangerous and unpredictable, livid a lot of the time. If he'd been born a woman, he'd be like Sylvie: driven by a need to swipe out at everything and everyone who stood in her way. She felt happy, capable and strong only when she was working with tools, with unmalleable materials, chipping against absurd deadlines and pressures, bullying everyone to do it her way, to do it better, to get it right.

She was tough as an old boot, and then, sometimes, so very frail. He loved the contradictions: she was like a wave breaking hard and loud on shingle but ending with a sob. She was a woman impossible to get used to, get bored with. She suited him quite perfectly.

Humphrey hummed to himself, liking to cook, liking best to cook for Sylvie, to look after her at the end of the day when she was tired. He wished he could have been like this for Beth, when she'd needed him in the past, he wished he'd known better then. He was cooking Sylvie liver and bacon, to build her up, with lots of almost burnt onions.

He remembered how, when he'd first known her, she'd turn up at his office in her orange Volkswagen van, and say, 'Come on, I'm taking you for a ride to the country, leave all that rubbish, it can wait, I've taken the afternoon off.' He went like a shot. It was the beginning of his boredom with work – frozen food just couldn't compete with Sylvie's warm flesh. When they were out of London, she'd stop, take off her jeans and chuck them in the back, driving along like that, the muscles in her strong brown legs flexing and flowing under his hands, the bottles of chilled wine clicking together beneath the red blanket in the back. They'd lie in the hot grass by the river all afternoon, kissing a lot, in a half-drowsy state, and then she would bash him on the arm and say blithely, 'You realize that this is only physical, don't you?'

'Of course, same with me. Who could be interested in such a mean little woman if it wasn't for her tits?'

Now, he could hear her key in the lock. She shouted his name as she came in, throwing a satchel of work on the floor. Then sneezed loudly from the plasterdust that was sprinkled in her hair and made streaks down her overalls.

'I must have a bath,' she said, throwing herself at him with some force. 'How are you, my little darling, and what have you made me for my dinner?'

He stood back from her and brushed the dust off his shirt. 'Kissing you is like kissing a navvy, you're disgusting.'

'Yep, I know, I'm going.' She turned back and winked at him. 'So you wouldn't take me up on my offer this afternoon, huh?'

'I will as soon as you're clean.'

'Forget it,' she said. 'Always grab the moment in case it doesn't return.' As she slipped out of reach, she said jauntily, 'Don't worry, I'll really give you a seeing-to later.' She smiled at him, then strode across the floor towards the bathroom, unbuckling the straps of her dungarees as she went and pulling her T-shirt up over her head.

As she lay back in the hot bath, she felt very happy: a big contract to do all the inside work on an old, grand hotel (probably one selling Humphrey's deceptive little dinners). It would require care and craft; it was something she could do better than any other builder. They were using Szerelmey for the outside restoration, but she'd bagged the rest, even the preservation work. She was trying to work out in her head just how much she was likely to make on the deal when Humphrey came in. He brushed the tendrils of a plant off the stool and sat down, handing her a large gin and tonic and drinking to her. Her success gave him the greatest pleasure, it was like revisiting his own early coups.

'Soon you'll be richer than me,' he said contentedly. 'Then I can retire and you can support me.'

'You'd die if you retired,' she said, sipping her drink.

'Oh no, not now,' he said serenely, feeling that it was almost as if her ambition had freed him of his own. He was totally relaxed with her. He felt he had nothing to prove.

So he sat back as she told him the detail of her day, how she had beaten off the competition: a lower tender, a guaranteed deadline and her exact plans for executing the job. He gave her a scrap or two of advice or caution, but she knew exactly what she was about. Then she went quiet for a while and he watched her face as she lay in the bath, still struggling with figures and deadlines.

'OK,' she said, 'that's it, now I can put it out of my mind and concentrate only on you. I shan't think about work any more.' And she wouldn't. He admired her this capacity to shut work out and wished he'd had it himself years ago.

She splashed water on her face and rubbed her skin hard. She never wore make-up. Her skin was pale and fragile, her mouth was a brownish colour. It was a full mouth with an odd dent on one side of her top lip where something had struck her long ago. She had thick eyebrows that had never been shaped or plucked and black eyelashes that always looked wet and spiky. Her hair was long and dark brown, yanked on top of her head so that the curls spilled down the back and front of her head and into her eyes. Her hands and feet were small, every part of her body was delicately formed: her shoulders had strong sloping planes, her hips were straight and hard. He looked at her body with pleasure, trying not to stare at her breasts. It was difficult, because Sylvie, for all the boyishness of her body, had these big beautiful breasts. When he admired them she became irrationally angry.

'I hate them, I always have, not a day passes when I don't hate them – I've even thought of having them off.'

'But they're gorgeous, Sylvie. People would pay a lot of money to have a pair like that.'

He found it very hard to understand the extent of her rage: 'OK, Humphrey, you try going out with a huge pair of knockers before you give me all that crap. Just try it. All my life men have been pushing up against me, as if they had a perfect right – in trains, in the street, anywhere. It's foul. What the hell are you grinning at?' She wanted to murder him.

He looked abashed. 'It's just that I can't think of your tits like that. I love them.' He was laughing and her eyes went mean with anger.

'Listen. Say you walked around and your balls were sort of on the outside, like tits, and women kept coming up to you and leering and grabbing at them and pressing up against you – you'd hate it, wouldn't you? Wouldn't you?'

He was smiling a little, trying to work out whether he'd hate it that much.

'Well, you bloody would! It's such a liberty. I feel as if people, or men rather, think that because I've got big boobs I'm a tart. That's the way they behave. Just like some people think that if you're a builder and work with your hands, you can't converse in words of more than one syllable. It's so unfair to be rated by your body. I didn't grow these things, I don't feed and water them every day, I just have them.'

'Oh Sylvie, couldn't you just like them a bit? Take some pride in them? They really are the most beautiful boobs I've ever seen.'

'Thanks,' she spat.

'Sylvie,' he said quietly, 'I've been thinking, for a while now – why don't we have a child?'

'Well,' she grinned, '*we* is a nice word, but it's actually my body that'll be used.'

'Well, wouldn't you like one?'

'Hell, no.'

'Why not?' He cupped the frothy water in his hand and poured it over her.

'Too busy.' She sat up and leaned forward so that most of her breasts were submerged in foam. 'Anyway, one abortion was enough.'

'I didn't know that.' He looked startled and stopped scrubbing her back; it seemed extraordinary that there was something about her that he didn't know.

She said tautly, 'Why should you? Talking about your sexual past is stupid, nobody wants to know.' She lay back and drew the bubbles over her like a blanket.

'I'd like you to get pregnant,' he persisted, taking up his watering again, completely at home with her spikiness, enjoying her bad temper.

'Would you?' She closed her eyes, her chin trembled imperceptibly.

'Hm, I might even look after the little bleeder, be a house-father.'

She roared with laughter. 'Yes, I can just see that. You bitch about your kids the whole time – they probably didn't recognize you when they were little and now you want to start all over again. But,' she glared at him sweetly, 'not with me, my little darling.'

'I always liked babies,' he said. 'They're nice when they're small enough to sit on your hand, they're still nice when they smell of pencils and plasticine; it's only later that they get revolting.'

'Go to hell, Humphrey,' she said amiably.

'OK, you little jerk, I'll just have to find someone else. Now get out of that bath, my ferns don't like all this steam, come on, move it.'

Sylvie stepped out of the old green tub and pulled a towel around her.

'Come here and give me a kiss, Humphrey, you're not such a bad old stick,' she ordered softly, wrapping him into her towel. And feeling her warmth, those boobs, the idea of a child seemed very good to him.

'Anyway,' she said, 'what made you suddenly talk about babies?'

'Oh, no reason.' But he thought – now he tried to figure out these things because if he didn't she'd make him – that death had begun to sprout its weeds on the spruce surface of his life, cracking it up. Beth's mother – a formidable and exacting old lady, but what life there had been in her: quite dead now. He'd refused to go to her funeral; he never went to funerals. And then, a friend of his snatched away at only forty-five – it was appalling, just snuffed out between dinner and bedtime. He felt it in himself, this seed of death. But he was going to do nothing to encourage it. He would dig himself so firmly into life that nothing could uproot him.

'A son perhaps?' he said lightly. 'Perhaps that's why.' He kissed her arm.

'Have it yourself,' she said brightly. 'Now where's my dinner? I'm starving.'

Fourteen

Sylvie, in her office in Seymour Place, sorted through neat piles of paper in front of her. At home she was messy and hurled her things around; at her office she was meticulous and could find anything she needed in seconds. Her walnut desk had been made by her father; it was sturdy and simple with a wonderful patina. It was all she'd wanted of his when he died.

Now she was waiting for her sister. Hilda came often, she lived nearby in a small flat in George Street. As children they'd been separated when their mother died. Hilda, the younger, had gone to Aunt Moira, Sylvie was brought up by her dad, an uncommunicative man who'd thought Hilda would settle better in her new home if they didn't see too much of her. Sylvie and Hilda had only got to know each other again properly after they'd left school. That time of rediscovery cemented them together as years of uninterrupted sisterhood could never have done.

Sylvie always felt that when her mother died life stopped like a clock and nothing was ever right again. Inside she hadn't changed, but the world outside had shifted utterly. Sylvie, the tough, unconventional one, had become oddly dependent on her younger sister. Hilda was gentle, with a pale, almost austere character perfectly reflected by the delicate sweetness of her face. She was married and had two little boys who adored their aunt. Sylvie pushed her papers aside and looked up and smiled at her sister.

'It always makes me proud,' Hilda said, as she came in and sat down, smoothing her skirt beneath her, 'to see the sign out there, in big letters: Sylvie Brown, Builder. How proud Dad would have been of you. How hard you've worked, you must be proud too.'

'I'm not really used to it,' Sylvie said, putting her papers into the top drawer. 'I suppose I never really thought I'd actually be able to start a business of my own, and have it work – and bring me in so much money!' She leaned back in her chair. 'Why didn't you bring the boys?' she asked.

'Oh, I was glad to get shot of them for the morning, they're playing next door.'

Sylvie hesitated and then said quietly, 'Do you think I should have a baby, Hilda?'

'Well, I don't know. When you were little you said you'd never have one. I can still see you laughing your head off because I was playing with a doll – you gave all yours to me.

'Is Humphrey going to leave her? Beth, I mean, will he, do you think?' She worried about Sylvie: wished she would settle down, marry, be safe.

'I hope not,' Sylvie said, tipping her chair right back so it balanced on two legs.

Hilda's brow puckered as it had done since she was ten. 'Oh, you don't mean that, Sylvie.'

'Oh, I do,' Sylvie said softly, carelessly. 'I don't want him to leave her. I don't want him all to myself. I'm not cut out for that, you know. And he likes things the way they are, too, we both do.'

'Isn't that a bit selfish of him?' She liked Humphrey, had often met him, but at heart she didn't approve of the set-up.

'Selfish of him? To whom?'

'Both of you. Perhaps more to her. You don't mind. She must hate it. I would.'

'Would you?' Sylvie said, curious.

'I couldn't bear it at all.'

'Hm. Well, Beth understands, so I'm told. And I wouldn't want to break up anything, even if I could. This way everyone is happy, no one is deprived.' She insisted softly, 'No one is suffering, Hilda.'

'Are *you* happy, Sylvie?'

'I'm as happy as it's possible to be,' Sylvie said with a guileless smile. 'No one could be happier than we are, really, I mean it. It might seem odd to you, but really it suits me, it gives me more than I ever thought I'd have with anyone. Humphrey is everything I want. You see,' her black brows came closer together, 'he doesn't love Beth in the same way as he does me. He's bound to her, connected to her by all sorts of ties and memories, I understand that and it doesn't bother me. She doesn't want what I have – his passion – anything like that, she doesn't want. I mean, if she did, she'd want to kill me, wouldn't she?'

'And you?' Hilda asked quietly, twisting her hands in her odd way.

'Kill her?'

'No ... I meant ... good heavens, of course not, Sylvie!' She laughed, a little nervously.

'I *have* Humphrey,' Sylvie said firmly, 'I know I have him.' He had said so: You will always be first and best to me, Sylvie, I'm always here for you.

'But how can you have him if someone else does too?' She had said these things before; she felt it was her duty to go on saying them.

'I've been through that, through everything,' Sylvie said patiently, 'there's nothing you can tell me I don't know. I have thought this through very carefully, Humphrey and I talk about it a lot, there's no lies, no pretence, it's all quite straightforward.'

'I don't believe that people can be "civilized" when their feelings are involved, I don't believe there's love without jealousy.'

'I know, I've felt that. But there are compromises in everything, any relationship, nothing is perfect, Hilda.'

'No,' she smiled at her sister, 'I just don't want you hurt.'

'Hurt is hurt, it doesn't improve your soul, it just hurts, you can't avoid it. Don't worry about me.' She stood up. 'Lunchtime, come on.'

Walking down the street to the Italian place with Hilda, Sylvie felt quite unruffled by the conversation. Beth and Humphrey: oh, she had watched them together – walking down a street, going to the pictures, walking through their front door. There was a phone box close to their house. She had watched them, she had checked. At weekends, when he left her, she had watched the two of them piling into the car with those massive kids and dogs. She knew how it was.

She had followed them to Oxford one weekend; had stayed in the same hotel and took the room next door (looked a little wonder in an auburn wig with a friend posing as her husband!). She'd watched them at breakfast and dinner; at night she'd listened with her ear to the wall. Love was shameless. Theirs was quiet. Yes, Beth had a kind of beauty, refined, elegant, but he was tired, distracted, hardly spoke to her. When they were driving down that country road, Humphrey had stopped the car for a moment and Beth got out. Sylvie considered killing her – running her down, she was close to the road. But there was no need to, she was so certain that Beth no longer had Humphrey. There was no need to at all.

Fifteen

Sylvie didn't for a minute believe in love at first sight; she wasn't even sure that she believed in love. But there he was – Humphrey – rushing up to her door at the small hours of the morning, panting, covered in sweat, his hair flying, his eyes glowing like a blackbird's, his pockets crammed with apples.

'I had to come, Sylvie,' he panted. Then shoved an apple towards her. 'Here, I brought you an apple from my tree.'

'Thank you,' she said, bewildered, and stood back.

'Oh, Sylvie,' he was breathless with running, with love, 'I had to come, I've been trying not to, I must've run about ten miles tonight.'

'You look a complete burk,' she said sternly, looking him over the way she had first surveyed his ceiling. '*What* is the matter with you, what do you want?' He was a mystery to her, she'd met him two days ago.

'Oh, don't say that.' He was crestfallen, but not for long. 'Can I come in?'

She yanked him in off the doorstep, almost angrily, decidedly irritated. There was something so athletic about her he felt she might fling him over her shoulder.

When he was inside, she said, not offering him a seat, 'What is it? Why are you here?' She gave him not a shred of reassurance; she stood there with her hands on her flat hips and glared at him.

'Have you forgotten last night?' he growled.

'What about it?'

'For Christ's sake, you rock-hearted little idiot, we had dinner together, don't you remember?'

'I remember. What of it?'

He grabbed her by the shoulders. 'Last night you loved me.'

She laughed. 'So I did. That doesn't mean you come leaping in here like a loon. I hardly know you.'

'Think I'm trying to seduce you, do you? Leave your heart out for the milkman?'

'Something like that.'

'Well, you're quite right, I am. Now, seriously' – he led her into the barn of her own home and sat her down on her sofa – 'I had to come and see you. Last night you said you weren't interested because I was living with someone else. So tonight I told her about you.'

'You did what? Who the hell do you think you are, taking things into your own hands like that?'

'I had to tell her.' And now he seemed to be appealing for her help, walking up and down, banging his hands together. She was appalled – that he plunged in like that with truths that barely existed – and yet she was mesmerized too, watching him as he wiped the sweat off his brow and rubbed his hand down the front of his leg. He seemed so angular, inside and out, like a man hoarding his youth, fighting off maturity at all costs. It was impossible for her to take him seriously but just as impossible to doubt his sincerity.

'Well, what did you say to her?' she finally asked.

'Oh, I just said' – and here he sat down, knees out, hands flat on knees – '"Beth," I said, "I'm going to see a woman, I have to."' He grinned. 'I was feeling so tortured and idiotic, I was quite embarrassed.'

'And she, what did she say?' She was fascinated, but cynical.

He walked off into her kitchen and ducked his head under the cold tap, letting the water pour over him. He suddenly felt a bit shocked: he hardly knew Sylvie. And yet he felt he knew her intuitively, in every sense, even sexually. He'd always felt love sprang directly from lust. And love had sprung him – no question of that.

'Well, what did she say?' Sylvie repeated, having walked up behind him. She watched him whap his hair back and thought what an odd nose he had: bony, individual, tweaked at the end.

'"Oh," she said, "if you have to, Humphrey, well, you have to."' He frowned a little. 'She's a remarkable woman, you see, she said that in a very precise way, as if she was finishing a bit of sewing and stopped, and bit the end of her thread. That's how she said it, d'you see?'

'No.'

'You're going to be difficult for me,' he said amiably, 'quite a pain in the neck.'

She went away to fetch him a towel. And stood in the bathroom for a while, flexing and unflexing her fingers.

Humphrey stood by the window, his wet hair dripping water into his eyes. The scene with Beth repeated, leaving him with a sense of shame and betrayal.

'If you have to, Humphrey, you have to.' He'd been a mess, in total confusion and had grabbed her hands, 'I had to tell you now, at the beginning, what's the point of hiding it, when you'll know, and when I know, already, how important it is.'

She didn't flinch. 'I'm glad you told me, I can't stand lies.' She had always believed one could survive the most awful knowledge if one had not been deceived.

Her courage shamed him further. 'It's just that I know how it will be, I don't need to wait and see and lie to you while I'm checking it out. I just know ... one does.'

'Oh yes,' she said coolly, with her civilized smile, 'one knows, one knows because one has been there before.'

He was lucky because he could misunderstand her and snap, 'What do you mean, we've not been here before, this has never happened before.'

'Not to me,' she replied quietly, 'but it happened to your wife, when you met me.'

'Is it so terrible, Beth?' he demanded, 'that someone can love more than one person, in a lifetime? Is it too much? Are we only allowed one?'

She hated him then, he knew it. He was asking for her understanding and she was refusing him.

'I remember my father saying,' she said, remotely, 'something like: women never understood that to a man any woman could be exciting, arousing, whether she was plain or middle-aged or dumpy. There was some indefinable aspect of any women, all women, that was sexually desirable to a man. I remember him saying that.'

'I'm not talking about sex, Beth.'

'What are you talking about, Humphrey?' Her grave brown eyes withered the insult he had felt at her words, the insult to him, to them both.

'Love.'

'Love!' She rose in agitation. 'Love. I never thought it was easy. I've always felt it was like farming, something you have to keep at every day, something you have to keep going over again and again, reworking the soil, nourishing it, taking no holidays, setting little store by the triumphs and failures because it was all part of an ongoing purpose. I'm a good retainer, Humphrey, I can keep love, hold it, keep it going. You slough it off, you slough me off.' She was furious with him. 'Your selfishness, this stupid boyishness, it will disable you, time and again,' she snapped. And then stopped.

'Don't fight with me, Beth.' He took back her hands and she sat down again. 'Nothing will change between us, how could it? You're my home, Beth, always have been, before I met you I was homeless, I knew nothing, I couldn't exist without you.'

He wondered if he loved her so tenderly at that moment because he had hurt her so badly.

'Go on,' she said, 'just go.' There was no tremble in her lip, her back was straight and he felt that had she been sewing, she would have taken it up again calmly.

He stood outside in the garden by his tree, deeply upset. He loved Beth with quite frightening intensity. He remembered her how she used to be, as a young woman, when he had wanted her with the same absurd urgency that he was feeling now – anywhere, anytime, but more. Always more. Remembering how they were then, he could cry for both of them, he missed them both desperately, loved them both desperately, for the way they'd been then.

'Sylvie?' he called, turning from the window.

'Yes.' She stood just behind him. He pushed his hands hard over her face, as if trying to erase her features.

'Sylvie?'

'Yes,' she repeated, her expression wide and anxious.

'Oh, nothing, nothing.' He laughed at himself.

For a moment he'd felt stranded, as if some solid security had left him, as if he had, recklessly and ruthlessly, tossed away the compass which for years had kept him straight and true – and that without it he would be quite lost.

Sixteen

Beth, when she first found the letter in Humphrey's pocket, dropped it, as if it were on fire. But it was too late, already the words were embedded in her mind: 'Today it's exactly a month since I met you. Do you remember how we . . .' She dropped it, knowing if she hesitated she'd read it all, satisfy and torture herself completely. So she picked it up, crushed it, uncrushed it and tore it to shreds. She tossed it down the lavatory, and after each violent flush, little laughing fragments remained stuck to the bowl. She didn't stop until the last shred had gone. But the words remained.

From the moment she read that letter, it became real. Their relationship had entered her home, lain in his pocket, her hand. It was awake and it was here. It had to be faced full on. It was a relief. But from that moment a pain started, a weight that pulled at her and never entirely left.

So she set herself against herself in battle. She made her days turn smoothly, for the children's, for Humphrey's sake. And because she understood Humphrey as she understood herself, and loved him better, she did not resent him for this. Understanding it made it tolerable, and yet, that way, one had to extend the understanding to its full length – that made it quite intolerable. It was like being given a view through a keyhole and forcing yourself to watch the privacies being enacted behind it to the very end.

But, oh, he was so vivid, she thought, so generous in his under-standing of how she must feel. He did not discuss it, but he made it clear to her that nothing between them had changed – that she was as cherished, as much his beloved as she had always been. She was quick to believe it. She began to feel that in fact she had lost nothing of him, that perhaps, even, there were benefits to be gained from the new knowledge that he was gaining about himself elsewhere. That he could see her more clearly, love her more tenderly, by knowing another woman intimately. As for the other woman, well, she'd have nothing to do with that – it was the effect on Humphrey that concerned her.

And Humphrey was clearly so happy. How could she begrudge him that, how deny him another, softer side of himself, when it had made him supple enough to encompass her needs also? He seemed closer to his responsibilities; his awareness of his children was keener than it had ever been. To begrudge another person, one you'd loved through many changes in a long time, would seem rather wicked. So she thought, as she watched him in the throes of his passion for Sylvie. And instead of turning away from it, from him, she began to see him with the sharp clarity that is preserved for strangers. He was a young man again. Looking at him in sunlight she could see that it ripped years off his face. She saw how appealing, how warm-hearted he was. It reminded her of how he'd been when he'd fallen in love with her. It made her fall in love with him all over again.

He horsed around with his daughters as he'd never done when they were little. He was a little delirious. Was she young? Was she beautiful? Was he just guilty? But then he would suddenly stop and throw his head back – and laugh as if he could not stop. He was happier, freer than she'd ever known him. He was quite irresistible. George was complaining that he had given his secretary six months off after having a baby. His generosity extended to everyone.

She found that rather than feeling censure or bitterness, she was actually taking his happiness into herself in the way she had always absorbed his deficiencies. She knew it was this that saved her, and ruined her.

Sometimes, late at night, she would lie awake listening for his footsteps. Without setting a deliberate pattern, slowly he began to be at home less during the week. She would take to wandering around the house when even her daughters were asleep. She looked at the house and felt dissatisfied: it was so finished, so settled, so over. It had shifted and adjusted to the needs of the family, and now it just seemed patient and resigned. It would be so easy, after all, for those it had nursed and sheltered to simply leave it.

She sat at the top of the wide sweep of stairs staring at a bright puddle of moonlight that rippled on the Oriental rug in front of the door. She remembered buying that rug. It was in those early days of living with Humphrey. She'd gone a bit funny: a languor, a dreamy happiness had settled on her and made her idle, made her wonder if she would care if she never saw her little office outside the ward again. She only wanted the days to end so she could be with him. Her laziness was a sensual and delicious pleasure – an allowable privilege no man could afford. A chance to rest, to pull the soft fabric of life closely about them. She cooked, picked flowers, she felt lush and brazen, thinking that now she was a woman, a wife, soon, very soon – a mother. Was Humphrey, in his own way, experiencing something of this in his idle happiness, in the way he tried to make each act of tenderness something unique and perfect?

She took herself back to bed, walking gingerly, as she had done during each pregnancy, and then the miscarriage – her arms extended a little in case she slipped or crashed into something. She put on Humphrey's dressing-gown and lay with her cheek against the soft nook of his lapel. It smelt devastatingly of him. Oh, if he came back, as he might, he just might, she would turn to him and he would gather her up. He would love her as he had always done, as he could love no other woman; their bodies would slip into those familiar and comforting rituals that had been born from such deep physical passion.

Seventeen

Sylvie, holding on to the bars of the scaffolding and squinting up, the sun in her laughing face, was trying to communicate to the young man making a mess of the wall that, if he suffered from vertigo, he should find employment closer to the ground. When Frank, her foreman, on the plank beside her, said, 'Hey, isn't that your bloke getting out of that taxi, guv?'

Sylvie whirled, letting go with one hand so that Frank moved involuntarily to save her from a twenty-foot fall. But, like an acrobat, she had landed on the next plank along. She waved wildly at Humphrey, who looked up and waved back.

'Thanks, Frank, my old love, I'll go down, leave you to it, OK?'

With relief he saw she was now on the ladder; really, she could do with showing a little womanly fear once in a while.

'And,' she said, jerking her arm up towards the boy pinned like a butterfly against the wall, 'get that wally down – without' – she looked menacing – 'taking the piss out of him about it for the rest of the day. Send him down to number twenty-one, there's some railings there he could paint.'

'OK, guv.' He stared down moodily at Humphrey, who was waiting patiently on the street below, not moving, his hands behind his back. 'What d'you see in that geezer, anyroad? He's not half as young and handsome as I am. And he hasn't got that posh Bentley any more either. He's got a face like a block of wood and eyebrows like a coupla well-used Brillo pads.' He flashed his cheeky green eyes at her. 'All this time I've worked for you, guv, never seeing you with a fella: too much work, too busy, Frank, you'd always say. I sort of got to think there might be a chance for me – before this one turns up and sweeps you off your feet. I'm quite disappointed,' he said.

'You'd be lucky,' she laughed scornfully.

Frank scratched his groin. 'So what's with him, then? Money? Bit of class, is it? Suppose he got it all from his old man anyway.'

'Really, Frank,' she said, trying to manoeuvre past him because he was now draped very close to the ladder, 'must we show our social envy quite so clearly?' Then she stopped and added thoughtfully, 'He was an orphan actually, didn't have a dad.'

'Oh, poor little bleeder,' Frank said with deep satisfaction. 'No dad, but left all the money to him, eh?'

'Frank,' she said patiently, and then gave him a shove so that he had to do a little quick-step to land back on his plank, 'if you must know, his dad was a rat-catcher.'

'A rat-catcher!' Frank had a laugh like a drain emptying. 'Oh, I love that! That's how he caught himself a wife, was it? And that's the result down there, is it?' The acid note of jealousy made the joke sink.

Sylvie's eyes flashed, she leaned forward. 'You leave him alone, Frank, or I'll chuck you off here. Call it an industrial accident.'

'Come on then,' he taunted her, grinning, knowing when to stop – no one else dared take liberties with her the way he did; she had a temper all right. She took a step closer to him, so he put his hands up in surrender: he'd heard about her Judo.

'Cool down,' he said cheerfully. 'I'd never hit a lady anyway.'

'Well I'd hit a man, you especially.' She began to climb down again.

If only, Frank thought longingly, there was a woman in the world who'd be so savagely protective of me, who'd punch a guy for putting me down – now that'd be a woman in a million, that'd really be a woman to have.

'Sylvie?' he called softly to her shiny head with the little brown feathers of curl about her forehead.

'What?' She looked up at him, quickly, dismissively.

'Aw, nothing,' he mumbled to his dusty boots.

'Well then,' she continued to descend, 'just make sure that they get these walls finished – every scrap off. By tonight, all right?'

'Right guv.' He sniffed and rubbed a hand down his leg, then began shouting at Mick up above, who was too scared to look down, let alone be thinking of climbing down. He began to blubber, 'I don't feel well, Frank, I think I'm going to be sick. Where's Sylvie going?'

'Just get your backside down here, you miserable little twit, you're not a bloody cat stuck up a tree. Get down or I'll help you down,' he bellowed, watching Sylvie like a hawk.

Humphrey, looking up from the pavement at Sylvie's blue-jeaned backside as it came bobbing down the ladder, wondered why he'd always imagined that the people who were the most serene were the wisest. Sylvie, with her vehemence and her tears, her furies, her selfish ambition, her bloody-mindedness and her sheer awkwardness in sexual matters, seemed to be on the threshold of knowing the secrets of life. They were hooked up somewhere deep and inaccessible inside her, but she knew them all right.

He walked over to her and she ran up to him. She put her arms about him and held him so – quite publicly – in front of all those scruffy workmen who had downed cups of tea to watch her. It was quite wonderful the way she did that; the way she greeted him with such warmth, wherever they might be. He could see how other men reacted to it, and this pleased him more.

'Give us a sec, my little darling, got to sort out this lot before I go.' She seemed to swoop down on her men as they sat or squatted on a pile of bricks near the pavement, drinking tea out of plastic cups, eating sandwiches out of paper bags. He looked with pride at her sign on the building announcing her trade. Then his eyes went back to the little group of men, who sat, relaxed, looking up at her, nodding, smiling. She pointed up to the top of the building, where Frank was dragging Mick to safety; they all laughed. She crouched down and did a quick sketch in some spilt sand. They moved around her, looking down as she looked up – she explained something that Humphrey could not hear. He was fascinated watching her – watching the ease with which she placed a hand on one of their arms; the seriousness of her expression breaking into a laugh. She waved her arm in a circle and then spoke directly to one of the older men. It was all a mystery to him, what she was organizing, but watching her, you could have no doubt that she was totally at ease – and that they were happy working for her. Then she stood, hands on hips, emphasized something again – and strode off.

How strange it was, he thought with affection, that though she was tomboyish, with a butting directness in everything she said and did; though without a single feminine wile, yet still there was nothing about her that wasn't ultimately feminine. There was nothing mannish about her handling of situations. Even when she cuffed them, she did so in a way that was effective because it was not as a man would have behaved. That lot over there, though they called her guv in a way that conveyed their amusement at the title, felt at home with her, not because she was one of the boys, but because she wasn't. She kept her distance, but they'd seen many different sides of her – in a way, they'd tell you, you never did with a boss who was a man. She could be a tyrant, but not a bully; a sister, a mate and a confidant. Most of all she was a generous and considerate employer. You knew where you were with Sylvie; she was quite straight: if someone made a balls-up, she'd yell at him and make sure he didn't do it again. But she was fair. And she kept her labourers a long time. She was OK.

She walked back to Humphrey in her brisk way and pulled him over to one of the vans. She took out her satchel, then locked the van and threw the keys to Frank, who had got Mick safely on the ground again and was teasing him.

'I'm off then, Frank. See you first thing tomorrow.' She walked with Humphrey over to the second van and unlocked it.

'Finished, guv?' Humphrey asked patiently, turning to kiss her.

'Not with you I haven't,' she said, raising her thick eyebrows. 'And what are you doing here anyway?' She frowned at him. 'This was OK when we were courting, but we're an old staid couple these days and you can't come and drag me off the site in the early afternoon.'

'We're going for a picnic,' he said, 'in Richmond Park. You've been working too hard. Hurry up then, move this thing,' he ordered, 'and we just have to nip into my office and pick up the champagne and food.'

'What's to celebrate?'

'Just you and me, Sylvie, just you and me.'

Eighteen

'Isn't this nice?' she said, lying on her back with her hands folded under her head. 'And to think everyone else is working.'

Humphrey chewed a bit of grass and squinted over the water at the trees beyond.

'You've got to learn how to relax, how to have a good time and not waste it working,' he said lazily. 'And actually, you work better for it. I take my staff on compulsory picnics sometimes, when the sun is shining. After all, it only happens once a month in the summer here – so why not?'

'I agree, everyone should be like you, Humphrey. If I could bear to work for anyone it'd be you.' She leaned over and kissed him.

'No, I'd rather work for you, I wouldn't have to lift a finger. Who taught you to be so efficient? I'll never forget the way you operated in my office: none of this drifting in for an hour and then disappearing for three days on another job.'

'I don't like the casual aspect of the building trade. It has to be efficient.'

'You've got a knack with those fellows of yours, Sylvie, that I can't quite work out. They eat out of your hand and I would have thought men like that would hate a woman as a boss.'

'Oh but I'm not a woman, Humphrey, not a proper one.' She grinned. 'I only know how to be one way with men. I suppose it's because of not having a mum or something: there was no one to watch to see how a woman was supposed to talk and behave with men, or how to dress, or flirt, or whatnot. There was only my dad and me, and Hilda, very occasionally. So I was just myself. That's how I am with them.'

'You don't know the roles, so you don't play them. Well, it's disconcertingly pleasant,' he said.

'You see,' she sat up, 'my dad was not ambitious at all, he was a quiet, dedicated sort of man. He knew no women. Once I asked him, "Will you ever marry again, Dad?" And he said, gently, "I've always thought one marriage was enough." After my mum died, he never looked at another woman, and I mean that quite literally. Sometimes I thought I'd like a woman around. I mean, I grew up with no *idea* – there was no one to take me down to the shop and say, "I think it's time we got you a bra, dear." My boobs were growing like anything and he didn't even notice. I only got a bra because I was being teased so much at school that I had to do something about it. I wrote a note asking him for the money for one and left it on the kitchen table. He put the money in an envelope and left it there for me. After that he gave me an allowance because he knew there'd be other unmentionables that I'd need.'

He flung an arm around her and said, 'Oh, poor Sylvie, you sound such a lonely little thing.' He felt protective of her in a way he never did with Beth.

'I was a bit,' she smiled, 'but I went to school with boys and they couldn't make me out either. They were always after me, after my tits. I was really scared of the little creeps. So I learned to fight. We used to have wrestling matches in the playground, me and the boys. At first they thought it a whale of a chance to feel me up, but soon I learned how to fight and began knocking the shit out of them, and then they began to fight me for real. It was then that I decided that the only way you were going to be taken seriously by a man was by kicking him hard enough to make him see you straight.'

'God, you're a little pest.'

'Well, it works doesn't it?' She stuck out her jaw.

'Well, for you it does seem to.' He moved so that he could lie with his head in her lap. 'God, I bet they were mad with lust for you all the same.'

'Oh, no, I scared them. I meant to.'

'It would have driven me mad with lust,' he said, turning his face into her thigh.

She brushed his hair off his forehead. 'There was this one boy I remember, he used to pull me behind the lavs to show me his thingy – he was one of the ones I fought with most. He seemed to think showing it to me might stop me beating him – or fill me with reverence or something. Instead, I knew just where to bite the bastard if he was fighting dirty or trying to sit on me. I could never win if they got me down and sat on me.'

'Bloody hell, Sylvie, I'm glad you've stopped all that, makes me feel positively squeamish.'

'Nah, served them right.'

'Humph,' she said softly, 'time we went. You were going home tonight, don't you remember?'

'No, I don't and I'm not going home, I'm staying with you.'

'You can't,' she said in an odd voice, 'you promised.'

'Did I? Why did I make such an absurd promise?' He was angry with the situation.

'Because of your birthday, you said you'd go home and do some things. Oh, come on, Humphrey, you know you remember.' There was a tremble, something unhappy in her voice now.

'I'll ring her and say I can't.'

'It's not fair, Humphrey,' Sylvie said, and he turned to look at her, quietly, strangely.

'She'll understand.'

'No.' Her voice was very firm. 'No, if you've said, then you must go.'

He put his arms around her and rocked her gently. 'OK.'

He was like a boy, she thought, who had built an ingenious structure, a house with two separate compartments between which he could slide freely. The structure could not fail, he seemed to imply, because he would love each woman so much that neither would feel denied.

Once she had said, 'It will never work, Humphrey, you know it won't.'

'Oh yes it will, it must.' He'd kissed her hand in his particular way, holding it in both of his and raising it slowly to his lips.

And this, she'd thought dreamily, this is how he must kiss her hand also. There was no pain in it, the pain had been anaesthetized, as so many moments were by his tenderness. Beth, she knew, in the same circumstances, would turn to him just as reasonably and let him go.

Nineteen

'I really can't stand any more of this excitement and palaver,' Cass moaned, sitting down stoutly.

The day had been spent in the most hectic activity since early morning. The butcher had delivered the meat, the wine merchant left crates of wine on the doorstep. Cass had been dragged to the market to get fresh fruit and vegetables with her mother, and now it had transpired that the strawberries were too squishy, so someone must be dispatched for more. And then the nonsense began: was there enough beef and would it be tender? And would the cake stick like it did last time and the whole effort be ruined? And Lord, I've forgotten to buy bread and where has someone put that pile of linen napkins? And how on earth am I to get everything done by eight-thirty?

All day long, the cooking, and Beth's impatience – nothing ever actually went amiss but the anticipation of disaster was constant. Bunches of flowers had been seized from the garden and had to be arranged, just so, in the best vases. Fran had been bellowed at for plundering two of the fattest ripe tomatoes from the garden when a ban on their consumption had been set three days ago by Humphrey. The dog's bones must be gathered up from under the sofas, cat's hairs be removed from the cushions, everything unsightly hurled into cupboards.

'Mother dear,' Abi said with disdain, 'I'm sure your friends must realize that we actually live here and this is not just a show-house.'

'And all for his bloody birthday,' Fran moaned, after a good hour's sullen silence about the tomatoes. 'Anybody'd think he was actually going to notice all the trouble we've taken. The silver's so old and heavy my arm's bent out of shape polishing it. Why can't she use plastic ones? Or hire a maid?'

Cass spluttered with irritation as she was pushed aside to make way for yet another display of roses. 'I'm going out,' she said.

'Get the strawberries while you're at it,' Beth yelled.

'I'll come with you,' Fran leapt up.

'No you will not,' Abi glared. 'I'm not polishing that lot for you, I've got the glasses to do.'

Cass escaped with a sense of relief. Sometimes the house, and family, were suffocating: it was like a hothouse where everything sprouted too quickly, where everyone's emotions got tangled and had to be ruthlessly pulled apart. All that revolt and laughter, boredom, bad temper (Beth saying angrily, 'Must you fight *all* the time? Why can't you get on together? Learn to tolerate each other? Do your father and I fight all the time? No, we do not. Can you just stop going for each other's throats? Just for one day? Just for today? Please?'). Beth, so perfect, so gentle, so much the eternal mother rushing around in search of the perfection she must create around her – driving them all crazy.

Oh, it was grotesque and ridiculous how they annoyed and exhausted one another; how they could not work together without hurling out the abuses and shames of the past.

Abi: 'Well, the last time we went through this procedure, Fran, you managed to do nothing as usual and then fell asleep exhausted at nine o'clock.'

'Oh yeh? And don't I seem to remember you pushing off before anyone had arrived and turning up at one in the morning – just to draw attention to yourself as usual and upset everyone. And then having hysterics when Dad had a go at you.'

'I suppose before the day is over I'm going to be reminded of the time I was sick on the carpet,' Cass said wearily.

But it was romantic somehow, and wonderful, and infinitely comforting to be part of this obnoxious collection of people and know that each was part of you. The same blood trickled through you, little bits of them cropped up in you at times, bits you recognized and bits you loathed. It was as restful as lying in bed late at night, hearing her mother and father's voices floating upwards, talking long into the night – there was such safety in that. And if you went down, they would turn and say, 'Come and sit down, have a cup of tea, we were just talking about . . .'

But some days, oh it was too much! If only someone would sweep it all away: the house with its memories, the family with its tyrannies. Emotion was flung against all the walls, every room splattered with it. Abi screaming in the middle of the night, Fran fighting her father about his intolerance and then walking down the stairs with a rope around her neck saying she was going to string herself up from the apple tree if he didn't improve. Humphrey barking at everyone because someone had moved something in his study and he seemed to take this as a personal insult. Cass herself sneaking into her bedroom with a boy and being pressed up against the cupboard – which, with a terrific shriek, had broken! The other two galloping up the stairs to find out what the racket was about – the embarrassment, the shame of it all.

And her mother and father presiding over it all: loving, tolerant, peaceful. Her mother, whom she adored more than anyone in the world, pulling it all together somehow, making a net into which she scooped all the misery and laughter, the anguish and tears, shook it about a bit until it settled again. But today she'd like to sweep even her mother away and forge a life of her own. On her own.

She slammed the door behind her. Once Cass had gone, Abi seemed to expand, as if her sister acted like a cord that restrained her. She sat chatting with Fran, polishing glasses, buffing each one with great care and holding it up to the light to see the cut glass shimmer and sparkle. She loved all the things in the house; the plates that had belonged to her grandmother, the silver that had been in her mother's family for hundreds of years, the things that had been collected and loved for as long as she could remember. Beth was not a believer in keeping things for best; all the precious and delicate things were used. When she was a little girl of three, Beth had placed irreplaceable china and crystal in her hands and said, 'Feel it, Abi, isn't it lovely? Rub your finger down that line, isn't it beautiful?' She remembered her father coming in and seeing her holding a decanter: 'For God's sake, Beth, do you know how much that *cost*?' And her mother: 'She won't break it, unless you frighten her.' She never broke anything.

Fran, on the other hand, presented with an antique glass at the age of four had had a good look at it, said it was pretty and taken a great big bite out of the side of it.

'Get on with it,' Abi said to her sister, 'or I'll never have time to do your hair.' She breathed hard on the glass. 'I can't wait to get out of here tonight.' Her family intimidated her with their ability to mesh, to knock against each other and recover. They could relate to one another separately, or together. She always felt excluded. She didn't seem able to be a part of anything or anyone, and then she wanted to smash everything up – like earlier – and over a pair of socks. She and Cass had actually gone for one another, fought like animals, trying to hurt and kill. Beth had come in and said in a furious low whisper, 'Have you gone mad, Abi?' Abi had fallen to the floor, while her sister looked at her in disgust.

'I think I have,' she'd screamed, 'I think I am mad.' Then she'd turned on her mother and yelled, 'Why is it always *me*?'

'Because it *is* always you,' Beth snapped. Oh, she was stern towards Abi, almost harsh, as harsh as she was on herself. It was as if she felt, she is part of me so she must be better. When will she be genuine, be undramatic, be true? And poor Abi, trying to pull herself up beside her mother's shadow, would shrivel and fail.

She watched as Fran yawned, pushing a pile of smudged silver to one side, in the same way as she discarded food on her plate. 'I've had enough of this,' she said, 'let's go upstairs.' And Abi was furious, knowing that Fran would get away with it – because she was the youngest, the most beguiling. Abi would not come until she had finished the glasses to her own satisfaction. And then perhaps Beth would say, 'They're beautiful, darling, you've done them so well, you always do.' Yes, perhaps she would. And would also forget about the cut down Cass's cheek where her nails had scored.

Fran nipped into the kitchen and swiped some sticks of celery and one of the warm rolls that had just come out of the oven. Her mother shooed her out and watched her stroll off, munching. Though she is lazy and fickle, Beth thought, she is utterly and only herself. She's the most distinct person I know. Fran sidled back in to get another roll.

'No, I said only one! Fran, put it back – at once.'

Fran wandered into the garden with the second roll coddled against her cheek. It was a most gorgeous day and the night would be magical, she just knew it. She was glad they didn't have to stay to dinner; more guests again. She'd had enough of all these people treating her mother as though she was theirs: Samaritan calls in the middle of the night and Beth going out to help Mary. Really, there was quite enough for her to do at home.

She went to her room and switched on a tape. She walked up to her mirror slowly. She stopped and looked at herself, long and steadily, lifting her arms luxuriously, and yet a little reluctantly too. It was all there in the mirror: some promise for the future, some wonderful anticipation, something that was hers alone to bestow or deny – her beauty. But, as if she knew somewhere that it was a burden too, she didn't want it yet. Could she not keep everything just so, as it was, for a little longer?

Twenty

But by teatime Beth had bound her children closely to her again. And the scratch down Cass's cheek didn't look quite so bad. She and Abi were reconciled to disliking one another. Beth felt she had everything under control – that the evening must be a success, that Humphrey would be surrounded by the people he loved best and would dazzle as only he could. It had always been her pleasure to provide him with the ambience in which to glow, to draw him to her by the strong tides of her domestic accomplishments.

She sat for a few moments in the drawing-room, drinking jasmine tea, making sure it was all just as she wanted it: the polished wooden floors with pale rugs, two plump sofas in a pastel pink, a long pine table inlaid with glass, upon which a pot of yellow roses stood. The glass of the conservatory was golden and sparkling and she went into it to check that all Humphrey's plants were watered. She set some lilies on top of his piano and walked back to her chair. A mark on the mirror above the marble fireplace drew her duster, a shoe poked out from under a chair and had to be kicked out of sight. But it was looking lovely. Green plants at the French windows brought the garden into the house and coaxed the room out into the garden, where the apple tree threw its majestic shadow over everything. Soon she must lay out the food in the dining-room next door. But she was waiting for Humphrey, who had turned forty-five at six o'clock that morning. Somewhere else.

He entered the garden a little later through the side gate. It was deserted. Beth had cut the grass the day before and a sweetness still hung in the air. He rubbed his hand along the bark of the apple tree and patted it. He flung off his jacket, shoes and socks, and began to climb the tree, making for the higher limbs. There were marks on the trunk where he had footholds and a curve in a particular branch that seemed to have bowed its shape to accommodate his. He lay back, his head cradled by a forked branch. He could almost have slept. He and Sylvie had spent the night before at the Ritz and he was exhausted. The emerald shade around him was restful; the Bramleys were dark and there was a spiciness about them already. In this small space of time before he had to enter the hectic life of his house and family, he tried to deal with his conflicts.

He hated leaving Sylvie on days like this, important days when they should be together. It seemed treacherous that she had to be excluded from such a large part of his life. It made him feel helpless. When there was a problem in his life he just brought it to ground – but in this case he had to suffer it. There was nothing he could do to make things better. Not that Sylvie had complained, she never did. Not that Beth hadn't understood; she was very conscious of the fact that he suffered; that he was always trying to make up to someone for something. That he absolutely hated for anyone to feel hurt and not be able to remedy it.

What he was doing seemed ruthless and cruel to him now. The ultimate in selfishness. But the alternative was worse. A choice no longer existed. He had tried to create harmony, to be all things to both women. He had tried. He felt rather sick. He had wanted to live with an arm constantly around each of them, sheltering and protecting them both. But then there were these times when one always excluded the other. In the jungle, of course, it wouldn't be that way: they'd all live together, it would be natural and right. That's how it should be. Sylvie should be here tonight as well as Beth. As, early this morning, when he'd woken, he'd missed Beth, missed not being able to turn to her and give her a birthday present from him: an old ritual of his, giving presents on his birthday.

It could tear you in half, thinking like this. Having left Sylvie in a quiet and forlorn mood, he could end up creating the same one in Beth if he wasn't careful. He had to be the strong one, he had to hold the structure together since it was for his ultimate benefit. He began to dislike himself in this honest frame of mind – but that wouldn't do either. So he remembered that he'd left Sylvie sleeping, with a huge bunch of red roses to wake up to, with her favourite chocolates and the promise that he'd ring her. More was not possible – though he wished with all his heart it was. Then he remembered his caustic youngest daughter and her remark: 'You ought to go back to your tribe, Dad, this isn't a polygamous country.'

He was glad to be home – that was always the difficult part – his own ease and pleasure wherever he was, whichever one he was with.

A little laugh of Sylvie's returned: 'You must be very insecure, Humphrey, to need so much love.'

'Yes, I do need it all, every scrap of it,' he'd barked. He couldn't do without it. But he wouldn't tolerate the suffering. Love must be made up of happiness, of cosseting and care; it could be done, it was being done. It was possible to love two women, and to love them both well enough that neither felt neglected.

'Just don't say it, don't tell me, I don't want to know, Humphrey, I don't want to *know.*'

He walked quietly into his house through the French windows and admired the room. It looked sleek and scented as a woman dressed for a grand dinner. Leaving his clothes at the bottom of the stairs to take up later, he padded in his bare feet down to the kitchen. And stood silently at one side of the door and watched. There they sat, around the kitchen table: his family. His wife standing, her dark head lowered in concentration; frowning and biting her lips as she squeezed an icing bag between her hands and lifted her shoulder to push back a tendril of hair. She was icing his birthday cake. His daughters pressed close to her like acolytes, watching the letters curl out of the nozzle and spell out his name on the smooth iced surface.

'Oh bugger,' Abi said. 'Look, the Y's gone wrong.'

Beth flicked it off and licked her finger, then pressed again. 'There, that's perfect.' Looking at it, her hands on hips, smiling with satisfaction. She swiped out at Fran who had taken the bag and was now writing on the table with one hand and eating the letters as they wormed out.

Humphrey watched her and a smile broke across his face. How lovely she was in her yellow dress with the white collar which showed up her tanned skin. He wished his children were not there; he wanted to grab her silently from behind and bite her on the neck. He wanted her all to himself. He wanted her to be alone, absorbed, waiting for him. But she was always so pulled and stretched. People were drawn to her and she had little time to focus on anyone for long. He felt it, his children felt it: there wasn't enough Beth to go round. And each felt exclusively entitled to more.

Then she saw him. She saw him and moved forward; she seemed to fling her daughters away from her in impatience. Because he was home. He had come at last.

Seeing them, Abi's mood toppled: a moment ago everything had been so round and warm and close and now it was all dispersed. She turned furiously away. She lived, as they all did, so completely in her mother's atmosphere that outside it everything seemed weak and thin. And there she was – Beth – stretching out her arms to him, as though she must save him from something. Oh, it was enough to make you sick.

But Beth was laughing her head off! And then they all looked at Humphrey and began to snigger. Cass rushed up to him and ran her hand through his hair.

'What have you done? My God – you look,' she laughed more, 'just look at him! Oh, Dad, it's wonderful,' she now decided.

For here was Humphrey with his dark brown hair cropped close to his skull like a skin-head. It stood up straight and spiky as cut grass. And beneath it his face looked bashful but unrelenting.

Humphrey could pull it off of course, Beth thought. He had quite a little talent for that. Even at his age he managed not to look ridiculous, his bone structure and personality could support this new outrageousness.

'Well, Beth,' he said, as if he'd done it entirely for her sake, 'what d'you think?'

'Well, Humphrey,' she said coolly, 'it suits you. It's bloody silly of course, but it suits you.' She turned him so that they could admire the back of his head.

'Poor old devil,' Fran said. 'I wonder how long we'll be able to keep him at home.'

'Listen,' he snorted at her, 'if you have any hair left, the way you keep bleaching it, by the time you're twenty, you'll be very lucky. So better button your lip, eh?'

'Yeh, yeh.'

He sat down at the table and ran his hand a little awkwardly through his hair. 'There's not a lot left, is there?'

Beth, covering the cake, which had been whipped out of sight when Humphrey announced himself, wondered about him. Of course, one never said to Humphrey: why did you do it? It never seemed appropriate. Humphrey just did things, everyone knew that. So she made some tea, and thought, not entirely with pleasure: yes, he had a masculine beauty still, his features were strong and now your attention was drawn directly to their sharpness. When she'd first met him she'd thought his nose was like the beak of an eagle who'd crashed into a wall early in life. Would he ever grow old? she wondered. Would he ever allow it to happen and stop fretting about it? Oh no, neither – not Humphrey.

'You haven't kissed me,' he complained. 'Don't tell me you've never fancied any of those yobs who come in looking just like this.'

'Is that why you did it?' She stopped to kiss him. Then she said, 'You've been drinking.' He couldn't quite place the tone of voice, only that it was different somehow, and she looked at him strangely.

'Yes, I've had a few.' He didn't have to lie about whom he'd been drinking with, because she didn't ask. She didn't ask because she knew. But her hand, putting down the kettle, shook a little. She stared at her husband, whom she loved to distraction, she stared at him and inside her something began to hiss. She thought, calmly, I could strangle you, I really could, I could choke you to death.

He was watching her: she pushed her tea to one side and began to roll out a little block of puff pastry with a child's rolling pin she'd kept since she was seven and always used. There was something about the way she used the knife that bothered him, he couldn't tell why. Then the apprehension passed because she was telling him what she'd cooked. He adored her cooking – the cake would be a miracle; everything would be perfect – to look at and to taste. That was Beth: she made you feel she loved you by feeding you. It was odd – but when Sylvie slapped a plate of salami and French bread in front of you, he adored her just as much. He loved her disinterest because somehow it made him feel he was the only thing she would spend time on, would be distracted by. She wouldn't spend hours cooking because it would take her away from him. She made him feel she was quite single-mindedly his.

He turned back to the woman he was with. 'You've done so much work, my darling. You've even cut the grass. I feel a rat.' He was a little in awe of her. 'What can I do to help? Give me something to do.'

'I've left you the wine to sort out, and I need some beans picked.'

'OK. I'll just change.'

She watched him as he left the kitchen; she couldn't make out what she was feeling.

She had asked him to do what he liked best. He set out the wine and then went into the garden. He dug in the earth for potatoes; pushing his foot down on to the bridge of the fork and raising it slowly. The smell of dug earth made his nose quiver with pleasure. As he raised the fork it hurt him to see that he had spiked one of the small potatoes. He crouched to lift them, letting the earth fall between his fingers; rubbing at the tender skin to expose the pearly potato beneath. God, they were little beauties. Tossed in butter, parsley and a touch of garlic they'd melt in your mouth. He put them carefully in the big square basket beside his foot, which was full of tiny French beans ('They're much too small to pick, Beth, they're not ready. Leave them alone.' 'No, I like them like that.' 'Squanderer.'). Yes, that was enough, lettuces, spring onions, radishes, his prize tomatoes – or what was left of them, and a bouquet of herbs.

Beth was coming out of the house. She had been a little angry with him earlier and he could detect a trace of reluctance in her walk and something unhappy in her face. He walked towards her quickly to reassure her, to make her happy again. He presented her with the basket of vegetables as though it were a child. She smiled; they walked off together towards the rose garden. Cass watched them from a window, concerned because she had heard them quarrel. It was rare and unsettled everyone. They all tried to find ways of putting it right: by tidying up or turning the music down, or even offering to help.

Now they stood facing one another and Beth's head was moving in a way that suggested she was still agitated. But then slowly their heads moved closer together and Cass could see that her mother had gone still. Humphrey placed an arm about her and they walked on, a man and a woman struggling, pitted against one another in a sunny garden. But Cass knew that they would resolve it, whatever it was, privately out there and that then they would come back united. In spite of it all they were a real, a perfect couple – her parents.

She watched as her father lifted Beth's hand in both of his and kissed it slowly. She saw her mother throw her head up again – she was righted. Watching them, Cass, who pitied anyone who was deprived, felt very sorry for that other woman. For how could anyone compete against her mother? How could anyone push against so much security, so many years of love and tenderness? And most of all, how could she, that poor other woman, succeed against Beth's extraordinary acceptance of Humphrey's – of everyone's – right to do just as they wished?

'I shall never be any man's mistress,' she vowed solemnly, 'and I shall never be any man's wife either. I'll just have children, one every year.' And she longed for that with all her heart. She pulled her head back into her room, closing the window softly behind her.

Twenty-one

Sylvie woke at seven p.m. with the certainty that someone was ringing bells in her head, and not just ringing them either, bashing them against the inside of her skull. She rolled over in her bed, crushing a red rose that Humphrey had left her, with a note scrawled in his large, loose handwriting: 'Loved you to bits at the Ritz. Will call later and miss you every moment.'

She touched her head gingerly, resenting the fact that Humphrey never got hangovers – he had the constitution of an ox. They took turns in out-drinking one another, but he never suffered. No, he never suffered, she repeated quietly to herself, banging the pillow over her eyes. Bloody sun still sprawling about in the sky, nothing better to do than keep the day going. Would he ring? Or would he become totally involved in the dinner party for his birthday? By the merriment of people she never met? No, no point in that train of thought – it hurt no one but her. If it could hurt someone else, well, that would be another matter. She stretched out her arm and felt the dent where Humphrey had been lying; no trace, no trace at all. It was such an insignificant dent, it seemed almost unreal that a man had lain there, loved her there, then gone. She looked at the phone; it looked back silently.

She had a bath and let her hair fall backwards into the water; it was dark and cool in the bathroom and she lay in the water a long time, doing her utmost not to think, not to get angry. Then rose suddenly, impatiently, dried, dressed and settled herself in front of a pile of papers. She couldn't even focus.

She thought of phoning Hilda, or one of her mates, but she hadn't the strength, and she'd seen them all very recently anyway. With Humphrey, as it happened. He could meet her friends.

Every so often she would get up and walk to the window restlessly, then back to the red sofa, then back again. Her hair had soaked through her shirt and she felt cold at the back of her neck. She sat on for hours, getting up, drinking coffee, going back, achieving nothing. She walked over to the window again and looked down at the street below: it was still light: nine-thirty and still light as day. It drove her mad, she was sick of it. It was still his birthday, would be still his birthday until midnight.

A man and a woman were walking together, hand in hand, laughing; the man carried a small baby strapped to his back like a papoose. And Humphrey had the nerve to want a child! She turned away from the window and glared at the phone. It looked back with no passion whatsoever.

'Oh, fucking hell.' She threw the papers violently to the floor. 'Oh, fucking hell,' she repeated in a whisper, 'fucking hell.'

Twenty-two

Humphrey, looking out of his front door at seven p.m. for his dog, slammed it again. He turned and glared at Abi and Fran, who were crouched on the floor whiling the hours away on his telephone.

'What's that revolting thing outside, draped over a motor-bike, in black leather?' he snarled. Then peered out again and shuddered. 'Abi, it actually looks as though it's crying!'

'Oh, I don't know,' Abi said impatiently, because she was trying to listen to the conversation her sister was having, 'it's probably one of the macho-poofs.'

'What did you say?' he asked. His voice was not raised, not now, not after all these mutants.

'It's Phil's boyfriend, he's sulking because they've had a row,' Abi said, returning to her address book while Fran continued to talk in a low whisper into the phone.

He took a cautious look out of the window; it was still there, but had untangled itself from the motor-bike and was now strutting up and down outside – a stocky body squashed into shiny leather, tight as a condom. Crying, yes, definitely crying – bawling, you could almost say. Fascinating, quite fascinating. Then the creature lowered the front half of his body carefully and looked at his face in the wing mirror of a motor-bike the size of a tank. He whipped out a comb, flicked back his sleek black hair, dabbed at his eyes, and with a sigh, leaned back against the Kawasaki with his plump arms folded petulantly over his broad muscly chest. He glared up at the house and then began to pat his Hitler boot menacingly on the ground.

Beth was looking over Humphrey's shoulder and she turned to Abi and said, 'You're being a bit rude, aren't you? Why don't you ask him to come in? He looks upset.'

'Beth!' Humphrey roared. 'Have you taken leave of your senses? It's my birthday ...'

'I know it's your birthday, darling ...'

'Human beings will be entering this house later, Beth, our friends are coming here, Beth. You're not suggesting that that overfed woofter, that black-leather sofa, stays for dinner? Are you?'

'Of course not,' she said with the slow impatience of a mother. 'Cass is trying to comfort the other one. They've had a row and she's trying to get them to make up.' She appealed to Abi, 'Do get him to come in for a minute, Abi, do.'

'I don't think he will,' Abi said vaguely.

'Why not?'

'He says he doesn't want to see Syph again – though God knows why he's hanging about outside.'

'Syph? Syph?' Humphrey reeled. 'What kind of a diseased name is that?'

'Oh, it's just Phil's little joke: he says Syph's been on penicillin since he was ten.'

'Jesus, now look here!' Humphrey asserted himself, or tried to as his daughters began to laugh at him. 'I am not having him in my house . . . I am not having him eating at my table – is that clear, Beth . . . I am not having him sitting on my lavatory.'

'Oh, don't worry, Dad,' Abi said with evil coolness, 'it's not catching unless you have it off with him!'

'ABI!'

Beth chortled and ran lightly up the stairs. Humphrey leapt up after her, protesting, moaning. His daughters giggled together and told him to try and be a little tolerant for once in his life. He was furious: after he'd given them all those record tokens, twenty quid's worth each, after he'd tried to talk to them properly. Well, he hated talking to them, really, they were so boring, all they could talk about was themselves. God, who'd have children? And to think he'd actually considered having another one. But of course a son would be a different matter. Of course. Jesus – a son – that thing outside was somebody's son!

'Could you,' Fran asked Abi, watching her father as he threw himself up the stairs, 'could you live with a man who blows his nose in the basin?'

Twenty-three

Humphrey, to calm himself down, went to organize the glasses and check the ice. Something uncomfortable was going on inside him: he was actually getting a bit sick of his own stupid behaviour. Abi was right: why couldn't he be a bit more tolerant? Why was he, as Beth had accused him, always drawing attention to himself with tantrums? He wished now that he'd offered the macho-poofs a drink – in the other room of course – but too late, they'd gone. Vrooming down the drive on that deadly machine, clutching one another after kissing and making up. But they weren't so bad, not really, not if you averted your eyes. Next time he'd be less of a pain. Next time.

He kept feeling this need to change himself, and he didn't know quite what to do about it. It had first struck him forcefully at Sylvie's; one night when he'd turned up unexpectedly and found her with a few of her friends. Three pretty women in their thirties, all with highly paid jobs. They were sitting and lying about Sylvie's room, drinking and talking. Sylvie had rushed up and kissed him; they had all welcomed him, but Sylvie hadn't made a fuss of him, not like Beth would have done. He had to get his own glass; she expected him to sit where he wanted to – she even seemed to be watching him to see how he might behave.

It was only afterwards that he'd studied his behaviour, as now, unfortunately, he had to study this evening's episode. That night at Sylvie's – he'd immediately had to find himself a central chair. They moved back to include him, but they went on talking, in a way he wasn't familiar with. They probed and pried at one another, protected, teased, laughed. But no one was in charge. No loud male voice guided the proceedings. Everyone had a turn to talk, no one dominated. He was baffled, and the chaos of it all disturbed him.

Then he got this maddening desire to take control. He took an imposing position in his chair, he began to dominate the conversation, mustering an artillery of good opinions, sound logic and deadweight theory. They had been discussing nuclear disarmament.

Well, they listened to him as he spoke, they listened with interest. But no one gasped at his brilliance. Then a quiet woman told him a small but quite riveting fact that reduced his argument to rubble. Conversation began to glide again, as it had done before he'd tried to take over.

He had felt very threatened. There was no Beth in the room to take him to one side and find a special nook for him. He was alarmed; it seemed he actually needed a woman to defer to him. Did he? Did he really? He'd never thought of himself that way. But none of these women would defer to him; they didn't need to. They simply let him be himself; but he didn't know how to. He was clueless.

After they'd gone, he and Sylvie talked about it. She had been a little awkward with him, as if he'd made her uncomfortable, but she didn't criticize him. How tolerant she was, he thought savagely, patiently waiting for him to turn into a human being. And then he thought: I am a bore, a pushy, aggressive fart. It was shattering to feel, suddenly, so dissatisfied with oneself, with the way you took on the world as though it were hostile, as though you must grab it by the scruff of the neck and batter it into submission.

Now, as he thoughtfully rubbed a finger around the rim of a glass, he felt it was time he tried something different, did things from another angle. Trying something else was what he immediately did if he felt he'd bungled. He now saw that he'd spent most of his life bungling, in this particular, very private, very important part of himself. Tonight it would end. If nothing else he was a man of determination, and a quick learner.

He went to talk to Beth about it. When he told her things that he'd clearly learned elsewhere, things about himself, she'd look at him sharply, as if he was trying things out on her that he'd discovered in someone else's bed. But something in her responded to the changes in him – couldn't not respond. As if, reluctantly, she had to accede that it was an improvement. Something she had not been able to bring about herself.

Twenty-four

Beth, presiding at her table, looked over the candles and she thought: Love, happiness, the minute you feel it it begins to die. Food was like that too. Here before her all that remained of Humphrey's cake were crumbs – but how beautiful it had been! A perfect sponge – the strawberries and cream, laced with Cointreau, exactly right. And each course a triumph, for once no disappointment; usually it was the middle course that let one down so, that seemed unexceptional. But the spiced beef had been so tender and so delicious that it had nearly all been eaten – barely a scrap for the dog. She smiled and pulled her shawl about her. She looked over at Humphrey and thought: Yes, he is different. He's still witty, but less brutal about it; he's quieter, he lets things find their own course. He is a fine man; I would have no other.

One of her dearest friends, Toby, a man whom she'd known since childhood, put his hand on her arm and said, 'I love that shawl so much, Beth, it's so you.' She looked down and touched it: it was thick, cream silk, large as a tablecloth, embroidered with deep scarlet roses and purple peonies with a central tracery of blue stems. Toby had been watching her, and he found her not beautiful tonight, she had lost a certain radiance, but very remarkable – about the eyes and brow. And curiously passive, as though she was holding herself in; holding her breath, as she'd done as a young girl before leaping into the lake at the bottom of her parents' grounds in Ireland. Or, on that one occasion when she'd taunted him: 'Go on, then, go on Toby, kiss me, do it now.' Though she knew his tendency, and adored it, as Beth had always adored misfits. She had been so majestic, so scornful that day, he'd almost done it.

Of course, Toby thought, Humphrey was not up to her, never would be. He'd once said to Beth, before she'd married Humphrey, 'He's a mongrel, my dear.' And she, 'Of course he is,' and smiled, 'but mongrels are always the most lovable, the best loved. Don't you remember old Sally and how you loved her much more than all your pedigree dogs?' After she said things like that, she would stride off; you knew you hadn't touched her, she was so secure with herself it was intimidating, you felt nothing could throw her. When you saw her on a horse there was no question of it. She never forgot how well born she was; she always made you appreciate the value of character.

He looked away at Humphrey, down the other end, doing his village boy bit, talking about the country. He was enchanting them all – he was witty, charming as hell. But then the phone rang. It startled Beth. It startled Humphrey. They looked at one another, in alarm. Toby watched Beth's face – it was anxious, almost pleading. How extraordinary, he thought, that she should look at him like that. And then he watched as between them a conspiratorial glance flew, back and forth. Then he rose and she stiffened. Humphrey was saying he never got a chance to answer the phone, only happened when the girls were out. He laughed easily and was gone.

Toby poured a little more wine into Beth's glass, she put her hand over it to stop him and he saw that her hand shook a little, and that, in a moment, a worn look had slipped over her face. A touch of defeat. It hurt him, for he idolized Beth as other people idolized Beth and Humphrey's marriage, as one of those flawless things.

They were sitting outside under the apple tree. In one of Humphrey's exhilarated moments, after he'd blown out his candles, he'd suggested the table be borne out into the garden. The night was as beautiful as Fran had predicted, a velvet sky inlaid with a sprinkling of very bright stars, no wind, just warm air that brought out the scent of the wistaria and honeysuckle and drew all eight people together far more intimately than the inside could have done. Beth was talking, explaining Humphrey's gardening technique. It was not easy, she said, to bring out the wantonness in plants and flowers; see that bush there, it had taken him years to break down its natural orderly shape and make it spill over the wall that way. She spoke of him, as she always did, with a touch of admiration. And yet, Toby wondered, what was it? What had shaken her so badly?

When Humphrey returned, Beth would not, on principle, cover his inexcusable delay. She would force him to lie, or test his honesty, but she would not help him. She saw how ruffled he was, unsettled, his hand going to his brow where his hair no longer flopped. And then, he lied. A business call, he said. She hated him for lying. For whose sake, she raged, for who's benefit? Why couldn't he have said nothing? Oh, he was full of secret pretences. He was unbridled, he wouldn't rest until he had annihilated all he had known and loved and enjoyed, until all memory and hope was crushed. But then, perhaps, it *had* been a business call? But no – look at him: he was in a tangle, all his earlier composure gone. He was being pulled about, this way and that. She did not pity him. She was not sure she even liked him.

But Maggie came to his rescue, lovely Maggie with her crown of titian hair and her rosy cheeks, she came to his rescue as on many occasions in the past she had drunk and run with him. Not so often these days, but still she would ring up and say, 'Fancy a sprint, Humph?' They'd run to the nearest pub and stay there. They were close as siblings with the same capacity for booze, late nights and long conversations. Now, as Humphrey tried gamely to chide her for not running more, she said, 'Too old for it now, Humph, these days I prefer the booze straight.' And she'd laugh with a strong, punchy laugh. How interesting it is, Beth thought, that she's always happy; she shies away from misery like a petrified horse. Just as Humphrey does. Humphrey has always been intent on happiness – everyone's happiness. Perhaps that's why he causes such bloody misery. Why could they not, both of them, desperate in their different ways, accept that it came and went – like everything else?

She could hear Humphrey saying, now, that unselfishness was a weakness, a definite flaw in the character ...

Maggie laughed. 'I think, Humph,' she said affectionately, 'you'd actually lose some self-respect if you had to be honourable.' She poured more wine for him. 'It's the selfish devils who do what other people'd like to: we love 'em for it – for getting away with it.'

'Do we?' He frowned. 'No, I think we hate them for it.' But he had recovered.

It was this that made something start snarling inside Beth: this satisfaction in him that should be grasped and pulled out firmly by the roots. She rose to get more candles and came back, pressing the creamy sticks hard into the wet stumps of the old until they had joined. A little hot wax dripped on to her hand. The pain she felt was out of all proportion to the injury.

She wanted to be just. It was true that he had been quieter tonight, less of a show-off, but now the booze and some unhappiness was moving in on him; she could almost smell it. Would he plummet into a depression later, as he often did? But no, he was getting up, saying he would make some more coffee. She was grateful; it was something he always did, but now she tried to stop him. 'I'll do it darling, it is your birthday.' But he insisted. She didn't want him to go, but she could not leave everyone and follow him. She began to play with the sugar in the little silver pot, stirring it round and round. She wasn't concentrating and once Mary had to repeat her question. She was sitting very straight, smiling, wanting to turn round; she began to rub her hand against her cheek until it looked quite chafed and hot.

Humphrey returned with a pot of coffee, brandy and port. He placed it tenderly in front of her, kissing her hair in that demonstrative way his friends always admired and envied him for. He is better, Beth thought sadly, he has spoken to her again.

'Toby, let me have your cup.' She put out her hand, there was a pale pink mark on her forefinger.

Ah, Humphrey thought, she is unhappy. She had a way, when she was uncomfortable or sad, of slipping into a role she must have learnt from her mother or grandmother. She would adopt a formal, almost Victorian manner; she became reserved and sympathetic, but she was not really present, just an aspect of her behaviour remained.

Oh, my poor Beth. For a moment he felt physically weak, quite disabled. We can hide nothing from one another. How painful that is.

Just as silently, she seemed to answer: It wasn't before. Her head bent and she poured the coffee from cup to cup with careful movements, like someone a little stuck. He couldn't bear it: there she sat, the deepest, dearest pleasure of his life – and she suffered.

When I fell in love I became unscrupulous.

You were always unscrupulous, her eyes answered him.

But then, like a transformation, he could see her girding herself with her maturity, her strength of character, her sense of place and occasion. She offered Toby a chocolate; she allowed him to amuse her. Soon she would have them all glowing in her warmth and the intimacy of her table again.

But Humphrey was furious. Everyone round the table, his friends, all of them, they seemed to him unsatisfactory. Now, when he needed them, they failed him. Here they sat, at the house of the ideal couple, the perfect partnership – and God, it was insupportable – this fraud and deception. And yet it was true also, his marriage with Beth was all those things they believed in; it did have all the virtues that they admired and cherished. But, if it was not a lie, it was only half the truth. He couldn't tell them the whole truth, as now he wanted to. He couldn't – they would not allow it. They all had their own reasons for believing in the perfection. But why can't we ever talk, he wondered, among our friends, about our true emotions; about the things that really matter to us? About the truth. About love between men and women. Why can't I tell them about Sylvie, without breaking everything else to bits? Why can't we talk together here, tonight, as women talk privately to women, or men talk privately to women, but not to each other? It's the men who are at fault, he knew that – they simply wouldn't allow it. They would shuffle uncomfortably, they would probably begin to be flip or to sneer. Or their unhappiness would make them vicious, or dismissive. They would pull it all apart, any talk of the emotions. How inadequate we are, he thought, the way we stoically stand by our fellow man, but never open our trap to ask him what the hell the matter is.

How inadequate I am, he thought, watching Beth, who recovered so fast: she is full-blown, beautifully at ease, she could talk deeply of anything, to anyone – she would reach the heart of it. She would take your confidence carefully, tend it, and hand it back to you. She was remarkable, there was no question of it, and loving her was a privilege that at this moment he wasn't sure he deserved.

She looked up and caught his eye – and read it. She smiled tenderly, but the smile was for herself. Because when she looked up she saw that all his devotion and reverence and passion for her was there, intact, in that look. It had all returned to her, it was quite safe, she knew it. He thought her a wonderful woman; she was the most cherished, the best loved. She was, after all, a perfect woman.

And with her smile, Humphrey was righted also. If he felt that her love faltered, he lost his balance; now it had been restored to him. And he was able to dazzle and charm them all again; he was safe. He turned to talk to Roger, his fishing companion, the only man he felt he could do things like that with. Roger was a good man to go fishing with; they went to West Wales, just the two of them, for the gentle lap of the waves on the boat and the good company of men together – something physical and hard, something he missed in a childhood without a father.

Beth watched her husband; she considered him again. When he settled on someone in that way, he seemed to grab that person and hold them hard against him. He centred on his choice of the moment so single-mindedly, boring his brown eyes into them, capturing them so completely, that when he put them down again they felt almost bereft. But now Roger's wife was laughing at him, at his ridiculous hair that suited him so well, that showed how confident he was.

As Beth talked and poured more coffee, half of her was always listening to Humphrey. He was talking about death now – what could be done about it? How to get round the problem? How to outwit fate? How revolting age was: an old man, full of gas and foul smells – who could contemplate it? Fifty: it gave him the willies just to think of it, there, over the horizon. He'd rather someone put a pillow over his face.

Lucy laughed joyfully, 'Oh, don't worry, Humphrey, you won't die – God wouldn't have you and nor would the chap downstairs.'

He leaned towards her, with his heart-melting smile, 'Then there is the possibility, Lucy, isn't there, that I might not ever die?'

'Definitely.'

He looked up to include Beth, his smile was so warm and deep, like a hand reaching across the table, like his touch on her cheek. She was quite restored now, they both were. Yes, she thought, there was honour in marriage and it could not be displaced. She must pitch her life above self-pity and pettiness; what was here, now, in this house, this garden – this only was real, was true.

Then the phone rang. She felt that the sound was attacking her. It was preposterous: how dare she? How *dare* she? Ringing here tonight – again? How could anyone behave like that? Humphrey's eyes had gone small and narrow. He looks like a crook, she thought, her hands clawing at her skirt. If you answer it, her eyes warned, I shall rip this evening to shreds. I shall smash the image that these people treasure, I shall expose your lie, your lie that I've lived beneath in order to protect us. The lie that you force on other people to deceive them also. It was shabby, it was vile. She watched the candle as the wax ran down, making a flat pool. It was impossible to look at him. When it reaches the bottom, she thought, when this glob of wax reaches the bottom – if he makes the wrong choice, I'll do it. He was looking hard at her; he was pleading with her, he was asking for her understanding, he was saying, I know you will not do it.

He wouldn't go, it wasn't possible. But then she found that he was rising. Around the table everyone stopped, they put their coffee cups down, they sat quite still. Humphrey pushed his chair back, his face was quite blank and then, as he turned to go, it seemed to rip. He could not throw down a light remark to amuse them, a bauble to reduce the suspense. And Beth had left him, she would do nothing for him. For a moment he hated them both, both his women, equally – he wanted to be rid of them both, because of the misery of moments like this, when they both asked for a sign. And he had none to give.

And, as he turned away from the table finally, as Beth lost sight of his face and saw only this unfamiliar shorn head, this naked neck that she could chop at with an axe, she said, loudly, with an incoherent sob, 'Humphrey has left me for another woman.'

Because for the first time, that is how it felt to her. For the first time she knew that she was heartbroken.

Part Two

THE RECKONING

*For everything we love flies
continually away from
us at a speed of exactly
one hundred and eighty-two thousand
regrets per second. And we too
are flying away from what we
love at exactly the same old
guilty spin off.* — GEORGE BARKER

One

Of course I knew it would all go wrong. I suppose Beth did too. But somehow you never imagine the worst, or you stop yourself thinking about it. Humphrey goes charging along, thinking he can hurl every obstacle out of his way, only stopping to pick one or other of us up when we got hurt. Of course that night I was hell bent on making trouble. And so was she. A crisis point had been reached and it was time he knew about it. When he came to see me, very late that night, or rather early morning after his birthday, I just stood and glared at him. I couldn't speak. I didn't know what he'd been going through and I didn't care. I couldn't even look at him. It was only much later that I told him.

'I've been pretending,' I said. 'I don't think I can stand any more of this. I just can't. I've had enough.'

He said he was grateful I wasn't screaming about it. He was black with tiredness around his eyes – and his hair – I've never seen anything so bloody ridiculous – just made me furious.

When I said that, he sort of slumped down. And for the first time I saw that he couldn't cope with it either, that he'd been pretending even more than I had, that it went against his grain too. It was just too exhausting.

Poor Humphrey, when things really began to crack up he was still trying so hard to keep everyone happy that he couldn't see straight any more. He was so desperate to keep his view of things: that he could manage it, make it all right, look after us both – that he'd ceased to see either of us as we were, or were becoming.

Strange things were happening to me. There comes a time, after you get over the rival feelings, when you really become obsessed by the other woman. You want to know everything. Only it's so difficult to get a clear picture of her, when all you're getting is Humphrey's view. I had built up this idea of a bloody marvellous, saintly woman. That's how he saw her, he didn't try to hide it. He worshipped her. That really gave me a deep sense of security.

There's another thing about Humphrey: he drags you into all his feelings whether you want to know about them or not. He did it to everyone, even his brats. He refused to hide a thing; everyone had to know the score. Nothing frightened him more than secrets, whispering behind closed doors, especially at night. No one was spared a thing.

And of course I began to get really tormented by that family of his, that other life I couldn't enter. Sometimes I thought I was a bit mad. I had this picture of her sailing around that house looking immaculate, being so domestic and perfect – all the things I'm not. I mean, I knew she wasn't a little drudge, but I refused to see her as Humphrey's business partner, as a woman who'd always worked, who had two professions. I refused to see her as being at all like *me*. I wanted to see myself as the exact opposite of her; I wanted her to be the stereotype of the little woman, dumpy and boring. I needed to think of her like that because then I could imagine that to Humphrey I was a woman of a different sort, more his own sort – I had to be more exciting. But he wouldn't allow such comforting fantasies. He made me see Beth as she was – it was his way of explaining to me why he couldn't possibly leave her.

I was OK until I saw that I was becoming dependent. I was changing. It hit me most when I saw that my rage against the world was going. That really terrified me. It'd kept me going so long, it was like petrol to me. Also, Humphrey liked it. He envied me my anger. He actually envies women their deprived status because it's made them get up and fight back. It gives them something to fight for. He lost his cause when he got rich, when he had everything. And he misses fighting for it. That kind of fighting's an addiction – getting your own back on the world is a big charge. He loved breaking the rules, every way he could – not just society's rules, but the rules of the human condition. He'd twigged that life was finite – and he couldn't stand it.

Love was making me mushy – his word – and I didn't feel I could show him that. He *needs* me to fight him, to make him look inside his head, to have a good look at what was there. And he wanted, all of a sudden, for women to have a new place in the world. Because that would give him a new place too.

Somehow, to him at least, Beth belonged to the old order of women. She'd never needed to fight, everything had come easy to her. I thought she wouldn't know where to start. That was my big mistake. She had great subtlety in the matter of fisticuffs. I'd never met anything like it and it made my defences pretty ridiculous. To fight Beth, I began to see, meant knowing every single thing about her, and everything that made her vital to Humphrey. I had to expand myself to include Beth, I had to be all the things she was in order to make her superfluous.

But then, quite spookily, I began to feel that Beth and I were actually changing places, swapping roles, and that in a way we were even in league together. I began to act in ways that weren't like me. And this made me feel that her character was slowly, in little ways, rubbing off on me. Or perhaps in my head I just gave her too much power.

But we were connected, that was certainly true. And not just through Humphrey. I can't explain it, but I was beginning to live through her, I felt we were sharing all sorts of feelings that we hid from Humphrey. I wanted to get closer to her. I knew how to do it. So I just waited for my chance. And sure enough, it came.

Two

I broke into her house. I always thought of the house as hers. And the garden Humphrey's. Breaking into houses is something I learned as a kid. A bricky, who I called Mr Smelly, taught me how to do it when I was ten. It was easy to get into her house. I knew they wouldn't be back until Sunday. They'd gone to stay with some friends in the country; the kids were on an anti-nuclear walk somewhere or other.

It was only once I was in that I got scared, I could hear my heart thumping away. It was like walking on a grave or something. I got in through the kitchen window and I looked around at the room I imagined she spent most of her time in, stirring those cakes and puddings, cooking roast beef – or whatever she cooks. I just know that she cooks – perfectly of course. It was a nice kitchen, though there was damp on the wall by the window and the guttering was loose. I noticed a pair of shoes in the corner, her shoes: she had bloody big feet.

Somehow, though the house was quite silent, I seemed to hear the music of it. You could sense what went on in each room by all the personal things flung about; you could breathe in an atmosphere of security, of family-ness. They all lived here together, ate at that table together, watched that telly together, talked and laughed and were happy together. I felt so excluded. I wasn't part of anything, as they were all part of one another. Part of Humphrey. I've never felt anything so painful before, such terrible jealousy, as in that house. It made me feel very small again with a big hole in me. I felt like the orphan Humphrey pretended he was. No mother, no father, no husband, no child. Not even a dog. I was just walking around another woman's house, spying on a life that I couldn't share.

I could have killed her. I didn't want to take her place there, not that, never fancied that, inheriting children must be worse than having them. I just wanted her to die – painlessly – in a car crash or from a massive heart attack. She seemed, in that house, to have such power, over Humphrey, over her children, even over the way my life could fall to pieces. I wanted to test that power, to check how much she really had. And to feel that as a person, a woman, I too had the power to hold him – without all these trappings of a long life lived together. Just because of me.

I did a dreadful thing in there. I couldn't not do it. I am sure it was something she would never stoop to, but in her house I couldn't raise myself to her level. I looked inside their bed. At the sheets. Immaculate bed-making of course, beautifully ironed sheets with hospital corners and all that – crisp and clean. Or almost. I covered it up like a guilty schoolgirl. I was shaking. And sweating. I began to look at her things: Chanel No. 5, perfume, powder, body-cream. Who gave them to her? A cut-glass dish with a rope of pearls, with sapphires breaking up the chain at regular intervals. I put them on, but they looked awful on me. I sat down at her dressing-table and looked at myself in her mirror. For one spooky second I thought I saw her face reflected in the glass, as if she was standing behind me. I cleared out of there fast. Into the room next door. Her study. Lots of reports stacked, with a letter from George on top. Humphrey had said they were working together on something. He didn't know what. He was losing interest in his business at an alarming rate. And because he was there less often, she began to go in regularly, which she hadn't for ages. Something bothered me about that letter from George to Beth, but I couldn't work it out. Something else interested me more.

There was a little black notebook with red binding. I opened it. It was a diary. I read it:

Most people in a situation like this would consider choice. Would be pulled back and forth, wondering which one shall I have? Which one can I do without? I'm certain now that Humphrey doesn't consider this, doesn't try to choose between us. He must have put that possibility out of his mind right at the beginning. Other people would insist on it, of course. They would accuse him of cruelty for not making a choice, of having his cake and eating it. Of being a law unto himself. But the fact is, the choice is not Humphrey's to make. It's mine. Or, I suppose, it's hers. It's we who have indulged him, we who have allowed him to dispense with choice. And why?

Who was this woman, I thought, who could think so calmly, so rationally, who was working it out like some strategy, like a balance sheet, in a book just like a ledger?

But then I began to consider her question. Why? Yes, why *have* we allowed him to get away with it? I've wanted him to choose, I've even tried to make him, but I've never pushed him. But she provided the answer, or at least the easy part of it. Here it was in her long, looped handwriting, beautifully clear:

> Though we suffer, we don't want to make him choose. The choice is only – having Humphrey or not having Humphrey. If he were to choose, one of us would lose. So we're prepared to share. Perhaps we even like to share. I've always believed in sharing, taught it to my children. Love, after all, should be magnanimous, not petty or tyrannical. It should give to the other what the other needs.

I thought, the woman's after canonization, or else she's screwy.

I didn't believe that stuff. I knew Beth, I knew that there was a side of her very different from that, whatever Humphrey said. And sure enough, here it was, written on a page all by itself: 'But, Humphrey, there has to be a reckoning. As a businessman, surely you must know there has to be a reckoning?'

I read the whole lot of course. It was pretty scary. Those great swings from tolerance and love to the most frightful anger and despair. The delicate way she had of expressing herself couldn't hide the rage and violence that was brewing there. I felt that not only was she a sister-side of myself, but that the two of us were actually living the same life. That there really was no difference between us. We had been made, by Humphrey, slowly and surely, into the same woman. And here she was, writing down my own feelings, all of them, good and bad. She was making me, or I was making myself by reading it, face up to the truth. The truth was that there was no difference between us – and for both of us to survive we had to believe that there was.

I went upstairs to the kids' rooms, I thought they would be safer, I had begun to feel that the house was mined. In one of the rooms there was an old teddy stuck away on top of a cupboard, all alone, sort of toppled to one side, neglected and forgotten. I took it down and held it. But when I did that, I just cracked up. It just made me cry and cry. All over that teddy I cried, and all over her spotless house I went crying. The last time I cried like that was when I walked into my mother's hospital room and she was lying there as thin as a twig, she hardly made a dent in the pillow. The wind could blow her away, I thought, my little mother is dying. And I cried as I could not cry when she died.

By the time I got back to the kitchen I was badly shaken. I drank some cold water, very quickly, and it seemed to rush to my ears. I stood there, looking at those photographs: there was one of her holding a baby; one of her and Humphrey laughing at one another on holiday; all of them together in a garden round a child's birthday cake.

No, I was not heartbroken. Guilt didn't throw me to the ground. I was absolutely livid. I wanted to rip those photographs down. I wanted to smash all her pots, all those labelled jars, all those pretty old plates. And I was going to do it. I had to. It was quite essential. I yanked wildly at a drawer and hurled it to the floor. The crash and the scattering silver stopped me for a moment. But then I pulled down the onion and garlic strings and kicked them. I knocked a tray of cups to the floor and stamped on them. Then I stopped because I thought my heart would explode. But I hadn't finished. Just as I was reaching for a pile of plates, the door opened and I froze.

She stood there. Her. Beth. Quiet. Absolutely still. She looked at me. I looked at her. She was quite beautiful. It radiated from within her, an illuminated calm. My face was mad and red. She didn't move. She didn't seem to see what I had done. Then she slightly turned her head when there was a sound like a door closing at the end of the hallway. She looked back at me. Something about that look: the gentleness of it, the kindness and understanding, it made me want to rush over and bury my face in her shoulder and say, I'm sorry, I'm sorry. She said, softly, even tenderly, but urgently, 'Go quickly, go out of the side gate.' She closed the door. And I ran.

Three

That scene in the kitchen turned me right round. It was only later that I realized precisely what she'd done. She had protected me. She had saved me, or saved herself, or more accurately, saved all three of us from something terrible. She had swept aside the chaos of that moment, the horror of a confrontation that none of us could bear. She had let me escape, and I was sure she would protect Humphrey in the same way. I was so grateful, and so awed by the generosity in her – she had a perfect chance there to expose me – that I almost loved her. I began to forgive her for being loved by Humphrey. I began to believe again that we could all continue in the same way as before. And be happy. All of us. I thought I could really learn to understand, on a deep and noble level, as she seemed to.

Somehow I couldn't maintain that. And it was she who undermined it. Just when I was feeling settled, I found the letter, it was among some music sheets of Humphrey's. He'd bought a piano; said that my room was acoustically perfect and that he wanted to play there. I used to listen to him play for hours. He played jazz mostly, and some classical music, but I liked the jazz best. He could sing; he said he wanted to sing as well as Sarah Vaughan. He sang all of her songs. He could pick up any tune if you hummed it to him and play it for you. He was so happy at that piano. I often felt a little sad listening to him, he was so good, you felt he should have done nothing else with his life but play the piano, play those sad old melodies, the Schumann and the Brahms.

His hair was growing, so now it had begun to flop forward again when he was playing. I loved that flop of hair, it made him seem so young. It was what he needed: to be always young. I used to sit between his knees and he'd try and teach me to play, but I was useless. He taught me how to cook instead. Well, we were sort of learning together, but he was much better at it, he enjoyed it and I found it a bore. I never felt that he was trying to get me to be a good cook, like she was; he was quite happy to do it for me. He was not a demanding man, and because he wasn't, you wanted to do your utmost.

Often I came home and I could tell he'd been there for hours, playing Ella Fitzgerald or Benny Golson tunes, drinking red wine and eating peanuts. He would look up and smile. He was so relaxed, all of that hurling about seemed to have left him. He'd go on playing for a bit. Then he'd stop dramatically and hold out his arms to me.

'I'm filthy, Humphrey, I probably stink.'

'Not to me you don't. Come here at *once!*' he'd bark. He'd sit me down, get me a drink, behave like a wife really: 'How was your day? Did you sort out that problem with Frank? Is the plastering done? I hope you're not going to work tonight, are you?' Then he'd start to send me up when I asked him how his day was; 'Oh, simply frightful, the cooker broke, the kids spilt water all over the floor, I have a terrible headache and you're going to have to unblock the sink.' The role reversal thing amused him no end. And it wasn't as funny as it sounded, because he was spending less and less of his day at the office and more of it at my flat. If I asked him about work, he'd flip it aside, bored. Often I discovered that he hadn't gone in at all. But we were so happy together that I didn't bother. It seemed to be something he needed to do.

It was after a few weeks of real contentment between us that I found the letter. It just fell out when I was stacking up the sheets to put them on top of the piano. It was a letter from her, from Beth to Humphrey. At first I thought it must have been written long ago. But Humphrey had brought that music to my flat only a short time ago. Then I began to wonder if he'd even seen the letter. I didn't dare show it to him. It was a quite terrible letter. It shocked me.

It was the most raw, and the most erotic thing I'd ever read. It detailed their most personal life, explored it so openly, so explicitly that I recoiled from it. I hadn't the strength to destroy it. I wanted to. When I first began to read it, I kept telling myself, tear this up, now, this second. Don't go on. But I took it instead to the bathroom and read it. All of it. All ten pages of it.

She seemed really to be screaming at him on those pieces of paper. But they were the people who never had rows. She seemed to wipe their sex, his and hers, all over him, rubbed it in with bitterness and anger. She wrote about a dream she'd had, about the two of them making love. There were things in it about her, about how he had been to her sexually. I mean, I never thought. I imagined that after years of being with the same person, that it wasn't like that – not for them. That it wasn't like it was between him and me. That letter made me throw up. Literally.

I felt deceived and dirty. I felt a sense of betrayal equal to hers. It wasn't quite that Humphrey had deceived me, he hadn't. It's just that I knew he'd tell me if I asked, so I never asked. I'd deceived myself. I desperately wanted to know if he'd seen the letter. If he'd read it. I couldn't believe he had. Because he would have told me. He couldn't have borne that sort of pain alone. He'd shown me other letters from her, from the beginning: calm letters asking him what he wanted to do, what he wanted her to do. She seemed to prefer, when things were very difficult for her, to write them down for him. She didn't do things head-on, as I did. Or he did.

I didn't show Humphrey the letter, I couldn't. Then slowly, the more I thought about it, the more I began to wonder what the purpose of that letter was. It had blown my security and trust. It had made me question and doubt everything all over again. The more I considered it, the more I thought that the letter had not been intended for Humphrey, it had been intended for me. It was an act of revenge, an act of warning. She had written that letter to me, from her to me. And from that moment, all her sweetness and under-standing that day in her kitchen seemed a lie, a manipulation for her own benefit. Beth was fighting back. And she was being dirty about it.

Four

Monday

To see that woman standing there in my kitchen – it was utterly shocking. In my kitchen, like a burglar, yes, most precisely so, a burglar. To be confronted by an enemy in so unexpected a way would dash the confidence of anyone. I could feel the tell-tale signals inside me – my breathing was shallow and harsh and the blood was rushing in my head. But I knew she would not detect any of this if I spoke very calmly; I felt she knew nothing at all about me. But just then I could not speak. We were just surveying one another – at last. She and me. We too alone. With Humphrey outside, quite unaware of it. We stood there for a while, in complete silence. So riveted was I by her that I couldn't even take in what she had done to my kitchen.

When the shock passed – it was surprisingly fleeting – I knew precisely why she was there. I also knew that she had read this diary that I've taken to writing to keep my thoughts in order. It was a despicable thing to do, to enter our home like that. But then I wasn't surprised. You could tell she was a shallow kind of person, someone of no real consequence. Not Humphrey's type at all, I'd have thought. You know how it is, there are people one meets and feels: now if I went up to her and if I pushed into her, I would find she was made of papier-mâché, my finger would go right through her and encounter air. That is what I thought of her.

Then other things struck me. First, she was not as young as I'd imagined her; she was over thirty, though she was wearing the kind of clothes that Abi favoured when she was going through her scruffy jeans and dungarees stage. And she was very small, dainty and sort of quivering, quivering so much that looking hard at her face, which was very flushed and desperate, I thought: there is something a little deranged about this person. Her smallness was startling somehow, because in my mind she had loomed so large. Her breasts were large. Strange that one's husband should be involved with breasts that size when he has always professed not to care for them.

She was hugging her arms just above her waist and she looked positively petrified – not just of me, but of herself and what she had done. I refused to pity her, it wasn't hard. By then I was looking at what she had done on her visit. She had completely destroyed my kitchen. She had obviously been at work for some time and had finished by the time I disturbed her, because the house was quiet when I'd entered the front door, and if she'd been hurling my mother's crockery about, I would definitely have heard it. Things that old and that expensive don't die quietly.

Then she dropped her eyes, as if she couldn't bear to look at me. Her face tipped down and became like that of a small child who has broken your favourite cup and doesn't know how to put it right. Cass still looks at me like that. She looked around her, dazed, at the devastation. All the drawers had been tipped out, the porcelain plates smashed to smithereens, the collection of old coffee cups, each one unique and specially chosen for some delicacy of colour or design, crushed under those little feet of hers. Feet small as an Oriental's. And now her face wore a mask-like pallor, almost a decorum, as she looked around her, rubbing her hands down her straight hips. She was a woman who had not had children. She had torn my children's paintings off the walls, had shredded the photographs. My jam was all over the floor, studded with broken glass; there was a horrible smell of onion and garlic, the silver had been kicked all over the place. She lifted her hand to her head as if she was confused. A shard of the mirror that was now smashed fell noisily, and we both jumped as it clattered to the floor.

For a moment I wanted to say, calmly, as one always hopes one would say to a vandal: All right now, you've got what you wanted, you've done what you came to do – now clear it up. But I had heard Humphrey coming in and closing the door. My mood was broken. Remembering him had thrown me into a panic. I couldn't bear for him to be a part of this. I could not allow it. It was far too dangerous.

She seemed to spin like a clockwork doll. She whirled about like someone trapped. She made no sound, but I could see large round tears rolling down her cheeks, one after the other, and her face was transfixed now with the deepest sadness I have ever seen. It was a sadness I felt she had lived with always; it was like the sadness of someone who has done something monstrous and then tasted the knowledge that it is something she will have to live with always. I'm not sure she knew she was crying; she seemed quite incapable of thought or action.

I wanted to hit her hard – right across her eyes, her mouth, her cheeks – and then I didn't want to at all. Because I saw suddenly what it was that Humphrey saw in her; helplessness, something fractured, something lost and bewildered.

But that was no business of mine. And she still stood in my kitchen, in the comforting, beautiful room I had made, and in which we all spent most of our time, contentedly, without her. There she stood, where she had no right to be. Surrounded by her havoc. Which I must explain to Humphrey, not lying to him, but feigning ignorance so he could make his own assumptions. After all, I had no idea how well he knew her. Perhaps she did this often. But I had to cover for her, so that Humphrey should not suffer, so that he wouldn't come up against the edge of reality. Because to Humphrey, this could not have happened. Everything he tried to do to bring happiness, and peace – would make this scene unthinkable. It was as if he kept a picture in his head: a perfectly composed portrait of a man with two women, one on each arm, smiling, happy. The tension and pain that might be found in the faces and postures of the women would escape him, the badly composed nature of the picture – incomplete or over-complete, would not strike him. He would catch only the hesitant smile on each mouth and concentrate on that with his kisses and his deadly kindness. But here, now, someone had got that picture and ripped it right down the centre. Such violence would have shattered Humphrey; I had to protect him from it.

In a low growl I shouted at her, 'Get out, get out,' and in that second, in that sudden loss of control, the kitchen knife, so snug in its rack, could just as easily have been pulled down to cut her throat.

'Get out!' I shouted again at her immobile stupidity, wanting to push her right through the glass, and terrified that Humphrey would come into the kitchen.

But what an extraordinary thing. When I yelled at her like that, she smiled, a strange knowing smile, as if my fury had comforted her, as if she was reading my thoughts and recognized them. Her smile stilled and chilled me. Because it was as if she had stolen that smile from me – it was my smile. It is how I smile when I have achieved what I set out to achieve, when I stand back in satisfaction and say, There, I've done it.

She turned her back on me and walked out of my kitchen carrying my smile, bearing it off like a trophy. She turned to look back at me once more and I felt that she thought she knew all about me, knew all my secrets, knew even when I had learned how to hang a smile on my face like that so no one could see behind it.

And with that look, any tiny bud of pity for her left me. I hated her in the most complete and horrifying way. I felt she had not only attacked me where I lived, but that she had also manipulated me – had seen my sympathy emerging and walked off smiling with it. It would have been the greatest pleasure to have killed her then.

Five

'This is bloody, really bloody, Beth,' Humphrey fumed, picking up the torn scraps of a photograph of himself and Beth last spring in Portugal. Before he knew Sylvie, just. 'This isn't a burglary – it's just wanton destruction, for the sheer hell of it. Who could have done this? What perverted, bigoted, tiny, crusted mentality could have done this? My God,' he was appalled at the possibility, 'could it be some of those yobs you're always having to supper?'

'No, it could not,' she said firmly, then added, 'People are very strange.' No one could have been more calm than Beth at that moment, picking up lumps of china, placing them, unmourned, in a large plastic rubbish bag.

'But you're the one,' he insisted, 'the sympathetic, mushy one – pass me the broom – there's nothing salvageable here. So explain it to me. What would the social workers say?' In his fury his voice had a brittle quality; his eyes were bright and hard and he was accusing Beth of complicity because of her sympathy.

'They would say' – she was staring at a coffee cup, which, by some miracle was intact. It lay in her hand, pale pink, with a little rosebud crouching at the pit of the bowl. 'They would say,' she said, 'that this is the work of a disturbed person trying to get back at their mother, trying to smash up the womb.'

'They would, would they?' he sneered.

'Yes, and they wouldn't recommend hanging, either,' she said archly.

'Anyway,' he spoke more reasonably now, 'it would be a man in that case, wouldn't it?' She wondered if she imagined it, or whether there was a tremor of relief in his voice.

'Not necessarily,' she said quietly, 'and nothing done here requires any great strength.' She was gathering up the knives and forks, to put them in the sink. Everything that was whole would have to be washed, very well. He looked at her and she returned his look, like a perfectly placed shot that skims the net and cannot be returned.

'Humphrey . . .' she began.

'Yes,' but his look was furtive, it said, proceed no further, let it be.

'Oh, nothing.' It was his defence which silenced her, it was the way his mind had circled the possibility of Sylvie and veered away from it – and now refused her any access to his thoughts.

'Perhaps,' she said thoughtfully, 'we should have locks put on the windows? It would be safer, wouldn't it?'

'Hm.' He hadn't even heard her. He was looking intently at a ripped fragment of a photograph, his eyebrows drawn so close together that they seemed like a hedge blocking her view of his face. She knew what he was looking at. A bit of the photograph was missing, the side with Humphrey on. Sylvie had taken him home with her.

'Yes,' she repeated, 'we will get some locks fitted.'

Beth was thinking that that person, that creature who was here earlier must be kept out at all costs – doors and windows must be barred against her, chipped glass be put on top of the brick walls, alarms set in secret corners. She was like someone carrying on guerrilla warfare in their back garden, in their kitchen. It was this that made Beth feel that there would be little difficulty in shooting her. She began to be quite drawn to a crime of passion. Humphrey would certainly enjoy it – he loved spectacular things, he loved to be the centre of attention.

'Perhaps we should get a gun,' she whispered, moving closer to him.

'Oh, for God's sake Beth!' Now what had shaken him like that? she wondered, watching as a muscle pulled at his cheek. She still held the little cup in her hand and she looked at him slowly over it.

'Do you remember where we bought this, Humphrey?' She wanted to caress him, to draw him back to her, to love him among the broken intimacy of all these things that she cherished, that had enriched her life as much as books and music, paintings and long summer days. 'It was in that odd little shop, near Haworth, do you remember?'

He nodded. He felt a great pain in him – a sense of his own evil. He was standing close to her, facing her. He took the cup from her and placed it carefully on the table.

'I remember everything, Beth,' he said quietly. 'I've forgotten nothing, you are as close to me now as you were then.'

'But it's so easy,' she whispered painfully, 'so easy, so quick, for things to get broken. It takes no time at all. They fall apart and you look at them dazed. Oh, Humphrey,' she clutched her hands and her eyes were wide and watery, 'you have to be so careful, people have to be so careful of one another, they have to stop and think and wait. Or all those years of building and growing, collecting, loving – they come to nothing. They become like this room.' She was crying, quite devastated by what had happened. She wanted him to comfort her as only he could, to put everything to rights again: wind the day back; scrub the kitchen clean of all discord. As only he could. He took her to him and held her tenderly; he turned her face and pressed it against his shoulder.

They made love on the floor. 'No, Beth, not here,' he'd said, appalled. 'Yes,' she hissed, 'here, it must be here.' She looked at him and saw how hard it was for him. So he did know. 'Here,' she repeated, 'it must be here.'

There was blood on her hand, a deep cut where a piece of china had cut the skin. She did not notice it then, but later she saw a streak of blood across the back of his neck, a straight line, like a knife slice.

Six

Tuesday

I know that in a few years' time, when this is all over, when I read this again, it will seem like another life – or like some terrible affliction that damages the power of love and hope. When you have put so much in a marriage, in a man, you cannot let it go; you have to consider all the means at your disposal.

There was nothing wrong with our marriage. That was the critical wisdom, that was what made the entire thing like a nightmare, that's why I couldn't deal with it, tidy it up and lock it away. It was why it was impossible to forgive him.

The weekend before, the one before that frightful scene in the kitchen, when we'd been away, had been so revealing. Perhaps it unhinged me a little. I felt ajar, not myself any more. Everything seemed sinister, seemed to be building up to some crisis. We were staying with old friends, in a cottage in Sussex. Anne and David had known us from even before the children, and she in particular was perceptive. She knew something was wrong. She said to me in the garden, 'What is it, Beth? Is it anything to do with Humphrey's business? I thought he was doing so well.' I couldn't possibly tell her.

Since my last dramatic outburst, at the dinner party on Humphrey's birthday, I have seen my friends discomforted, awkward and absent. It was as if we stood up and struck one another in front of them. They went to ground, after the obligatory thank-you phone calls. No one, not even Mary, would ask me to explain. They were angry with me, as if I had betrayed them. Our marriage, by being so openly discredited, had soiled, not only their relationship with us, but it had frightened them with the possibility of disaster in their own alliances.

So I did not tell Anne; I said we were tired. That I was working much more in the business now, more than I had for years – which was true – and that Humphrey seemed disenchanted with it – which was true – and yes, this could be turned into an area of worry. How clever of her to divine it. And so on and so forth. She very quickly flung these ingredients together into the concoction she found most digestible. She nodded, she was reassured.

I felt vacant, detached and my smile began to weary me. I have smiled that smile – gentle, sympathetic, calm – for so many years, it's stuck to my face. And suddenly it seemed dreadful to me, as if, for years, presiding at dinner tables, entertaining business contacts, entering rooms on his arm, that smile had gone before me like an announcement to the world: see how happy and successful we are; how proud he is of my beauty and grace; see what a perfect couple we make. I wanted to put my hand round it and yank it off my face for all the falseness and conceit of it. But it had become so automatic, I wasn't aware of using it any more. Besides, as long as it lasted no one believed any harm could come to us.

Sometimes, I cannot make a move towards him because I am in such disarray. He will hover around me, almost fuss; he'll ask me if I'm hot or cold, if I'm feeling well; do I have a headache? I never have headaches. But he cannot actually say, 'What is it, Beth?' He can't ask for the truth. I look sharply at him, and then a look of – what is it? – obligation? burden? settles on him, which I cannot endure. So I have to find some odd or end to tell him, to bring him back from that marooned place my displeasure leaves him on. Because I know he cannot bear the thought that he is hurting me. And I do know also that all our life together, what he has always wanted to do is to surround me with comfort and ease and security.

I don't know how she can do it: I couldn't live a hole-in-the-corner life, with no mutual circle of friends, no security, no constant companionship. I couldn't bear not to be Humphrey's wife, because being that has made up the best part of my life, the best part of me. It must be hard for her. As for him, I can understand that he loves another woman – I understand love and there isn't a lot you can do about it once it's got you. I understand what he's doing, though I couldn't understand a succession of women from a man who couldn't mature. It's jealousy I don't understand; what it does to you, how it breaks down character. It's like an illness, progressive and untreatable.

Last weekend we were dressing for dinner. I like the formality of such things; Humphrey doesn't – the most he will do is change his shirt. But I like this about him, as he likes the way I will dress up.

We don't expect to be the same. He watched me as I put on a blue silk dress and smoothed it across my throat. I let him choose the jewels I would wear with it and bent my head as he fastened the amethyst chain around my neck.

'Humphrey, make sure the clasp is centred at the back, I hate it crooked.' I reached my hand up and stroked his cheek and asked him what he was smiling about.

'I was remembering how long it took me to get the money to buy you that first tiny emerald ring.'

'I love it more than any other jewel you've given me.' His hands came down lightly on my bare shoulders and he looked at me in the mirror, standing quietly behind me, just looking. I turned my face and kissed his hand.

'You are still so beautiful, Beth.'

And yet I felt he was remembering me as I was, long ago, and that there's a sadness in it for him.

'Shall we go down, my darling?' I asked and he nodded.

We walked together, arm in arm, down the stairs and into the drawing-room, where people were gathered. As they greeted us, that feeling of being a unit, of being whole and at peace, came over me. Whenever I am with him, where there are other women, he never lets them feel that there is a possibility that he could be drawn from me – he charms, but doesn't flirt; he never appears available.

I feel that, as much as it is possible for one human being to understand another, I understand Humphrey, and he me. And this loyalty of his, this public statement about our marriage, has always given me the greatest happiness. And it's why he's never been able to talk to me about my public statement at his birthday dinner – it cut him to the quick. He didn't understand how I could do such a thing.

And yet something keeps eating at me. I've always believed that one only fell in love if the possibility was there, within one. Otherwise, you close it off – nothing happens because you have put it away from you. Humphrey has fallen in love – and he will remain so for many, many years. For him the possibility existed. It's the why that does such damage to me – that he could be open to it – how could he?

Perhaps it's just that he cannot bear to think that there are experiences in life, big ones, involving important emotions, that he would never know, that he would have to put aside? Does this make him morally slack – weak? – a bad person? Or just selfish? As we'd all like to be?

I looked across the room; he was talking vividly and for effect. I saw him move his hands with that quick grace and throw back his head and laugh. Being a witty man, he loves wit in others, he pounces on jokes with the greatest pleasure; he always laughs first. But then the man he was talking to, turned, was pulled into another conversation. Humphrey moved away. How lost he looked! Oh, how like a small boy. How it hurt me. I watched his face, his mouth had turned down at the corners, he looked tired and yes, he looked a little old. I begin to feel, as he does, that it's the cruellest thing in life to age, to grow old, and yet to feel just the same inside.

It is dreadful to wonder if he too wears a clamped-on laugh – if he too walks into rooms on my arm playing the same elaborate charade. Oh no, it's unthinkable. He fastened his eyes hungrily on the telephone, he moved towards it and then away. He looked around him guiltily; his smile flashed at a preoccupied audience. My heart contracted: he's like a boy playing a game that can only hurt him and he doesn't know when to stop.

I walked over and threaded my arm through his. Relief flooded his face. For a moment he seemed actually to believe that it was me he was missing. I started to tell him something that joined us together, but there was a distracted look about him. I lost heart. I am aware always now of a third person; that as he listens and talks to me, another woman is beside him too. We are never alone, he and I, any more.

Seven

Humphrey was worried about Sylvie: she was unhappy, something had undermined her confidence and she wouldn't speak to him about it. In her unhappiness she dug herself into her work, spending more and more time away from him, and when she was with him, being preoccupied and quiet. He couldn't stand it. He felt quite lost without her love and support, her rages and aggression. It was as if she had become a compass, keeping him happy and on course and without it he didn't know quite where he was.

He turned back to Beth and found her as she always was. She had divined his misery, even its cause, and she comforted him – by being happy, by being unchanged. When she was like this, knowing and giving him precisely what he needed, he found her magnificent. Her steadfastness humbled and awed him. And it was at times like this, at the height of her power, that he would come upon her working at some tear in one of her daughters' dresses, or scrubbing vegetables in the sink, and be amazed that none of her magnificence was dimmed. It was as if she had made of her life an art, a flawless thing that nothing could reduce.

But he was reduced, daily, by Sylvie's distance. His life could not be composed without her happiness. He had to restore her because without her he could not be restored. It seemed to him that there was only one way to do it.

He asked her to marry him.

Eight

They were married at Kensington Registry Office. Walking out into the sunlight with Sylvie, Humphrey remembered Beth at their wedding, in Ireland, all those years ago. His feelings on this day were no less inspired than they had been the first time. He remembered Beth in her white silk dress, her face harder than it was now, but quite lovely. And giving her his arm, precisely as he had just done to Sylvie, and finding in her raised face all the containment, the modesty, the happiness that he now saw in Sylvie's.

He felt no sense of treachery. It seemed now that things were absolutely fair and equal and that the affairs of his loves could be managed with the minimum of recrimination and upset. The fact that what he was doing was illegal bothered him not at all, but nor did it bother Sylvie. Their marriage did not seem devalued because he had done it before, or because he was still married. Some men, she thought, had a string of women and married them, one after the other. Three or four times. That was all right it seemed. What he had done seemed no less honourable than that. It seemed more honourable, more loyal. He was ending no vow, he was merely taking on new ones. It did not make him less responsible, just more so. So she convinced herself.

They went to Paris and spent a romantic weekend near the Opéra. And on Sunday night Humphrey went back home. It seemed perfectly acceptable. Quite fair. A redress had been made, a civilized understanding. It was now much easier for Sylvie to let him go back to Beth. There was now no difference between them. Or so she convinced herself.

Nine

'I'm packing it in, Beth, I've had enough,' Humphrey said, looking directly at her.

Her dark brows closed ranks, and her mouth, a small pink dent, straightened into a line.

'Oh,' she breathed through her teeth. He saw an expression on her face that he'd seen only once before: when she had gone into hard labour with their first child – a fierce, stripped look: the look of someone who will go through it whatever the cost. When she lifted her face, she was in command again.

He knew what she was thinking. He knew that what he said was a cruelty and a test, but he had to know. It was clear then that if he left her, and gave himself entirely to Sylvie – that would be the greatest cruelty. She could survive it, but she would grow bitter, she would hate him. Nothing would survive between them. Quickly he said, gripping her arm, 'I've decided to give up the business,' he said, 'that's all.' He made it seem so trivial; indeed, it was trivial compared to her imaginings.

They were sitting under his apple tree; it was late afternoon. The apples above their heads were full and heavy, he had even picked a few for her and they lay on the ground, fat and perfectly shaped. The summer was wearing on, but taking its time about it. Sunlight flitted across his face as she watched his thoughts darting about, much like the insects between the leaves of the tree. From the upstairs windows music roared.

She said, 'I just feel so wary of you.' She noticed that the garden had begun to look a little neglected; that there was something ragged about the roses. The dead-heads had not been cut off – Humphrey couldn't bear anything dead in the garden – the sound of his secateurs cutting through the stems came back to her and it reminded her of some woman in some film, who'd cut off her nipples with the secateurs.

'Why are you wary of me?' he asked anxiously.

'Oh, you are so full of these quick decisions.' She pulled at the grass. 'You never hesitate or question, you just say: "I have another woman," or, "I've decided to give up the business." Just like that. As if it had nothing to do with me.' Her face was hot, but she was willing it not to flush. She shook herself. She knew that what she had said had silenced him, and she must, again, bring the thing round.

'What do you want to do?' She was weary of it all. To endure such agony at the hands of a man who gave you days, months, years of unsurpassed happiness – and then to feel, as it floundered, as it pitched upwards again – oh, only the most overwhelming fatigue. Like the fatigue she felt when her daughters romped all over the house, spilling their enthusiasms in her lap, demanding her attention, her involvement in all of it – and yet, at the same time, making her feel curiously unnecessary, as if their real interests lay so far from her own, from the home, that she was just a laundry bag into which they hurled each used-up article as they tired of it.

And here he was, her husband, about to thrust on her his new enthusiasm, his desire for change, at a time – she felt it furiously now – when he should be consolidating, putting down roots for the future. She looked at him, she wanted to be hard on him, to force him to something more befitting – but no, pity flooded her. Poor Humphrey, he is older than he wants to be – too much water has rushed under his bridge and with his bare hands he wants to hold it back.

'Beth, I want you to have my shares,' he declared, knowing he couldn't go into all these emotions she was feeling. At times like this it was better to stick to the facts, they were reliable. 'I've talked to Harry, just to check out any complications. I want you to have the business.'

'So that you can get out?' she snapped. Her hand rubbed the grass flat with a movement that suggested she was wiping her palm of something unpleasant.

'I have been getting out for some time. There's no point in doing something that has lost all its appeal.' He was remote.

No, she thought, he won't do anything that is difficult, effort is offensive to him, things must glide, must fall into his lap. He had reached a point when he didn't know how to handle George, who was becoming boisterous in his discontent, who was determined to snatch some of the power.

'I don't want to burden you with it,' he said. 'I thought I'd just give it to you – all the shares – you don't have to run it of course. We'll get someone to do that.'

'But not George.'

'No, not George.'

'I see. And you want me to have all the shares?'

'Yes.'

'So that it will still remain yours, even though you give it up?' Oh, that was like him.

He sighed. She would not understand, she was going to pull him over the coals of it. Why couldn't she understand; she'd lived through it too. How tired he was of the whole thing, of the long, lonely years working to death on that stupid business. And now, at forty-five, feeling utterly bored by it all. Tired of the success of it, the way the figures expanded, the share price rose and contracts accumulated. It was so predictable. Whatever he did in that office, he did so easily – it actually made him feel useless. And to put up, each day, with the demands of George – like a child asking for an allowance, like a woman nagging for some token of affection. The same ritual of complaints and demands, and each time the bastard demanded, the tighter Humphrey's refusals grew. He had begun to hate to go to the office the way some men hate to go home to their wives.

'No,' he said, 'I don't want to keep it. It's a gift, for God's sake.' Beth was difficult on gifts, awkward and embarrassed. 'If you don't want it, you can sell it, if you'd rather. I don't care. It's simply that I don't want to do it any more. I don't need the money. I can afford to choose, and I want to get shot of it. You knew this, Beth, we haven't talked about it much, but you did know.' Why was she being so difficult?

'You don't need it. But I suppose I do?'

'Well, you've been going in a lot lately, every day. You've been more or less running my side of things.'

'You haven't been there,' she said tartly. 'When you aren't there, Humphrey,' she said it patiently, 'things go wrong. You've seen in the past how wrong they can go. People were phoning me up at home all the time, so I began to feel I might as well be there. To make sure the clients are happy – and that George doesn't get out of hand. People get crooked when the boss is playing truant, you know.' Had he forgotten how his last 'partner' – the one before George – had actually tried to steal his clients from him and set up on his own? Pulling the rug from under him had given Humphrey one of the greatest triumphs of his life.

She was reprimanding him, he felt. And it didn't anger him, its effect was more deadly. It reminded him of how much she had always done for him, cared for and loved him through the restless procession of his life. But even as he thought it, as if to save him, a second vision blotted it out: a round, sweet face laughing up at him, a throat flung back as Sylvie slaked down gin and tonic. She was so free – Sylvie – she made him feel the same. She exhilarated him. When he'd told her he was packing in the business, she'd laughed and said, 'Hoorah! You're a free man at last. It's time you did something else. It's time you had a good time. Don't worry, I'll support you: you can lie in bed till eleven and then go and play on the stock exchange or gamble on the horses. Nobody should work beyond forty – it's immoral, it's disgusting. You stick to it, my little darling, don't let anyone talk you out of it. You do what you want to do.'

'To success,' she'd said, raising her glass, 'to real success. To getting out of the rat race.' He'd remembered what Graham Greene had said: 'Success is only a delayed failure.' Well, now he knew that it was possible to delay for ever. And for what?

'I don't want the business,' Beth said. 'Half the shares are enough. They represent the work I've done there. It's quite enough.' She never mentioned her financial investment in things, ever. He thought now with pleasure that there was no greed in her. There were a few, rare people in life who didn't want any more, who were happy with what they had and could turn more away. He couldn't really claim to be among that select band, because, although he wanted no more of his business, it was because he wanted something else more urgently: his freedom from it, the right to be himself.

'Well, that's all right. I'll bring someone in to run it. There's a whizz-kid I met a year or so ago, we've kept in touch, he'd jump at the chance. I'll ring him tomorrow and get him over.'

'But what about George?'

'George?' Why couldn't she see George as he was? Or was it just her idea of fairness?

'George,' he said, 'can do what he does perfectly adequately, but if he ran a business it'd go phut in no time.'

'Why do you dislike him so?' She was looking up at the window where Cass was looking out; she waved.

'I don't,' he said patiently. 'He just doesn't have any flair. He gives clients the creeps, I've seen him do it. When he tries to be charming, he ends up oily.'

Of course, she thought, Humphrey would never bring in a partner who he could work with, who was brilliant or oozing with charisma; he always ended up with men he disliked. That way he didn't have to share what he had. It was this possessiveness, she felt, that spoilt the generosity in him; that made him petty at times.

'And you?' she said, looking straight at him, 'what will you do, once you've handed it over?' How strange that he could care so little for it now that he could hand it over to a stranger. Would he sell him shares, she wondered, do the thing properly?

He pulled himself up from his sprawled position on the grass with an athletic jack-knife movement that snapped his arms around his legs. 'I'm going to buy some land – acres of it,' he announced. 'I've seen it already – in Wiltshire: farmland and pine forests.' He looked at her with excitement. 'I want you to come and see it, Beth, it's marvellous. You'll love it.'

She watched him, almost bemused, as he began to entice her with his enthusiasm. It never ceased to amaze her how he could stir her up with his plans. Now, it was long weekends in the country overlooking tumbling meadows full of fat cows; streams full of trout – all that land – all that dirt and space. She felt his hunger to possess it – it was quite Irish – she recognized it: her father had had it. He'd had a territorial resistance to giving up his land, even when he was desperate for the money; he hated, in the end, letting other men farm it – renting it had spoilt it for him. Now, here was Humphrey, putting away a sensationally successful career to own land – because he wasn't going to farm it, he wasn't that foolish – he just wanted to have it. Wasn't this the height of boredom? This surely could only be a diversion. It couldn't be called a new career.

But she listened to him. Talking about it – his eyes bright, his hands moving in that emphatic way, as if they would sweep you up and carry you to the summit of his vision – she remembered sitting in meetings, watching him bewitch clients with his trenchancy, his repartee, his brilliant way of turning a negative question into a positive benefit. Oh, he was so good at it! Never mind that he was pulling things out of the air, improvising, inventing, downright lying – to watch him you had to marvel at his sword-play. Given ten minutes, he would disarm any opponent, flick the poor devil's sword into the air, catch it with his free hand and then laugh and say, 'There, the game's up. But I'll spare you dishonour; I'll just kill you cleanly.' It was the observers, the Georges who watched this procedure with hatred in their hearts; his opponents fell at his feet.

'Humphrey,' she now said, 'if that's what you want, then you must have it.' She moved a little away from him because the leg of her chair seemed to have fallen into some rut in the dry earth. She knew he wouldn't regret it. He had no time for regrets: he was never one, if things went against him, to say: If only I hadn't done it, if only I had done such and such instead. He did what he did. Finish.

She had become infected by his mood. Now, what he wanted seemed to be what she wanted too. She turned to him and said eagerly. 'Why don't we just sell it outright? I don't want it. Nor do you. Why can't we both be free of it? So we can start again?'

'Yes, perhaps,' he said vaguely. 'I did think of that and perhaps we will – in a little while. There's just one deal going through at the moment that I'd like to feel was secure before we did.'

'The banqueting chain?'

'Hm.' He was looking thoughtful; he realized he'd have to get back into that deal to bring it off. George had done all the ground work, but if he wasn't careful, the wally might try and take over and ruin the whole thing. It was a delicate situation, needing a cool approach, which was why he'd left it on a back burner: you didn't push people with great expertise, you let them come round to you as if it were their idea in the first place. That was the way to handle Mowbray, but now he couldn't afford to sit on it too much longer. A lunch, perhaps, in the director's dining-room with the Homard à l'américaine and one of those delicious Gâteaux Margot that the factory had finally absolutely perfected. Perhaps introduce the new man at the same time? No, unsettling, best leave that.

'How will you buy the land? Through the firm?' she was asking.

'No, I've sold some stock.' He leaned back, straightening his long arms and pushing them firmly into the ground almost as if he was doing an exercise.

'Which?' she said, her voice worried.

'No,' he laughed, 'not that' – he knew she was referring to the first stock they'd bought together. 'I couldn't anyway. It was just some shares I bought recently, Harry put me on to them. Came on the market six months ago and galloped up in value. If I sell now I'll have made a killing.' When he spoke like that, she thought, he always sounded shifty; the deals he did on his own were never, well, quite, ones that he was prepared to discuss in detail.

'Goodness, Beth, you're shivering.' He moved towards her in alarm. She had barely shivered. It made her aware of how acute was his sense of the small kindness – his arm was around her in an instant. Now, worrying that this talk might have distressed her, he put out his hand and took hers and said, 'It'll be fine, you'll see, we'll be fine, darling. How about a cup of tea? Shall I make it?'

Ten

When Beth entered the kitchen, she found Cass sitting on the table, painting her fingernails.

'Must you do that in here, Cass? Wouldn't the bathroom be better?'

'Yeh, I know, but Fran's having a bath and I can't stand the way she ogles her body in that mirror and sings, "I'm so perilously close to perfection". I mean, she's got even worse since she's convinced herself she's a reincarnation of Marilyn Monroe – her room's like a bloody shrine, you can't move for posters and deathanalia of Marilyn.'

Beth laughed and wiped her daughter's large and grimy footprints off the table.

Cass went on grimly, 'I mean, what future has she got? It was much better when she wanted to be a vet. Now all she wants is to be famous – that's it: just famous. Not famous as a singer, or a dancer – just famous. You can't be famous for *nothing*. And when I yell at her and say I'll be famous too, what does she say, the little twit, but: "Yes, Cass, of course you'll be famous – one day everyone will know you're my sister!"'

'Oh, Cass,' Beth laughed, 'the most this will last, God willing, is another month or so.'

'Yeh, you're probably right, Ma.' Cass's good humour was quick to return. She surveyed her long red talons with satisfaction; at least her nails were beautiful.

'Are you going out, Cass?'

'Hmm. Why?'

'Well, you said you'd help me do up that room – did you forget?'

'What room?'

'For Jimmy. He's coming round later. Mary's bringing him. I was relying on your being here; you're so good with kids.'

'Oh, shit. Never mind. I'll be back before he comes, then.'

'He's coming at seven.'

'Well, in that case, can I ask Antonio to come here?'

'Yes, of course.'

Cass crossed her legs on the table and her mother surveyed her with a little alarm: Why must she look conspicuous, whatever the cost? Today, it was streaks of red through her brown hair; black outlining around her purple lips and what looked like a layer of tar above and below her eyes. If she felt herself ugly, why did she make herself more so? It was Humphrey's characteristic, she decided, this desire to be particular, to be noticed, singled out – all her children had it. Even Abi, as a child, had made herself into the difficult, bad child, the victim, for this very reason – to draw attention to herself. It was greed, she supposed, insecurity and greed.

When Cass had left to make a phone call, Beth began to fret about the small boy she had agreed to foster for a while. Humphrey hadn't helped, of course, though he certainly was much better than he would have been a year or so ago. Then, he would have tried to bully her out of it. Was this new tolerance in him Sylvie's influence? If it was, it was infuriating, because it meant that all her years with him had left him unchanged – and then, the minute he cares for a new woman, he bends and mellows. Oh, it was so infuriating and so unfair. With the bitterness up in her she was horrified to find that the strength of her feeling was actually chipping away at the essential structure of her character. She, the stronger, the straighter of the two, was being broken down because of the violence of her emotions. While he, in the strength of his feelings and his love, was becoming more kindly, more noble even. It was positively sickening.

Still, it comforted her that his mockery had been left intact. He had asked her how long the boy was to stay and she'd said, 'Oh, I don't know. It's up to Mary and his parents. He's been pushed around so much: his mother's had a breakdown and his father can't stand the sight of him; he's been to six different foster homes in the past year – with violent spells at home in between.'

'Is he house-broken, Beth?' He'd looked at her over his glasses.

'For God's sake, Humphrey! It's not his fault. Of course he's going to be difficult.'

'So you realize,' he looked at her with amusement, 'that he's going to come in here and break all the chairs and kick in the telly?'

'Humphrey,' she said patiently, 'he's nine years old.'

'So he'll be wetting his bed as well?'

'If he does, we'll put your mac under his sheet,' she said crisply.

Humphrey shrugged with mock-indifference, 'Still, we can be like everyone else I suppose, and kick him out if he's a pest.' His eyes were racing with amusement but there was none of that caustic quality to his wit that had carried disapproval with it in the past.

'Take him on appro, you mean?' She gave him a withering look even though she knew he was teasing her.

'Listen, darling,' he said gently, rubbing her cheek and seeing how she leant it against his hand. 'Why'd you need to do this? We've got a house full of juvenile delinquents as it is. What's it about, eh?'

'I don't know.' She flinched at his scrutiny. 'It's just that Mary said that at the last place he was at, the woman often forgot to feed him, he used to go next door and ask for food ... it seemed so pathetic.' She looked pathetic thinking of it, and God she could be so mushy in her thinking, in her politics and conscience.

'You can't be the world's conscience, my love, you can't be so raw to what the world does out there.'

'Humphrey,' she was severe now, 'we all have to help – we can't just let the social workers be scapegoats because we don't give a damn.'

He held up his hand. 'You're absolutely right. I know you'll be marvellous and of course he must stay as long as he needs to.' He smiled. 'I might even teach him a thing or to. When's the little chap coming then?'

When the little chap came, he had eyes like drills and a mouth that rightly belonged on the face of a street-fighter. He wore jeans and a short T-shirt and his left eye had a bluish scar beneath it. He clenched his fists at his side and seemed to rock on the balls of his feet. He gave one the impression that if you made contact with him, you did it at your peril.

He said nothing when Mary brought him into the kitchen; he didn't even look around, but he stood close to Mary, and when finally he looked at Beth, it was with deep suspicion, she felt, with distrust, and certainly, dislike.

'Hello Jimmy,' Humphrey said, remaining seated at the table, but looking up. Not a word.

'Want to come outside and look at the garden?' Humphrey suggested a little later.

The boy turned his eyes on him and said sarcastically, 'Listen, cock, I've seen gardens. When I want to see another flaming garden I'll tell you, OK?'

Catching just a glimmer of humour there, Humphrey jumped on it. He said coolly, 'OK, kid, if you want to see this particular garden you just walk out that door. That suit you?'

The boy looked at him with a bit of interest, then his expression fell flat.

'Cup of tea, Mary?' Beth asked, a little daunted by this tough, wounded boy.

'Yes, love one. Jimmy, do you want some tea? Or some orange juice?' She pushed back her hair. 'Hell, it's hot, isn't it?'

Jimmy shook his head, but then watched them drink as if he was thirsty. He wouldn't sit down.

When Mary left, there was an uncomfortable silence in the kitchen as Humphrey went on reading the paper. Beth said, 'Shall I show you to your room, Jimmy?' She smiled. 'And where everything is. We're very glad to have you, you know. Come.' She tried to take his hand; he stuffed it into his jeans' pocket. It was curious how old his mannerisms were, it was as if he'd never been a child, let alone a baby. Beth remembered her children at his age and they'd seemed so innocent and small in comparison. He followed her up the stairs, walking behind her, dragging his feet. Humphrey watched him, a peculiar, touched expression on his face.

Cass came back with Antonio a little later. 'Is he sweet?' she crooned, 'I bet he is. What's he look like? Where is he?'

'Listen,' Humphrey said, 'this kid has probably never even heard the word sweet. He's more like an active member of the IRA.'

'Ah, poor little bleeder,' Antonio said in his gauzy Italian accent. 'He's had a bad time.' He and Cass exchanged looks of sympathy.

'Come on, Ant, let's go and find him,' Cass said.

As they left the room, Antonio called back to Humphrey good-naturedly, 'Hey, Humphrey, I've got a job now.'

'Good God!' He put down the paper. 'Doing what?'

'Sweeping the streets.'

'Excellent,' Humphrey said, his voice just hovering on the edge of sarcasm.

'Hey, what's wrong with him?' Antonio said. 'He's not taking the piss.'

'The way I see it,' Cass said, 'he'll be out of work soon himself.'

'Ah, poor bleeder,' Antonio said, concerned. He called back, 'Hey, Humphrey, if you want that fiver you lent me back – you ask, hey?'

'Certainly will, Antonio, only I wouldn't like to take a week's wages off you.'

Ah, now that was much more like him, Antonio thought with relief.

Eleven

'Hey, Antonio!' Humphrey called down from the centre bough of the tree, 'give us that small plank – no – that one with the nails in it. But I don't want the nails in. OK?'

The boy, Jimmy, moved across with awkward speed and began knocking out the nails, his face bent over the work, intense and savage. He handed up the plank without its nails like a soldier trying to please a favourite officer.

'Thanks,' Humphrey said, straddling a thick branch and easing himself backwards. 'Now get up here, Jimmy, will you? I want you to hold these two steady. Hurry up then. Antonio, can you get the chain-saw, from the shed?'

Beth, standing by the honeysuckle framing her kitchen door, watched them. It had been dreadful: her tenderness with the boy, her mothering, her attempts to be simply kind to him, had all ended in failure. He wouldn't take her kindness. Or food. He had found one of Fran's old teddies and disembowelled it. Fran had behaved very badly. But fortunately that slap across the face seemed to appease him; though it was dreadful, she felt, that violence should be so familiar that it was welcomed.

Humphrey had gone charging upstairs to see what the shouting was about. Jimmy had run like a terrified creature to the corner of the room, his arms and hands up to protect himself, crouched against the wall. But Humphrey had stood quite still, waiting for the boy to unfreeze, then he had turned away.

'Downstairs,' he'd ordered Jimmy. 'Work, that's what you need. Here, come with me – at once – I'm afraid it's in the garden. I know you've seen gardens, but this one needs a tree-house. And you're going to make it. That suit you, cock?'

The boy had followed him in silence.

Now Beth watched them. If his father was the bad one, she thought, then maybe Jimmy would need Humphrey more than he would her. And Antonio was so good with him, treating him like a kid brother. And look, now Humphrey was carefully and patiently explaining to the boy exactly what he was doing – getting Jimmy to make suggestions. There was such harmony about the three of them out there that she felt excluded. Their heads were close together, they were intensely occupied, by the work, by one another. Oh, he has won himself another convert, she thought, smiling, he has captured another heart.

She felt that the sun would go on pouring itself through the leaves of Humphrey's tree – his tree that he was actually sharing – for always. That her house, with its good nature, Humphrey's garden with its work and discipline, would draw even the most rebellious to its breast. She could, after all, make a circle here, that would include anyone in need of a home, would give them a sense of belonging. And she and Humphrey, as a couple, as a fixed point, could be the focus of peace and balance that she'd always longed for.

She looked again and felt that perhaps Humphrey had missed a son, and that perhaps, inadvertently, she had brought one to him – one he seemed peculiarly well equipped to father. And with a sense of achievement, happiness even, she put away the curious feeling of disorientation that often came to her these days, and went to her cooking. Mealtimes, she knew, would be the hardest with Jimmy. She must get all her strength back to deal with him. He was a foundling. In the fairy stories a foundling always had a most specific purpose. She felt that about Jimmy, most strongly.

Twelve

'Well,' Sylvie said, 'you've really landed on your feet here, haven't you, my little darling?' She was looking down a long sweep of land which ended in a valley threaded by a narrow stream. To the left, stiff pine trees stood out against blue sky. Behind them, a derelict stone house looked defiantly out across its ancient view.

'So you think it will do?' He was aware, even guilty, that she was the first to see it – but after all, she was a builder.

'What I think doesn't matter,' she said, looking into the distance, then jolting her head round to him. 'You've bought this for yourself.' She understood it, it didn't bother her. He'd bought a retreat, and yet, because he was Humphrey, he wouldn't retreat to it, he would turn it into something active and working. Nevertheless, it was his.

'I think it's wonderful,' she said, 'but you'll have to pull it down and start again.'

He came and stood beside her, putting a hand on her backside, 'You would think that – just pull it all down – that's just like you. As is that stuff about it being for me. I bought it for us, as it happens. And' – he kissed her on the side of the mouth – 'it needs rebuilding, that's all – and you can do it.'

She turned and looked at the house – it was long fronted, twelve windows, the panes cracked and broken, ivy feasting at the stone and birds whooping in and out of the roof, carrying in their beaks little bits of twigs for nesting; nettles and brambles pushing in at the door; one wall leaning as if tired of supporting so much that was bound to fall.

She blew out through her nose. 'It could be done, I suppose.'

'It *will* be done.'

'But not by me,' she said firmly. 'You get yourself a good architect from the nearest town and he'll get you some local builders.'

'You won't do it?' he asked quietly.

'No.' She shook her head. 'My business is in town, and I've four contracts to do in the next six months. I'm not building a house for you in any case. People have been building things for you all your life one way or the other. You're lazy. You just get on and get this done yourself. Give you something to do, stop you hanging around the house all day with a headache.' She hit him on the arm.

'My God, I love you,' he said. 'When I hear you say things like that, I think, there's oil here and I'm going to drill.' He beamed at her with pleasure. 'But just look' – he pulled her forward – 'just look at all that land, that grass, those trees – just look at it all.'

'And all *mine*, that's what you're thinking, you rat. You're so possessive, it's disgusting.' She looked angrily at him. 'And I bet once you've got this piece of land, you're going to need another lump, aren't you? I mean, you can't manage with one of anything, can you?'

'Well, I don't know,' he said, turning up his nose, 'I could try. Matter of fact, I was meaning to talk to you about that.'

But she was off, nipping round to the side of the house, interested in spite of herself, mostly by the magnitude of the task that lay before anyone who was brave enough to restore the house.

'It's going to cost you at least forty thousand pounds to put right,' she sang out, 'and you know what crooks these builders are. A new roof – Jesus – most of these outside walls are caving in. Perhaps you'd better get a caravan.'

'Sylvie,' he menaced, 'I don't like this negative streak in you. Now, look at it properly and tell me exactly what needs doing.'

'You'd better take notes,' she said, walking to the back door.

Later, sitting down on the edge of an old well, she frowned and told him, 'Yep, it's worth doing if only for all those beautiful fireplaces and the wood – which needs treating, but isn't too bad. You need a damp course throughout and most of the ceilings upstairs will need to come down and be redone. I suppose, considering it's two hundred years old, it's not too bad. It hasn't been too badly vandalized either.'

'Plenty of Durex lying about.'

'Yes,' she laughed, 'and did you see that scrawl that said, "Peter was here, with Jane, Martha and Linda"?'

He laughed, then said, 'The tiles are wonderful, in the kitchen.' He was remembering how Beth loved quarry tiles.

'Hm, but there's a lot of damp in there, it really stinks.' She looked at him. 'Humph, can you afford all this?'

'Sure.' He looked at her, puzzled. 'You don't know how much money I do have, do you?'

'No, and I'm not interested, either. What's yours is yours.'

'You're not much of a one for a shared life, are you?' He grinned.

She got up, pressing her hands into the small of her back, leaning deeply backwards so that her front became round like the brow of a hill. There was something quite strikingly reminiscent about the movement, the posture, the way she turned and smiled at him – triumphantly.

'You're pregnant,' he said, feeling his blood roar.

'You're right,' she said, walking slowly towards him.

'What makes you think such things should be unilateral decisions?' he asked sternly, but quietly, noting something nervous in her for all her devil-may-care.

But she rose, of course, to the attack in all her bludgeoning fury and said, 'Now look here, Humphrey, I'm having a baby because I want one. I'm not asking you to support the little blighter. I can perfectly well do that on my own. You don't have to start working out how much longer you have to go on making money to support a new offspring. You're free, you don't have to do a damn thing!'

He grabbed her roughly by the arms, 'Well, thanks a lot, how perfectly generous of you. But it happens to be my kid that's wriggling around in that armour-plated stomach of yours. And you're not about to deny me the outcome of all these months of fucking you. That is *my* son in there and since it's mine, I'm going to take a very active part in its upbringing.' He let her go and threw up his arms in disbelief, then pointed his finger menacingly at her. 'Now, listen to me, you little, independent, feminist twit, sometimes I can hardly believe you're a woman at all – you're more like a scrum-half. You've learned nothing, have you? You persist in this tough, snooty, taking-care-of-yourself nonsense, getting your own back for having a dead mother and an inadequate father. I'm sorry, but you've got to pack it in. How do you think that poor child is going to survive being looked after just by you? Or were you going to cut his balls off the minute he got out? Hm?' His head was jutted forward aggressively and his eyes were like needles.

'I can still work with a child,' she said, looking surly.

'Oh yes, of course you can. Just fling the carry-cot in the back of the van and lug it around the building sites – no problem. You call that planning?' he roared.

'Humphrey, stop shouting, for Christ's sake.'

'All right,' he said, more calmly, 'what I was meaning, peanut, was this: you're not too strong on looking after people, and you need some help ... as a matter of fact you need me. Now, does that astound you? You need me to be the father of your child and that's what I'm going to be. So you can just get rid of this notion that you're having a child for yourself, by yourself, because you're having it for me too, we're having it, had you forgotten we're married?'

'My God,' she said, sitting down on the edge of the well again, 'you've really got a nasty little temper there, haven't you?' She scowled at him, the black thickness of her eyebrows and lashes quivering. But she was quite happy. He came leaping across and lifted her off the well and high into the air.

'Listen,' he said, 'I can just hear the bricks and mortar coming together in your stomach.'

'Don't do that, put me down.'

He replaced her. 'You know,' he said, and knelt in front of her, 'all my life I've been a romantic. I regard Beth – always have – with deep romanticism. But you – oh, I have that for you too, but what I have for you is a deep, quiet passion – no awe, no hopeless idealism, no madness – just a quiet passion that needs the rest of our lives to explore.'

She smiled, she looked over his shoulder, she began to fidget with her hands. After a moment, she said, 'I'll just go back in and see if I can get right into the roof.'

'Jesus!' he said with disgust, 'you just can't manage any kind of declaration, can you?'

She looked at him, her bottom lip trembled and her sharp teeth bit into it to bring it into line. 'Humphrey,' she breathed ... But then she stopped, and then she laughed, and then she said with her old sarcasm, 'You'd better sit down while I go up into the roof. I'm going to have to be very gentle with you from now on.'

'You're a shit,' he said quietly, getting up and following her into the house. 'It'd really kill you, wouldn't it, to say something wonderful to me?'

She stopped. 'Humphrey?' she said, looking back at him.

'Yes ... go on, say it ...' he said impatiently.

'I love you,' she whispered, letting her hands fall, as if she gave in, suffered a defeat.

He laughed. 'I love you, too.'

Thirteen

'How long has this been going on, Beth?' Mary asked furiously. Beth shrugged, her oval face dipping, a lost and confused look on it.

'About a month, I suppose, but the attacks come and go, and in between I'm perfectly all right.'

'You don't look perfectly all right.' Mary's green eyes narrowed menacingly. 'And why do you always think you have to manage everything on your own?' Mary had worked with Beth at the Westminster Hospital. Such a waste, Mary always thought, that she spent her life in the service of Humphrey, who was a lovely fellow, of course, but did any man warrant such attention? And had it done her any good? The revelation at the dinner party was quite shocking. Beth, of course, would not discuss it, any more than she would ask for help when she was ill.

'Well, I *can* manage,' Beth said firmly. 'It's just not knowing what it actually is that bothers me.' She began rubbing her fingers along the edge of the table. 'I've been to two doctors and neither of them know what it is. Sometimes' – she pulled her hair back from her face with both hands – 'sometimes I think I'm going mad. Everything seems unreal to me: I look at the girls and I think: who are they? No, really, they don't seem to have anything to do with me. It's the same with Humphrey. The other night I wanted to ask him who he was. I can tell by your face,' she said quietly, 'that you think I'm dotty.'

'Of course I don't, it's just a bit difficult to understand: is there anything physical about it? Do you feel ill?'

She frowned. 'I feel it coming on, just slowly, I begin to feel dizzy, my head hums and I feel a loss of balance. That's all, but it's frightening. But the other things are much more frightening.'

'What other things?'

'Things in the house, they don't seem real either, and they're sort of menacing. I have to touch everything obsessively to assure myself that it isn't a figment of my imagination. I was cutting some meat the other day' – she suddenly looked very tired – 'and I found myself cutting my own hand, quite deeply, to see if I was dreaming. Or if it was real.'

'Oh, Beth.'

She was now very distressed, she went on, 'The pain was real, the blood was real, but that's all.' Her face was plaintive and small. But, in a second, that look vanished and was replaced by a detached face and an odd smile.

'Oh, poor Beth,' Mary said again, taking her hand and noting the deep cut down it. 'I hate to see you like this.'

'Oh, I'm all right today,' Beth said, ashamed of the mark now. 'Often' – she smiled – 'I'm fine for a week and then I think it won't come back and it's a quite marvellous feeling. But then it does.' Her voice was empty.

'Can you *do* anything when you feel like that?' Mary asked, 'I mean, can you go on as usual?'

Beth smiled in a puzzled way. 'Well, the thing is, Mary, the only thing I can do, perfectly, absolutely easily, is to look after Jimmy. I've got so attached to him. I go and fetch him from school, I bring him home – I can drive without difficulty. We have tea together and I get him to talk to me about his day – you know how bad he is about talking. He does his homework. Even when he plays up, when he becomes what he calls a little shit-head, even then I can manage him perfectly. He's the only person I can. When I sit with Humphrey, late at night, if we're working together or he's reading, I look up at him and this amazing feeling of – of not knowing – who he is. To say it now, it seems so strange, but at the time, that's all I know. That's all that's real. And Jimmy.'

'It was wonderful,' Mary said gently, 'how Jimmy was today – when I came. He rushed over to you and just hung on to you for dear life. I think he thought I'd come to take him away again. He's settled very well, Beth, oh, I know you've had quite a time with him, but really, it has been a remarkable adjustment. You've done so well.'

'I really think it's Humphrey more than me. He's so patient with Jimmy, I'd never have believed it. When he smashes something up, Humphrey will sit down with him and slowly put it together again – time and again. He calms him out of tantrums and seems to know instinctively what to do, as if he actually knows how the child *feels*. We all love him.'

'Well,' Mary said, 'I won't disrupt anything for now, then. But if you feel you can't cope, you must tell me, straight away. And, are you taking anything for these attacks?'

The word, attacks, upset Beth. But then Mary noticed that she was smiling that dreadful smile, and talking quite calmly, as though she were discussing a patient's illness.

'Yes, I was given some Lentizol and then I went to see Dr West, not for analysis, but for some sort of assessment, you know. He prescribed Anafrenol, but it hasn't done anything. I think this is something I'm going to have to deal with myself' – she laughed ruefully – 'which is why I'm talking to you. Of course the natural thing is to wonder if it's because of Humphrey and me – whether I've represssed it all the time. I do let my feelings out' – she spoke as if she had none whatsoever – 'on paper anyway. What bothers me, though, is that I think Humphrey knows that something's wrong. He keeps asking me what the matter is. I can't tell him. He hates me to be ill, you see. Men do, don't they?'

'Do they?' Mary asked sarcastically.

'You know they do.'

Beth shrugged. 'Anyway he's very involved in the business now, in getting out of it, I mean.'

'Has he got someone to take over?'

'Yes, a new man starts next month. But that's made George absolutely livid, of course. I think he might resign. I'm trying to persuade Humphrey to let them run it as joint MDs. It's a real hornets' nest at the moment, made worse by the fáct that Humphrey doesn't take an active enough part in it all. He's no good at things like that. It's a wonder the company has done so well with the kind of management problems there've been.'

'You sound resentful.' Mary watched as Beth plunged her spoon into the sugar and stirred it about angrily.

'I am angry' – again the mild smile. 'It means I have to try and placate George, who's stirred up Harry – and oh, it's all become very political and unpleasant. I've always tried to steer off things like that before they get out of hand. They're well out of hand now. Humphrey had the cheek to roar in there yesterday and yell at George for not sending him copies of all his memos. After he'd made it clear he wasn't interested. He's still insisting I keep all the shares – so that shifts the backbiting to me. I feel in a very difficult position.' And with exasperation she added, 'As if this wasn't bad enough, yesterday Humphrey went charging round the office like some demented bull to find out who had swiped some of his precious plants! It was George, of course, and very funny, I thought, but they nearly came to blows about it.'

Mary, reaching for her handbag, took a firm line. 'Beth, listen. Humphrey's baled out of that office. Now, you've either got to get out and let the thing sort out as it will, or you must stay and do what *you* think is right. He's handed it over to you, and since he has – take it. Don't let him play this game of leaving it, but still keeping it. You're quite capable, Beth.' Mary laughed. 'The only thing that's holding you back is some silly sense of duty to Humphrey. Well, to hell with it. He's lumbered you with a situation you didn't want. Talk to – what's his name – the financial man? Harry? Yes, well, talk to him. And talk to your solicitors and get the thing sorted out – the way you think is fair. Send Humphrey off on holiday or something.'

Beth was looking thoughtful, and thankfully, the smile had left her face.

'Now you will do that, won't you Beth?' Mary insisted. 'It's not knowing what you should be doing – in any area of your life – that's driving you crazy. Take control of your life, get things back into your own hands and I'm certain you'll feel better. Really.'

Beth touched Mary's arm. 'Thank you, Mary.' The smile returned.

Mary got up. 'Right then, another call to make, then back to the cat.' She sounded relieved. 'Come with me when I go and say goodbye to Jimmy. And Beth?'

'Yes?'

'Stop smiling like that.' It was such a set smile, stretched and painful as a grimace, and yet it was so close a relative of that sweet smile that had been Beth's most dear characteristic that it was frightening. It was as if, all those years, that smile had concealed a falseness, a lack of involvement – even an emptiness – and now it stood out stiff and menacing.

'Stop it, Beth, stop smiling.'

'I can't,' Beth said in a thin, child-like wail, 'I can't.'

Fourteen

Beth watched Humphrey as he worked in the garden, putting his back into it, something furious and sexual about the way he crammed his spade into the earth, which was black from the long rains of the night before. As she watched him, she found that the watching was of a different kind. Something was letting go, receding. She could feel it, almost as hands will slide away in parting as if trying not to acknowledge quite that that was what it was – a parting. A flick of pain, and then, a moment of rejoicing. Yes, it was that, she felt it was. There was pleasure, joy in it. A current of warm air blew over her and she saw Humphrey as a favourite room that you know and love most intimately. A room in which all her deepest feelings had been played out; the sun had come in and out through the curtains, tender and loving physical encounters had happened there, her children had been born there. There was a great richness, a fullness of purpose. And she was withdrawing from it, not just with relief, but with rejoicing.

She was sitting under the trees, a book in her lap, but she couldn't concentrate, could feel no sympathy with the lives of the characters in the book that day. Around her the sun shone warm and voluptuous – pouring, she saw it as a clear vision, like cream over a summer pudding. And then, just as suddenly, the vision altered – oh, horribly, horribly – it was as if it was all fraying at the edges, breaking up into a red ugly mass. A bird pecked at a fallen apple, pecked and pulled at the brown flesh with its sharp wild beak. The tomato plants were long and scraggly, they hung dejectedly between the fallen canes. There was a touch of decay. It was unbearable. She got up, knocking the book off her knees, and ran into the house.

Humphrey, with his back to her, seemed to shudder. He turned, he saw her – the most elegant, the most graceful of women, running clumsily into the house, weaving as if between obstacles, crashing into invisible obstructions. He saw her run past Fran, who turned and looked after her miserably. He saw her avoid the outstretched arms of Cass, whose face fell into a panic.

Beth, beautiful Beth, was scuttling like a frightened mouse into the darkness of the kitchen. He knew she would be wearing that smile, that wide and changeless grimace. His daughters came out and looked at him; the three of them, he felt, watching him with reproach. Abi said something to the other two and they turned away from him. He knew that the house would be silent when he entered it, that an unnatural atmosphere would fill all the rooms. Each of his daughters would be tidying something. Abi, trying to set things to rights, Cass making tea, feeling helpless. Fran would scowl, she would be the only one who could make a wall around what each of them felt with her harsh gift for honesty.

How long was it now since the punks and fancy boys had come? How long since those big dinner parties, when she had cooked for her children's friends? How long had it been since she had left them all to their own devices? And when would Jimmy return from his visit to his mother? Why did the child have to endure it every Saturday? They had come to need him, Beth particularly. What he wanted more than anything was to see her face light up with that luminous smile, that smile she had spread like honey for her children at teatime, for him when he came home from work. It was excruciating, missing her.

He looked up and could see Beth standing by the window on that part of the stairs overlooking the garden. How forlorn her face seemed. He wanted to go and fetch her shawl with the scarlet roses and place it about her shoulders. He longed to be able to climb up and through the window and find her standing there in the long white nightdress as she had done the first time, her hair falling about her shoulders and that quiet triumphant smile on her mouth. She vanished from the window, her breath made a little mist on the glass for an instant, then was gone.

He couldn't go to her yet, he didn't have the strength. He went and stood by the apple tree. He reached out for it, putting his arms around its trunk and pressing his face against the rough bark, feeling the sharpness of it, as he had, long ago, as a small and lonely boy in a very bad time. The time came back to him as if it were yesterday: the day of his father's desertion.

Fifteen

With Beth ill, he was desperate for reassurance and sympathy and he went to Sylvie for it. It was unfair, he knew it, but who else could he tell, who else would understand? He sat waiting for her to come home, drinking, deep in thought. When she saw him, she went immediately to him and knelt down beside his chair. She held him in that vice-like grip of hers and demanded, 'What is it, Humphrey, what on earth's the matter?'

He shuddered. In her face he saw fear. She was afraid he'd come to say that he couldn't go on with it, that he was leaving her. He looked at her and said, 'Beth is ill, Sylvie, and I don't know what to do.'

He waited for her to stiffen and turn from him – what was it to her? He expected her anger or her withdrawal, but instead he began to feel all that strength of hers, that character solid as masonry, gather itself together. She held him fast. She treated him with such tenderness that it humbled him, filled him with the sense of her goodness and generosity. And so often he doubted her, questioned her capacity for love. She comforted him in a way Beth did not – Beth would make him face it, would bring him up against his best qualities. Sylvie looked after him. He could be weak with her. She would muster her guns to protect him, to bring him back to the top of the hill again.

She listened to him as he explained how Beth's illness had started and when he'd first noticed it; the day Jimmy had come into the garden and stood silently behind him for a long time before finally saying, 'She's bad, Humphrey,' as if he blamed himself. That had made him, forced him to think about it. He couldn't bear Beth to be ill.

When he'd finished, she took a deep breath and said firmly, 'Now look, it's quite simple, you must take care of her, Humphrey. That's what she needs. She's always looked after you, all these years, stood by you when you needed her. Now she's asking you to take care of her. It's that simple. That's what she's been trying to ask you for, but doesn't quite know how.'

He looked at her and knew she was absolutely right. It was as if she understood his wife better than he did.

She came and sat upon his knee and curled her legs around his. 'Now listen to me,' she said. 'Instead of sitting round here, you go home. And stay there. Take care of her, nurse her and be with her. You've nothing else you have to do. We must get her better. Everything else is ticking over for you: the new man starts next week, George seems fine, though I don't know why, so he's no trouble. So all you have to do is be with Beth. OK?'

He looked at her and she saw how exhausted he looked. He said, 'You're not such a bad stick, after all. You're not as tough as you think.' But his voice was thick with emotion. He asked her, 'What about you? Is it what you want, or will you boil up in a froth of resentment in a day or two?'

'Allow me a little decency, can't you? I'll be fine.' She stroked his cheek. 'Just nip across the river and see me now and then. But stay with Beth and make that home of yours happy again. From now on we're all going to look after Beth, as she's looked after all of us. Oh yes, she has. She's the one who's kept us all together. Don't think I didn't know it. Beth has made it possible for me to have you without your agonizing about it too much, without her making you guilty and unhappy. And this is my way of looking after Beth – by giving you back to her for a bit. So go on – hurry up or I'll change my mind.'

Her small face, he thought, with its black brows and lashes, was quite beautiful. He watched her with wonder as she moved now as a pregnant woman moves. She seemed to him rather noble. She seemed to him quite definitely a perfect woman.

Sixteen

It was Saturday, Sylvie got out of bed and lifted her arms high. She was naked, her body, so taut and well-tuned, was touching now because of the round hard belly. She put her hands to her large breasts and felt them, womanly and large, but with reason now for being so. She was complete. For the first time in her life she felt tranquil, she felt it was allowable to be idle and cosset herself. Later, she would go and see Hilda and walk in the park with the boys, but for the moment she was quite content to be alone, to think of the future. Soon it would be the autumn and after that, her child would be born, hers and Humphrey's.

She missed Humphrey, but not as in the early days when his absence seemed a desertion and a neglect. Now, being where he was, with Beth, it was a labour of love. He did it for her as well as for Beth, he did it to heal himself. And Beth, slowly, was getting better. It was more than a fortnight since she had had one of those strange attacks that frightened her family and Humphrey so much.

She found Beth's illness fascinating, the way it had disturbed the rhythm they had all three fallen into. She had a peculiar influence – even now in what seemed like her decline – what she wanted you to do, you felt compelled to do. She had wanted Humphrey back for some purpose; she seemed to have made it happen through Sylvie. How insidious that power was; you were not aware of it until it was too late. If there was a triangle-player among the three of them, then certainly it was Beth.

Sylvie, always an early riser, crawled back into bed. Now she folded back, neatly, the cotton sheet and pressed it down with her hand so that it lay flat and sharp as the crease of an envelope. She smoothed the apricot blankets and ran her hand up against their fluffiness. Then looked around her with pleasure at their bedroom with the silky blue curtains blown fat by the wind, the pine table that Humphrey had bought and covered with plants and delicate ferns; the pots of fuschia, the Oriental rugs that warmed the once-bare floorboards of a flat, which, because of Humphrey, was at last becoming a home. She turned the gold band upon her finger, she stretched out her hand to see the emerald wink and sparkle in the morning sunshine. In the corner of the room stood an old-fashioned rocking horse with a red flowing mane, and in the drawer, a white baby's nightdress with blue smocking.

She fell asleep and was woken by a terrifying dream. She dreamt a woman's hair was on fire, dark hair, long and curly, exactly like her own, sizzling, leaping into red and violet flames. And someone was laughing, some woman was laughing, quite beside herself.

Seventeen

The eight-o'clock light showed up the lawn, threadbare beneath an apple tree quite weighed down by heavy pale green apples. The yellow roses, having their second blooming, swayed before a wind – a wind that was brisk, that began to swagger, full of the warnings of change: the season was rolling over, making way for autumn. A few leaves had fallen and lay like neglected toys on the grass. Beth shivered as the wind blew again, but not entirely without pleasure. Her daughters were about her, Jimmy sat quietly beside her. She was better, things had returned to normal, Humphrey was at home, where he always was these days.

A light went on inside, and from her position at the top of the table, she could see Humphrey in the kitchen, moving quickly between stove and table. Her eyes roamed over the house with its wistaria and honeysuckle and she thought again: it always was the perfect house, the house for us. She remembered when she and Humphrey had decided to buy it and the jubilation when they'd entered it, each child trying to be first through the door, until Humphrey had barked out, 'Back, you little wretches, your mother and I shall enter first' and she had taken his arm to walk through the door, but he had scooped her up and carried her across the threshold – 'We'll be so happy here, I know it.'

'Jimmy,' Beth said touching his arm, 'go into the kitchen and see what Humphrey's doing – hurry him up.'

The boy, his hair dark and shiny, his face filled out and his narrow mouth less likely to snarl, went – reluctantly.

'What's he cooking?' Fran asked suspiciously. 'He's been in there for ages.'

'Interesting, isn't it?' Abi remarked. 'Now he's not selling that frozen crap, he's finally learned to cook ... or' – she smiled with a trace of malice – 'perhaps someone's been teaching him.'

Cass wanted to hit her – she was so vile, so cruel. How could she with their mother still frail?

She looked at Beth, who was smiling calmly, with no trace of anguish, lifting her hand to rearrange the branches of wistaria in the vase in front of her.

'How well you've done these, Abi, I do love tall branches, it always reminds me of a restaurant we went to in Paris long ago, just before you were born.'

I hate her, Abi thought furiously, she's back in charge, she's forced us all to bow to her again. Nothing I say touches her.

Beth was thinking of her dream of the night before – how much more vivid it was, than, say, that expression on Abi's face right now. Dreams really were more vivid, more tangible than life – how strange that was. She dreamt she was crossing the sea to Ireland, on the old mail-boat. The air was clammy and when you licked your lips you could taste the salt. The mist became so dense that you felt you could take a big handful of it and roll it into a ball. She was walking back and forth. A man was following her and she wanted him to. Below in her cabin a sleeping child was waiting for her. She turned and looked at the man – he was very tall. He said, 'Come to our cabin, my friend is waiting, there are two of us.' She knew she could go because she had left everything behind her.

She wondered now if she wanted what Humphrey had – if everyone did; if two men could fulfil her more than one. It was the most erotic dream she'd ever had, erotic and also tender. She shivered a little. Cass, who always noted her mother's feelings and sensations, rose without a word and fetched her shawl.

Jimmy had not returned. Fran and Abi chattered excitedly as if the things they were discovering had never been stated before. And as she watched them, she thought, with relief, my time is nearly over, they don't need me, not as they used to. They can manage, even Fran, tough and dependent as she is, she will manage. But oh, she has no grace – she'll go out into the world wielding a club, I have taught her no grace. And Cass? Well, Cass will always understand and be wise. And she is transferring her need to adore to the boy with the black lacquered hair. Abi, with her determination to suffer, she will have to find her own way out – find others to blame. And perhaps along the way she'll find something to do well and that will make her happy.

She smiled: my daughters – you look up and see a sticky face above a bib, look up again and a schoolgirl stands awkwardly in a purple tunic; you look up yet again and a young woman is walking away – running away, desperate for a life that in no way resembles your own. She loved them quite painfully at that moment, as she saw them pull impatiently at the anchor and prepare to sail.

'Humphrey!' she exclaimed, 'oh, it's quite beautiful!' She was gazing in admiration at a perfect soufflé.

He was looking at her face, unworn again, the flash of her beauty intact. He kissed quickly the side of her mouth. 'Couldn't have got the ruddy thing out of the oven if Jimmy hadn't been inventive,' he said.

Beth looked at Jimmy with approval, with interest.

'I was about to take the top off, but Jimmy managed to pull the rack from beneath it and I caught it as it fell.'

'Heavens, you could have dropped it.'

'But we didn't,' Jimmy boasted.

'Well, I think that's really a success.' Humphrey beamed.

Fran watched him with a patient sneer: really, the little things that pleased his tiny mind; you'd think no one had cracked an egg before. And there was her mother treating him like a hero again. Any minute now, as soon as he'd settled down, he'd start: Have you read all the books you were meant to during the holidays? Did you do that essay – finish that project? – as if he seriously expected her to destroy her holiday in this manner. And worse was to come, bound to – they were all together and it was an occasion: the beginning of fresh starts. He'd want a three-month family discussion on everyone's plans for the coming months; he'd want his ground rules laid down. She recognized that look on his face: that look that announced: I, the father, am about to utter, hold your breath.

'So,' he said, in his casual, commanding voice, 'everyone back next week, eh?'

Each of his daughters groaned loudly. It was sickening, Cass thought, like on the very first day of the holidays when he must ask you when you were going back.

'Abi's off to university,' he announced proudly.

Much to everyone's amazement, Abi thought savagely.

'Cass to college for her A-levels, and Fran into the last year of her Os.'

Fran turned up her eyes and passed her plate to her mother for more.

'And Jimmy – well, Jimmy is staying with us,' Humphrey said gently. 'We've been told he can stay.'

'Because my mother's in the funny farm,' he snarled, 'and my dad'll beat me to death if she isn't around.' A small tension settled on them all, then Cass turned to him.

'Listen, sweetie,' she said firmly, 'surround yourself with trouble and you'll only get more of it. Think of the good side: you can stay with us!' She knocked his arm in a friendly way. He tapped his knife on the plate for a minute; they all waited for him to smash it. But after a hesitation he put the knife down.

'Yeh, big deal,' he said grimly, appeased.

'Right,' Beth said – why did it disturb her so? No one else bothered any more, if he'd smashed the plate to smithereens Cass would have picked it up, Abi would have got another, but she was frightened by his misery. She pulled herself up and said, 'Who's doing the next bit?' She had taken no part in tonight's dinner. Humphrey had done the first course and the girls had done the rest, one course each.

'Me,' Fran said morosely, 'and I don't want any stupid complaints.'

'Why d'you always expect the worst?' Humphrey demanded, passing his plate to Jimmy, who was stacking them.

'That's what families are for, aren't they? To complain and bitch about one another?' Fran sauntered out.

'Do you think there comes a time,' Beth asked thoughtfully, 'when one's had enough of a family? You know, like after the age of fourteen you really can't send a girl to boarding school any longer? Is there a point when family life is just suffocating?'

'Beth!' Humphrey was horrified.

'No, I know what she means,' Cass said, 'I mean, you must feel the same, Ma, not just us. You've had enough of all this running around after us, bringing us up and slaving away for us – and we, we want to run our own lives too, to try things out alone.'

'Yes,' Beth said quietly, 'that's exactly what I meant.'

But Humphrey cut in with annoyance, 'You'll always need your family, Cass, you need a base, everyone does, whatever their age. Your mother is a point of safety – more than I, I admit. You can't just chuck it all out because you happen to be sixteen.'

'I wasn't knocking her,' Cass said sharply, 'I was meaning that we don't need looking after in that way, we don't need the constant care, any more. She knows what I mean.' She was desperate for him to agree, to let her go, but his face, she saw, had closed.

'Until you have babies,' Beth said sweetly, 'then I'll come back and take care of you again.'

Cass looked at her, and a great flood of emotion, of loss, hit her, hard, in the middle of her stomach: my mother, she thought, my dear and lovely mother. Will I ever be, could I ever be as gentle and as good as that? Could I let my children free when they wanted it? Could I let everyone be and do as they want to, as they need?

'One day,' Fran began grandly – once she had handed to each person a single fish finger (well, if you make me do the fish course what do you expect?). She would not put herself out, stretch herself, for anyone; it would demean her, she felt.

'You might at least have added a slice of lemon,' Abi said with disgust.

'Jimmy likes it,' Fran said, giving Cass's fish finger to him. 'As I was trying to say,' she continued, 'one day, this will be a rare occasion, me, sitting here with you lot, without the cameras and the journalists, the fans outside the door, the autograph-hunters . . .'

'You'll need more than that hair and those eyes as capital to live on.' Beth laughed.

'Well, if you're ever world-famous,' Humphrey said lightly, 'just remember that I have one or two little stories to tell the journalists. We'll skip this fish finger course of yours, but what about the time you and the dog had a farting competition? And do you remember who won? And I haven't forgotten the time you went into the gents' loo and nobody knew the difference and . . .'

Fran walked out, swinging her hips.

'She's screwy,' Abi said.

'But she is,' Jimmy said adoringly, 'she *is* very pretty, isn't she?'

'She's a pain in the arse,' Humphrey said, 'and that fish finger was raw in the middle.'

When Abi brought in the course she'd prepared, Beth and Humphrey exchanged a glance; it was a glance which said: there are things at which Abi will always excel, make herself happy, make us proud. For look, she brought in, on a beautiful blue plate, pieces of golden chicken smothered in a rich sauce and garnished with coils of bacon and plump mushrooms. She set it down in front of her mother and turned to go to the kitchen for the vege-tables.

Beth took her arm and said, 'Abi, this must've taken you ages – did you follow a recipe?'

'Penguin Cordon Bleu: Chicken Sauté Bourguignonne,' Abi rapped out in her flawless accent.

'Perhaps you should run a restaurant,' Beth said. 'Make a stand against your father's dreadful practices.'

'Would you give me the capital?' Abi said eagerly to her father.

'Certainly not, I'm giving you nothing, you can do it by yourself or you'll be a spineless little devil. Besides, you've got to find something you can train at before you start off with any grand ideas.' Her face fell; she didn't want to train, she just wanted something handed to her, why must he make things so difficult?

'None of that sauce stuff for me,' Fran said, 'scrape it off, I just want the chicken.'

'Oh, for God's sake, you're a heartless little brute,' Humphrey said, swiping her with his napkin.

'Yes,' she said, closing her eyes with ecstasy, 'and I shall drive young men to despair, crack their hearts between my teeth like nuts, offer them the hem of my dress for their soaked eyes, send violets to their funerals . . .'

Cass was wrapping her hands around her sister's neck and about to squeeze there finally, but Humphrey said, 'Don't make it easy for her, Cass, let her find out the hard way: let her live.'

Beth, after approving the chicken, said, 'Will someone tell me what's happened to all the punks?' It was as if she'd forgotten that she'd been ill.

'Oh, we still see them, down the benches,' Cass said, but there was something about the way she said it that denoted a lack of interest.

How soon things change for them, Beth thought, they barely need to adjust, they just get swept off in another direction.

'But what's happened to Joe?' she asked Abi, who shrugged and would not answer. When Abi's short enthusiasms with one or other boy ended, she would have no truck with them again: that way, her mother felt, she could pretend it hadn't really happened. Abi's expression as she glanced at her mother was hostile. Yes, Abi thought bitterly, she sees herself as an unchanging example to us all – but she's a tyrant really, and we're all longing to be free of her. Perfection, after all, was so uncomfortable.

Humphrey was watching Beth; he was aware that she was not quite there still, her concentration wandered off, she was a little distracted. But he wasn't worried about her; she was quite better, altogether herself again. Perhaps more herself than she had ever been. She sat there, very straight, as she always sat, her fringe had grown out and now her hair was swept to the top of her head in a shiny knot, single strands of white here and there just made her more appealing to him: she was too graceful to try to cheat on the small encroachments of age. And that dreadful smile was gone. She was wearing her true smile now, the one she had worn all the happy years.

But later, in a striking moment very close to shock – as they sat quietly, having finished the chocolate mousse that Cass had prepared – he realized that Beth was not there at all. She had retreated into her own thoughts and feelings and he could no longer read them. She had dispatched a child for candles and lit them, and now sat demurely contemplating the wisps of flame. He felt desolate. He felt he had lost her entirely. He had to call her back.

'Beth?'

'Yes?' She raised her head dreamily, patiently; she saw he was troubled. 'What is it?'

'I must just check something,' he said bleakly. He vanished into the house, away from her absence.

She smiled to herself, wistfully, but reassuringly at the same time, so that no one should know what she was thinking. She had left them. She was remembering that the autumn was the time she liked best to be in the country, to be in Ireland, in the house left her by her mother, and watched over in her absence by Mrs Nolan, with her round rosy cheeks and placid nature. And when she was there, how interesting it was, Beth thought, that it wasn't the house that bound her, beautiful and stately though it was – it was the land, the black earth that nourished the people and animals on it. It was this that she longed for now. She took Jimmy's hand a second – touch, gentle or protective, still startled him. She let it go and asked him if he was tired. He shook his head vehemently and she passed him the empty mousse bowl to scrape out. 'You can lick it if you like,' she said.

A little later, when Humphrey returned, he found that the table had been abandoned; only his half-full glass remained and the candles were extinguished. Something troubled him, something was wrong, somewhere, but he couldn't place it; the surface was as it always was, but something was wrong. And Beth – where was she?

Eighteen

Beth closed the black book with its red binding when Humphrey entered her study.

'I wondered if you'd like a brandy,' he said, sitting on the green chaise against the wall. He filled a small glass and passed it to her. 'Where did you disappear to?'

'Oh, we just cleared up. They wanted to go out. And you?' She smiled at him tenderly. 'Where did you disappear to?'

'I had to make a phone call.'

'Ah,' she breathed, putting the top to her fountain pen and pressing it down hard.

'Beth,' he said, 'is anything the matter? I feel that something's not quite right between us.'

She turned in her chair so that she faced him, so that her knees touched his. 'Of course not, my darling, I'm fine, I'm just a bit restless, it's the time of year.' She could hear the wind getting up outside and slapping at the branches of the tree. It was very dark, there was no moon.

'The apples are going to come down in this wind,' he said morosely.

'Yes, we'll pick them up tomorrow and I'll cook them.' She was thinking that the blackberries would be getting ready in the lane on the sheltered side of her mother's house; you could always collect enough for a pudding at this time of year. She pulled herself back to him by taking his hand, 'I am better, Humphrey, you know.' She felt that it was he who had made her so: she had needed him and he'd been there, all the time, quietly, dutifully taking care of her. In the end she had spent most of the day asleep, but he'd made it possible for her to do that. He shopped, he cooked, he looked after Jimmy. The two of them had grown very close. It was odd, at times it seemed as though Jimmy was their child, his and hers. Which was it? the illness or Jimmy which had bound them so closely during those weeks? A combination, probably. He had nursed her in a way that had surprised them both and reassured their daughters. He had abandoned his own projects, bought her little presents and cooked her light meals.

Thinking of it all now, with that wonderful distance that returned health brought so quickly, she smiled at her doctor's verdict: a chemical imbalance, hormonal changes. The poor man had no idea, she thought sceptically. But what did it matter? Humphrey had got her better, it was as simple as that. She looked at him and gratitude and love rushed over her. She took his hand and rested it against her cheek, but her emotional balance had been upset; she was easily overcome these days, so she got up and went to stand by the window, looking out at the garden. He stayed where he was and played with the fringe on her shawl.

'Is there something the matter with *you*, Humphrey?' she asked incisively.

'No.' It wasn't quite true, but he waited until she'd come and sat beside him before he went on. 'No, nothing's wrong with me, at least not unless it is with you – I was just wondering, if it's all right with you, if I could go off for a couple of days next week? Say Monday to Wednesday? I've held up the architect in Wiltshire. He wants to pull things down and I want to be there. Would you mind? Could you manage without me for a couple of days?' He half wanted her to say, no, stay with me. He would have felt safer then. There was something unpredictable about Beth now which frightened him.

'Of course I can manage,' she laughed. 'It's all over now, I'm certain.' She touched his knee. 'You go, take a week if you need it, there's so much to do and you can't discuss it on the phone.'

He was happy, she thought with relief, his enthusiasm whooshed back, he was boyish with excitement. 'All right, then, if you're sure. There's something so marvellous, you know, about doing something utterly different like this. I want to help build this house myself, really get stuck in. To rebuild something that's old and neglected, it's such a challenge, how it will look when it's done . . .'

'Humphrey,' she warned, 'don't get up that poor architect's nose, don't take over.'

'It's my bloody house!'

'Yes, but it's his job.'

'I will endeavour not to be a pain,' he said sarcastically.

'Good.'

He began to talk about it, about how he wanted it, how the barn would be a music room, how he would widen the hall, put in new staircases, restore the ceilings – and of course his plans for a garden. She listened to him and thought him just like a silkworm – he spun a web around you, silky and close, he wrapped you up in it, he seduced you with that soft voice of his, that need for your approval – yours alone, your trust and interest. How interesting it was that his voice, when he spoke to different people, always took up a touch of that person's accent. How that had embarrassed their daughters. But he wasn't aware of it, it was just his way of wrapping himself around different people, making them feel at ease with him. Now, listening to him, she was bound hand and foot. He was telling her about their future together in that house, on that land – he was filling her with security, a sense of permanence, so that she almost forgot, she almost believed it was as simple as he said. When suddenly she demanded, 'Are you taking anyone with you, when you go down?'

He was devastated. He couldn't answer. Then he was furious – why must she do this? Pulling him up so roughly? Pulling the whole thing to bits? His loyalties began to tug him this way and that, so fast, so painfully, that he was dizzy. If she'd stuck a knife in him he couldn't have done a better job of hurting him.

'Yes,' he said. It wasn't true; perversity and anger made him say it.

A knocking began inside her head, furious and violent.

But Cass had come in, looking for her mother, needing a safety pin and a length of black cotton. Beth rose to get it and as he watched her walk over to the cabinet, he felt something slip and fall between them, it was so clear to him that he could almost hear it break. Shaken, he went out of the study and made his way slowly to his piano – which he began to play, very fast and very brilliantly, with an addict's need for forgetfulness.

Nineteen

'Cass,' Beth was saying in a hard voice, 'if he doesn't ring when he said he would, or the day after, or the day after that – it's not that he's been in a fatal accident, or put in jail, or lost the use of his fingers – it's just that he doesn't want to. That's all. There is no other reason. That is the one you must take because it's the only one.'

She was in a rush; she must take Jimmy to school. He was nervous to go back. He needed all her love and attention. The change from holidays to school alarmed him, was almost too much for him. He wanted to stay with her and she wished she could indulge him, give him what he asked for – it seemed so cruel to impose on him structures that ignored his own desperate needs. But she took him all the same. A scene at the door; she, more upset in the end than he was. Slow, so slow it all was.

When she got home, she went to bed. Not because she felt ill but because a chill had got into her – her bones felt cold, they felt loose in her body. Once in bed she felt better. The house had a chill to it too; the central heating would need to go on soon. She lay there, stretched out beneath the cool sheets and warm blankets. She found that she kept thinking of the past. Ever since Humphrey had gone early that morning to the country, she could only seem to think backwards.

She wanted the past back. When the children were little, under her feet, when she and Humphrey were struggling for a common success, a shared future. It had been hard. She'd often been angry, quite dreadful some days, but she'd do it all over again – gladly. She thought how many meals she had cooked – those nursery lunches with roast potatoes and sponge puddings with custard. The dresses she had cut out and sewn – beds she had made, the nights she'd sat up wiping hot little foreheads, walking back and forth, back and forth with a wailing baby. Now, the edges of life were tucked in so tightly, so smooth and neat that, thinking of the past she wondered sometimes, did I live it, or dream it?

174

Now there was something else that she must do – something brave, foolhardy, maybe even mad. Fear was manifesting itself in her as calmness. What she wanted to do was savage. Oh, she knew that. But how wonderful it would feel, to drop the temperate mantle she'd worn all her life and to see herself for once in wild vibrant colours – the colours of a passionate, not a perfect, woman. Perhaps these, after all, were her true colours, and the other plumage merely a ploy to keep enemies away, like a dun bird hiding in pale grass?

Was what she felt, what she was planning, the result of envy? An envy of that other woman's life? Of her freedom without children, her ability to devote all of herself to her work, free of a husband and his colossal needs? Sylvie had a freedom that Beth had thrown away without even realizing what it was she did: so conditioned had she been by what she'd thought she'd wanted. Perhaps both she and Humphrey were suffering the results of losing their freedom too soon. Perhaps they both wanted to be delinquent. But only he had had the courage to do it.

But lying there, she also knew that she had had all that she'd wanted. She had had the husband she'd wanted, the children, the home. And that business world that had seduced her with its closed mysteries, she'd had that too. She'd felt once – how laughable and peculiar – that she could never manage it: that world of banking and interest, stocks and shares, borrowing, building, mergers, deals that collapsed, partners that crossed. But how easy it was once you'd barged in. It was her world now, as much as any other; she had proved that in her dealings of the past weeks. She had turned those handles and levers and used them to her own ends; she had made them work for her as Humphrey had always made them work for him. Now the deal was almost through.

There was only one more thing to be settled and this – though surely more her territory, more a woman's domain to deal with another woman? – this frightened her the most. Once she had taken that step there would be no going back, ever.

Twenty

Sylvie lay flat on her bed, twisting her hands angrily: she wanted to wring Humphrey's neck. She needed him and there was no way to reach him. She was frightened. Hilda was away and she was the only person Sylvie could bear to be near her at a time like this. Not that it was an emergency, exactly, no, it wasn't, she counselled herself. It was just bleeding, when she should not be bleeding, when bleeding was the last thing she should be. And why did these things always happen at night? She considered an ambulance again, but it seemed neurotic. The doctor's nurse had said to lie still and call again in the morning; she didn't seem perturbed. Why the panic?

It wasn't really so much blood, not when you thought that the body had eight pints. But what did it mean? It often happens, the nurse said, in a pregnancy there's often a loss of blood here and there, in the first four months particularly. Not to worry. Lie still. Sleep. But this much blood? The nurse had wanted to know the colour of the blood. Well, blood is red, damnit. Bright red? Of course bright red! She looked at it from time to time. There was a thick wad of cotton wool between her thighs, but it was soaked now. Any pains? she'd asked, filing her nails no doubt. No, no pains. Well, that's good, she'd said.

Sylvie's back ached. She longed for Humphrey and took back all her angry thoughts in a fit of remorse and shame. She wanted desperately just to speak to him, to hear him say: Don't be such a stupid twit, there's not a thing to worry about, why must you be so darn dramatic? But she couldn't speak to him because he was stuck in the middle of the country messing about with an old house. She didn't see why he had to actually *sleep* in the house. Why not, like a sensible person, stay in a hotel? With a phone. Now she'd have to wait until he rang her. He was so obsessional. He couldn't do anything by halves, he had to fling himself right into it, had to go down there and rebuild the bloody ruin of a house himself, with his bare hands. He had to spend every minute there, and when he did ring from a call-box, he was like a kid with a new toy: she had to hear every detail of what he was doing. He was trying to pull her into that house with him when she'd rather he just got on with it.

Her anger returned. At the beginning, she thought, I tried to make it easy for him. I said, Keep it for yourself, let it be your house, a place you could be free of both of us and be alone and peaceful without all the splitting, the trying to share, the trying to be fair. But he wouldn't agree to that. Really what he'd like best would be for all of us to live there together, both his women, both his families, in one containable place. It would be exactly what he wanted, then he could take care of us all so easily. There's a sense of responsibility in Humphrey that's really quite sick. Very sick.

But right at that moment Sylvie could see the benefits of such a set-up. Bountiful Beth, who had birthed so many times, would be able to look after her. She'd know precisely what to do. Like the elder wife in a tribe. What a creepy thought. All the same, she'd rung up Humphrey's house in Chelsea. Stupid really, knowing he wasn't there. Perhaps she'd wanted Beth to answer. Not that she could have spoken to her. Anyway, there was no reply. And then a certain doubt arose as to where she might be – but that was absurd.

Sylvie's feet kept getting hot. She pulled them out from under the covers, looked at them, and then put them away again. Soon she'd have to get up and get something more substantial than the cotton wool. Keep still, lie down, don't move about – the nurse said. She'd pulled the phone as near to the bed as she could, in case he called. He would sense something was wrong. The warm leak between her thighs began to disgust her, it was revolting. And she was getting more scared.

The phone rang. She answered it. No reply, no one there. She kept saying, hullo, hullo. Nothing there. Then a click. She was so angry she could have hurled the phone across the room. Instead she just cried. She tried to lie calmly and relax. Who was that? Just a pervert? But no heavy breathing. Just a silence when she could hear someone listening, then that click. And nothing.

Twenty-one

Beth had put Jimmy to bed. Her daughters were out and the house was quiet. She kept pacing up and down. She kept returning to watch Jimmy as he slept, lying on his front, his face to one side and his arms all twisted up under his head. He looked so uncomfortable, but wouldn't be rearranged. School was not so bad, he said. But he'd been clinging, then disturbed and violent and she wondered again whether it was the right thing to make him go. Or whether it was the right thing to let people do as they wanted, not to rein them in? Not to make them see the value of restraint and hardship.

All day long these things had tormented her. And then, how clear it had become, in a flash – like a conversion. Her dishonesty couldn't be avoided any longer. For she had never believed in what she'd been doing with Humphrey, not for a single moment, not since that moment he'd said, I have met a woman who is wonderful, whom I love. Not for a single second after that had there been any truth between them. Humphrey, she thought, furiously, has broken all the rules. And I never tried to stop him. Because once it was done, it was done. She'd had to accept it or change the whole order of their lives. She couldn't do that, so she became cowardly and weak; she became something she wasn't. Oh, how clear it was now. She resented this most of all: that she'd been turned into a different kind of woman, the kind Humphrey had needed at that time: indulgent, understanding, compassionate, generous to the point of lunacy. She'd bent herself around his requirements like a reed. And even felt honourable at times. She even felt she was a perfect wife to do it.

How long I've hated him, she thought quietly, caressing the thought, holding it against her. How long I've wanted to hurt him, to punish him – to kill him. How long, she whispered. And her too. Both of them. How quietly I could kill them both.

She straightened her back; she let her thoughts run their true course at last. Fidelity, she thought, is the backbone of marriage, break it and the whole nervous system is paralysed and slowly the body will fall into decay. There are prohibition clauses in love, as in life. We lived in an enchanted place, Humphrey and I, but he forgot that there is always one tree you shall not eat off, one box that must not be opened, one glance backwards which lost Orpheus his entire world. Once that happened, the thing was finished. And now she wondered cynically: Perhaps I was right there beside him at that tree, like a cowardly Adam egging Eve on to eat, to try, to experiment? We were in it together. I was always intrigued by the lax side of him.

But she knew also that in spite of it, she still loved him. She loved him so hard. When the phone rang, she ran like a girl to answer it.

When she answered the phone, it was not Humphrey. It was no one. Or perhaps she got to the phone too late, for there was just a little silence, like someone listening, and then a far-off click.

Twenty-two

Sylvie was feverish but wouldn't look again to see how much blood there was. She was beginning to imagine all sorts of things and didn't feel at all like herself. She wanted to ring the doctor at his home, but it was very late and she was almost too scared of what he might say. The night seemed so long, each half-hour stretching further. She wondered if this was what it meant to need someone? It was a terrible feeling, like loss. She'd had moments with Humphrey when need was wonderful and inspiring, but this wasn't; this made her feel her own frailty and dependence. This time her fear was not just for herself, another life was leaking away and there was nothing she could do to stop it. Her anger had all evaporated; she lay there, using all her energy to try and sleep, to remain calm.

The phone rang. She forced herself to move slowly to the other side of the bed, to lean down, to reach for it.

'Hullo? . . . Hullo?'

The silence was a sinister, purring thing.

'Jesus Christ, what's the matter with you? Who is it? Are you some kind of pervert? What do you want?' She was yelling into the phone.

The silence washed back to her.

'Just fuck off! Get off the line and don't ring back or I'll call the police.'

A pause, then a slow click. A finger pressing the button, not the receiver being replaced. A slow click then that buzzing sound.

She couldn't stop crying. But decided if it rang again she wouldn't answer it. She was very scared. Jesus, what a mess, what a mess, she kept whispering. It was the disappointment, each time that it rang and wasn't Humphrey, that was the worst. Worse than the fact that there was some mad wanker out there, some creep who she'd like to strangle with the telephone cord.

'Oh hell,' she whispered, 'what was that?' More blood, more. 'Oh Humphrey, oh Humphrey.'

Twenty-three

Beth was studying herself calmly in the mirror. She had dressed herself carefully. It was ten o'clock but it felt much later; it was all the thought and determination that had gone into the hours; eighteen months of her life had passed in two hours. Eighteen months that now seemed a frightening farce. Cass had come back so she could go out, knowing Jimmy would be looked after if he woke. Music came down to her from the floor upstairs – old Ella Fitzgerald songs, Humphrey's records appropriated by his daughter. A car slowed at the corner of the road. The dog thudded up the stairs. So everything was just as usual then?

She sat on her bed for a moment, her face very serious, very composed. Her hand cupped her chin as it always did when she was thinking. She hesitated, she took off her shoes, then put them on again. She stood. She went back to the mirror and brushed her hair quickly, then peered into the mirror at herself. She was aware of her heart. She got up and walked to the door, turning round to look back at her bedroom once more.

As she did so, the phone rang in the hallway. She froze, her hand clutching at her dress. It continued to ring. Cass thundered down the stairs to answer it. Beth waited. She could hear Cass. 'Hullo?' She repeated it, 'Hullo? Hullo?'

Beth thought, If it's Humphrey, I don't think I could bear it.

The phone was put back on the receiver noisily.

'Who was it?' Beth asked from the top of the stairs.

'No one,' Cass said crossly, 'one of those stupid calls when no one answers. I hate people who do that.'

'Oh,' Beth breathed, fastening a button on her cuff. She walked down the stairs towards Cass. 'Was it a call-box?' she asked.

'No, why?'

'Oh, nothing, just wondered.'

'Will you be long?'

'No.'

'Hope it goes OK,' Cass said, plonking a kiss on her mother's cheek, believing her to be going on a Samaritan errand as she sometimes did late at night.

'I hope the phone doesn't ring again,' Beth said. 'That's the third time with no one there.'

Cass looked at her mother anxiously. 'Are you all right, Ma? Is something wrong, you look, well, sort of strange.'

'Do I? How?'

'No, it's nothing. Just don't be long, I hate it when you're not here at night.' She thought to herself how selfish that sounded, when she herself was so seldom there at night. 'Ma?'

Beth turned; she smiled, 'What is it, Cass?'

'I love you, Ma.'

Twenty-four

A muscle twitched spasmodically in Sylvie's left leg and now and then she shivered uncontrollably. She was lying on the floor with a sheet over her. She lay very still with her eyes closed, and then shivered, then lay still. She had been lying there for some time. The phone hadn't rung, but if it did she was closer to it. There was no way she could not answer it. Now she almost willed it to ring.

She was nearly asleep when the doorbell rang. She looked at the door with disbelief, which quickly turned into hope.

'It's Humphrey,' she breathed. Of course he'd know, he'd sense it. He knows these things. He's come. She had to restrain herself from leaping up. She pulled herself up and then made herself walk slowly and carefully across the wide floor and to the front door. She walked like someone who carries a bowl which is too heavy and full, holding her body steady not to spill a drop. She got to the door and opened it. It did not occur to her that Humphrey never rang the doorbell in that way, he used his key.

She opened the door, the light fell on a tall figure standing there. A woman in a dark blue dress with a high collar – an elegant woman, her hair pulled away from her forehead with combs and then waving and curling around the back of her head. Sylvie stared, speechless, suddenly feeling the cold whip through her.

'I'm Beth,' the woman said, quietly, not moving, 'but of course you knew that.' Her voice was low and melodious, it presupposed an intimacy between them; and it calmed the haggard woman clutching at the crumpled sheet who looked so ill, whose face seemed almost grey in the light, whose features seemed uncannily like Beth's during her illness.

Sylvie took a step backwards, in alarm – more than alarm. And as she did so, Beth saw her body sway a little. She put out her hand involuntarily and took Sylvie's arm, to steady her. Sylvie started as though she'd been scalded, and Beth saw, to her horror, that the face she'd remembered from before as being predatory and tough was flushing, the eyes brimming with tears, the little sheeted body seemed about to collapse.

'What is it? Are you ill?' Beth asked quietly, walking in, closing the door behind her. The room opened itself to her view: so this was where he came, this was where he lived and slept when he was not with her. This was where he played his music, the music that he hardly ever played at home. That piano there was obviously being used a lot, she knew the signs, she even recognized the sheet of music on the stool. Gershwin. It caused her pain.

Sylvie had now righted herself. Beth's arm was withdrawn. A gulf had opened up between them. They surveyed one another with curiosity and apprehension. Beth was very calm, she held the situation in both her hands, feeling a sense of power over the other one.

'I have to go back to bed,' Sylvie said, her voice pleading for something, but unable to ask.

'You must tell me what the matter is,' Beth said. How seductive her sympathy was, Sylvie felt, it made you feel you could not hold anything back from her. Beth placed an arm – as a nurse would, it was efficient, not tender – around Sylvie's waist and helped her in the direction she was moving towards so slowly. Beth could tell by the way her breathing stopped and started, by the odd rigid way she held herself, that Sylvie was trying very hard not to cry.

The bedcovers were flung back and Beth could see the towel upon which Sylvie had been lying, it was stained with blood. She looked at the blood, stunned, her body going cold. For one wild moment Sylvie wanted to rush and cover the bloodstains – she didn't want Beth to have any part of it. It was monstrous that she'd come, at this time, how could she do it? How could anyone behave like that? What did she want?

'Have you had an abortion?' Beth whispered with difficulty.

Sylvie flung her head sideways furiously, violently. 'No,' she yelled, her voice breaking. She wouldn't look at Beth. She sat down and gingerly lifted her legs on to the bed, then pulled the covers up. She didn't lie down. Beth could not move or speak. Sylvie thought cruelly, Well, this has shut you up, hasn't it? This has wrecked your cool composure, swanning in here – for what? Breaking into my life as if you had the right. Perhaps now you will go. But she didn't want her to.

It was only then that it registered fully with Beth: this woman had

Humphrey's child in her body. She was carrying Humphrey's child. Humphrey had put it there, willingly, knowingly, he had done this. Humphrey had done the unforgivable, committed the final betrayal.

'I'll just wash my hands,' Beth said, very quietly, 'you might be having a miscarriage.' Her voice was outside her body and her feelings; her voice had brought itself back from the ward, it had armed her against herself. She left the room. Her legs were quite wonderful the way they supported her, the way, of their own accord, they transported her to the kitchen. She held herself from falling by holding on to the sink. Her knuckles were white and the veins stood up large under her skin. The pain swept over her again and again. She made herself repeat it: in the next room, another woman was carrying Humphrey's child. They had done it, they had intended it. This woman was carrying her husband's child.

She thought – it was not the time to think, but it rushed in on her: the recollection of a night many years ago, when she had miscarried, before Fran was born. The one they lost. How frightened Humphrey had been that night; how awestruck by the pain and the blood. How he had gone into the garden and wept when it was over. How he had come back to her and said, in a voice soft and wonderful with emotion, 'I love you, Beth, how I love you.' He had taken the little wrapped bundle and buried it, deep in the ground, under his tree, because it must be buried, however little, however ill-formed, it could not be thrown into some hospital disposal. It deserved a burial, it was theirs.

In the other room, a woman lay pregnant. A woman who was terrified, who was bleeding as she had bled, another life stemming from Humphrey could be lost as she had lost her child. The woman was alone and crying. And she, Beth, had asked her if she'd had an abortion. And perhaps, after all, these things were happening every day, every minute, in all the civilized corners of the world.

She washed her hands with the Fairy Liquid and let the hot water scald her. She thought quietly, Let her bleed, let it die, let them both die. What is it to me? She dried her hands slowly on the cloth, waiting for it, willing for it to happen.

Twenty-five

When Beth returned to the bedroom, Sylvie opened her eyes and looked patiently at her. Beth's eyes wandered briefly around the bedroom, the technical books, the chest of drawers with plants on it; the photograph of a couple in a silver frame: Sylvie's parents perhaps? Then her glance moved across to the other side of the bed; there was a small carriage clock on the bedside table. Humphrey collected carriage clocks. Collected children too, it seemed.

'How long have you been bleeding?' Beth asked, placing her fingers on Sylvie's pulse and pressing there lightly.

'A couple of hours, about three or four.'

'Why didn't you call an ambulance?'

And how to explain, Sylvie now wondered numbly, how incapacitated she'd felt without Humphrey, without his moral support, the way he would have pushed her into some action. 'I didn't think it was that bad,' she said feebly.

'How much blood have you lost?'

'Quite a lot' – Sylvie turned her face away – 'but it has stopped a bit, it's not as bad as it was earlier; lying on the floor might have helped.' She was exhausted, so exhausted she didn't care about anything any more. There was something so dreamlike and unreal about the situation, but neither now questioned it. It seemed inevitable – even right. Beth's cool hand went to Sylvie's forehead and a feeling of wonder filled Sylvie: she looked up at the serene face. The mouth, though tightly drawn and terribly sad, was compassionate.

Beth left the room and returned in a moment with two thick cushions off the sofa.

'Brace yourself,' she said, 'I'm going to put these under the end of the mattress.' She did so; the mattress tilted upwards so that the lower half of Sylvie's body was raised.

'Now,' Beth said, 'I'm going out to get some pills to stop the bleeding and some sanitary towels. But, I could get an ambulance if you'd rather.'

'No,' Sylvie said, 'it's stopping, I'm sure.'

Beth looked at her hard. What dark brows she has, she thought, what a fragile little face, and I imagined her such an Amazon. It almost amused her. 'I won't be long. Do you want anything?'

'No' – her lip trembled – 'thank you.' What could she say? You are quite extraordinary, Beth, no wonder he adores you, no wonder he couldn't contemplate leaving you. And more than that, she thought: don't leave us, Beth, any of us. What would we do without you? You give us all a sense of belonging, even me. And what would Humphrey do if you left us? He'd go berserk without you and I couldn't manage him, not without you.

'Are these the keys?' Beth asked, picking them up off the table.

'Yes.' The voice was humble and child-like.

'Lie very still,' she said as she closed the door. 'Try to sleep.'

In a few minutes, Sylvie was sleeping peacefully, her face clear; she lay there quite trustingly waiting for the other woman to return.

Twenty-six

Sylvie lay completely still, so still she did not appear to breathe. In the far corner of the room, on the chest of drawers, a small brass lamp made a soft glow which lit up the floorboards; the window was open a little and a wind blew in and made the curtains swell. Sylvie's eyes were closed, her face was white and peaceful, her thick dark hair was bunched up under her head. The soft apricot blankets were tightly pulled around her. She seemed very small lying there, small and flat.

Beth sat in a chair on the other side of the bed, watching her; she was very tired. She had fallen asleep and a dream came back to her: the dream of the woman with her hair on fire – but this time there was no laughter. She felt confused and lost and every now and then she would get up and walk to and fro in some agitation. But she was so quiet that her movements didn't disturb the body in the bed. She went and stood by the window a long time, she pulled it closed, it was cold now. There was nothing else to do, but she couldn't go. She didn't know why she stayed. It was all over. But still she stood, thinking, almost dreaming; smiling her strange fixed smile, a smile that seemed to be clamped to her features like a vice.

Then she walked to her chair like a nurse returning to duty. She pulled the combs out of her hair, raked them through two heavy strands of it, then thrust them in place again. She placed her hands in the dark blue silk of her lap and sat calmly. There was nothing more to do. Presently she looked up; her eyes fell with curiosity on the table beside the bed – the one with the carriage clock. It was four a.m. It was getting colder all the time. She went over to the table, it had a little drawer in it and very quietly she pulled it open. What did she expect to find? she asked herself, hesitating. Then she looked. There were some photographs of Humphrey's house in the country, taken from the pasture below. And one of Sylvie, laughing. There was a fountain pen she'd never seen before. This prying – it didn't seem the wrong thing to do – not now. After all, it was

Humphrey's drawer, this was his side, he always slept against a wall. And how could it matter, now? There were some restaurant bills and a few telephone numbers on slips of paper. A few seeds in a twist of paper – how like Humphrey – he would have stolen them from some garden somewhere. She looked at them: foxglove seeds. She folded them up again.

And then, under an empty envelope, she saw a piece of paper that looked rather familiar, the way official things do. It was a marriage certificate.

Twenty-seven

When Beth returned home, at four-thirty in the morning, everything had changed. It was quite extraordinary how it had changed. She looked around the garden the way a stranger would look. Her eyes wound round the loops of wistaria that circled the house; the drying honeysuckle with its dusty flowers, the leaves no longer green but russet. She walked down to look at Humphrey's vegetables. She remembered his baskets of vegetables and the time he had said: I love your body, it'll make a whole wheelbarrow of children for us. Her hands moved down her body and clenched, as if she was following a woman in labour, moving her body to those same rhythms, exacting a last birth out there among the leaves and flowers that had withered, their scent vanished; their heads hanging listlessly in the cold air.

In the autumn morning the bluebells, the violets, the orange blossom that snuck into the wall, the wallflowers and roses – they had had their season and would not come back. The garden with its uncut lawn looked sad, it harboured no more children's voices. Over there, beneath the pear tree, Abi had made her little gardens, the gardens of Abilon she called them – surrounding a neat square of earth with pebbles, sticking flower heads in the earth, laying it out so neatly – and then forgetting it. Once Cass had come and trampled one of the miniature gardens under her bare feet and Abi had looked up with her serious, uncomprehending face, and said, 'Oh, why did you have to do that? Why did you have to?'

Beth shivered at the echo. So many echoes, but no clear chords. There had been a sandpit in the corner near the old lilac tree where childish laughter had broken the afternoon quiet. Where had it gone? Why wasn't Fran still lying on the long branch of the apple tree like a lazy cat, with her black brows and Siamese blue eyes – for ever trying to avoid school? Or Cass, cutting out cardboard crosses to sanctify the mounds of earth over the corpses of her bees and beetles? That day the dog had raised itself up and covered the bitch from next door, and Fran came screaming in fright: the dog's stuck, he's stuck up another dog and can't get out.

She sat down under Humphrey's tree and pulled her skirts close around her legs. Memory, desire, happiness – it was all there, intact. The garden, the house, though they seemed like strangers this morning, they had been loyal and good to her. As Humphrey, too, in his way, had been. And then it swam over her like a great wave of relief, soothing as a quiet sea. It was, after all, over. The death she'd felt in the garden, it was her death, the death of the past. And with it came exquisite relief. Oh, it would be temporary, it would be closed in by bitter, searing feelings again, but it was here now and she used it to carry her from the empty garden into her house.

She sat quietly in her kitchen for a while and then walked up the stairs. She remembered how, when her daughters were little, she'd woken them up in the morning, one by one, from the oldest to the youngest ... Wake up, it's nearly dawn, it's the first day of summer. A ritual, every year. Their plum-cheeked faces had woken instantly from sleep and grown excited. They pulled their legs from the covers, took a blanket from the bed, wrapped it around them and headed for the garden, whispering, shivering, laughing softly, taking hold of the dog and leading him out with them. Hush, don't wake your father. Then, on the grass, they sat huddled together waiting for the sun to rise; three nestlings in blue blankets drinking cups of sweet tea and eating fingers of bread and butter.

Now, as Beth woke their older selves, dazed from a long night of dancing and flirting, they got up trance-like and followed her, too exhausted to know that it was the wrong season. Jimmy, too, sleepy and silent, followed Beth into the garden. She sat them down under the apple tree, she brought them bread and butter and hot tea. She pulled them close to her and spoke to them, earnestly, all of her heart showing in her wide brown eyes. She spoke to them in the same husky voice that had once told them fairy tales and Greek myths, in this very same spot, such a long time ago. But now she told them the truth.

An hour or so later, when they had settled back to bed again, a splintering, shattering explosion split their sleep again. It was as if an earth tremor had struck the house and shaken it like a rag.

Twenty-eight

Humphrey left his house in the country at dawn and went straight to see Sylvie. She was sleeping peacefully, very pale and tired looking. When she woke she smiled at him, and told him what had happened. She was curiously calm. She wasn't angry with him for being absent when she'd needed him, not a word of reproach. She wouldn't let him panic or fuss, or call the doctor.

'I'm fine, Humphrey, really, everything is all right now. I must just take things easy.' She put her hand on his arm to calm him, to reassure him, he seemed so vulnerable to her. But he was perplexed; he felt things had been happening which were beyond his control, even his understanding. He couldn't understand Beth, he didn't seem able to believe in her goodness the way Sylvie so unequivocally did.

She seemed surprised that he must question it. 'What do you mean, why did she come in the first place?'

'Well why? It's not the sort of thing she would do.'

She looked at him patiently, as if he was a child. 'But Humphrey, she came because I needed her. She came to look after me.' She said this with an inexplicable smile, it gave him the willies. He was quite startled. But he said nothing. After all, Sylvie had sent him to Beth when she needed him; she was the one who had understood Beth's need.

He looked hard at Sylvie; what was it about her that seemed so altered, and yet so strangely familiar? Her face had mellowed and softened, it had a calm radiance for all its pallor. Her smile had a look of triumph, something that said, I have brought it off, I have done what I set out to do. He was puzzled and disturbed. She sat up in the bed now, pushed her hair back from her face and lay her hands quietly in her lap.

He went to make her breakfast and she tried to restrain him. 'No, my darling, you must be tired, let me do it.'

'Don't be daft. You can't get out of bed, don't even think about it, I'll wait on you hand and foot until you're better.' She picked up his hand and laid it against her cheek and smiled at him with a smile that seemed to announce her happiness, her contentment, her utter approval of him. But he didn't like it, it disturbed him, she disturbed him.

When she had had her breakfast, she said to him quietly, 'I've been thinking, Humphrey – perhaps I should give up my work, perhaps we could do something together? I have to do less, perhaps even give up for a bit, I'll have to once the baby is born anyway.'

He was appalled. He felt he'd had this conversation before, in another life, with another woman.

'Nonsense,' he said firmly, 'you mustn't do that, you mustn't give up what you do best. It's ridiculous. You always said you'd go on when you'd had the baby.' He became exasperated. 'Sylvie, what has got into you? I don't understand all this. You of all people can't tell me this is all the result of having a baby, for God's sake.'

She said quietly, 'I wasn't thinking so much of the baby, but of you. I'd like to be with you more. I spend all my time working, away from you, it's stupid.'

'Sylvie,' he said in a level voice, 'what is this? What's happened to you? You seem so changed.'

'Am I?' she asked dreamily. She rubbed her hand down the blanket and smoothed it, she looked up with grave eyes. 'I feel as if now, for the first time, I know what you need.'

Suddenly, it was clear to him: he could feel Beth's presence in the room, he could feel her power. His eyes flew to the drawer with the marriage certificate – it was slightly open. He moved round the bed, towards the drawer, towards the handle, with a feeling of cold dread. He opened the drawer. Inside he saw the certificate, ripped into shreds.

'I've got to go, Sylvie,' he said, shivering, 'I've got to go home.'

'Yes, of course,' she said, 'you go, I'll see you later, stay as long as you like. I'll be fine.' Her smile was tolerant, quite demure.

Once he was outside, he knew he couldn't go home and face Beth. He just couldn't do it. He was too shaken. He went instead to his office.

Twenty-nine

At his office, still reeling from his visit to Sylvie, Humphrey sat with a stack of papers in front of him. He was furious. His body literally vibrated with rage – his bushy eyebrows, the dense weight of his hair, which he kept flicking back impatiently, all were quivering as he read, flicking the pages over with quick, slapping sounds.

George, who was strolling down the corridor at that moment, was cursorily summoned. The clipped voice lowered George's high spirits, reminding him how peaceful it had been without Humphrey and his tyrannical rages for the past few months. Funny how it was that that voice could reduce George, could fill him with a sense of failure, a sense that he'd had on football fields, in locker rooms, in boardrooms and bedrooms, all his life. Yet there was no need for it now: things had changed in Humphrey's absence. How they had changed!

As he walked in, Humphrey noticed that he was wearing a new suit – looked quite expensive too. It was a source of pride and confidence to George, as he sat in his new Austin Reed suit, that he'd bought it himself.

'What's the meaning of all this?' Humphrey snapped, indicating the papers in front of him; no preamble, no good morning, no explanation of his long absence.

George glanced at the reading matter: three thick folders of proposals and figures. A lot of hard work had gone into those, so he replied firmly.

'They're the final plans, the agreed ones.' What was Humphrey in such a lather about? He was acting as though he'd stumbled upon a conspiracy.

'How can they be agreed when I haven't agreed them?' He was cool now, leaning back in that stupid chair.

'They've been on your desk for a month.' Here we go, George thought, here we ruddy well go . . .

'George' – it was difficult for Humphrey to control himself – 'if

194

you seriously think you can pull this off without my approval you're more of an idiot than I thought.'

George was patient. 'Humphrey, you agreed, in principle, months ago, that we should go into the consumer market with the new range.' It was his chance, his first real chance to deal with Humphrey, and a difficult situation, in a forceful and potent way. The expressions: shilly-shallying (his wife's) and tit in a trance, complete wally, his head up his arsehole, (Humphrey's) all came to him now and he kicked them clean out of court when he said, 'Humphrey, this was my project and I've gone ahead and brought it off.'

'And what precisely have you brought off?' Humphrey's disdain had moved down from those fearsome eyebrows to his mocking mouth.

'As it says here,' George reached over and pulled out the green folder, 'by the end of the year we should be on stream to have our brands in three major supermarkets in the London and Southern areas.'

'I read that, George,' Humphrey said dryly, taking the folder back, but seeing, to his annoyance, that George had sat down, with some arrogance, on the edge of his desk.

'So you've been through it all – sorry.' George was non-plussed. 'So, what precisely is it that you don't see?'

'What precisely I don't see,' Humphrey said, his voice like the sound of something very hard and sharp hitting ice, 'is what made you think you could go ahead with this – you and Harry – and get a massive, bloody massive, loan from the bank to cover your attempt – without my approval on any of it?'

George remembered what Beth had told him years ago: If you don't fight him, George, you're finished. He's ruthless. He can, and has destroyed a lot of people because they weren't smart enough, because they were sloppy. If you're sloppy, even once, you haven't a chance. And if you don't fight him, you're dead. Now he remembered the fiasco at the time of a minor merger – a takeover that Humphrey had wanted to give him better factory space and distribution – and how he, George, had hesitated, not having enough information, not having the nerve to make the crucial decision quickly.

'You've blown it,' Humphrey had roared. 'That man was scared to do anything but creep into the woodwork and go bankrupt, and you've scared him off by pissing around and he's backed off.'

Trying to explain at the time that he had needed Humphrey's agreement, he'd been chastised with a: 'To hell with that. You move when you have to move, at that precise moment. Trust your instinct. Fuck the facts. You'll never get anywhere if you're afraid of shooting in the dark. If taking a chance, a loan or a gamble makes you squeamish, you'd better clear out of the business world at once.'

These memories, far from intimidating him as they'd always done, now gave him confidence: he hadn't hesitated, he'd taken the opportunity when it came, he'd pulled the thing off.

'Humphrey,' George said firmly, 'the time was right. We have the salesmen, the warehousing, the distribution. The market research was very promising, the packaging's complete, the advertising and PR are nearly done, we've gone into a test area – it's time to get the thing off the ground. When the bank agreed to the loan, I put everything into motion.' He wasn't protecting his back by bringing Harry into it, he was taking full responsibility.

'The thing is, George, you can't do that,' Humphrey said quietly, 'not without my authorization. I own this company, George, and I could about-face everything you've set up here.' In fact, he was puzzled by the mechanics of the deal: how could it have gone so far? Why had faithful old Harry kept him in the dark? It was beginning to feel like a coup, and a coup that had been planned quite some time back.

'You haven't been here, Humphrey,' George said. 'I've left all the information on your desk, every stage of it, you just had to read it. The fact is, Humphrey, that you've left this business, you washed your hands of it months and months ago.' He got up off the end of the desk and went over, voluntarily, to the Chesterfield. 'You can't go off to play a new game and keep the balls of the old game in your pocket so no one else can play it.'

Humphrey moved over to the window and his plants, which all seemed to have flourished and bloomed with disgusting infidelity in his absence. He walked over to a pot of cyclamen and lifted one of the pink blooms carefully by the chin.

'Something puzzles me, George,' he said, his deep voice becoming very even and slow. 'Obviously Beth has been working with you on this' – his ignorance, which was galling to him, had to be flushed out now – 'she holds all the shares and could authorize the whole thing, but, all the same, it puzzles me that things should have reached this point ...'

God, George thought in triumph – he didn't know, he actually didn't know! She didn't tell him. She's done it all off her own back – what a marvellous bloody woman. She's done for him, she's really done for him; she's actually called his bluff.

George, with the timing and balance of a tom-cat negotiating a very high wall over a stranger's garden, said, 'The shares have been reallocated, Humphrey.' The cat placed one foot in front of the other, delicately, seeing the ground below, but certain he could not fall. 'We all hold twenty per cent now, Humphrey: you, Beth, Harry, John and me. A clean split.'

'Very clean,' Humphrey said, and began to laugh. 'So clean that it has the marks of the housewife all over it. Oh, bloody marvellous,' he laughed, 'bloody marvellous, what a woman she is.'

Thirty

Beth, leaning her arms on the railings of the ship and looking out across the Irish sea, felt her mouth pull into a small, victorious smile. Her left hand rested on her arm; she no longer wore the plain band of gold. But now, where it had been all those years, a pale indentation, a place where the skin would always be worn down, remained. It would never go, she felt. The small boy, whose head touched her arm, broke in with a: 'How long will we be gone? How long can we stay?' The wind tugged at his voice and hair.

She let down her arm and wrapped it protectively about his shoulders, giving him her smile. 'Oh, as long as we like, there's no hurry, we can stay as long as we want to. But' – her smile faded – 'there will be school, Jimmy, there are things in life that are difficult, but they must be done.' Her chin was raised as she looked out to sea, but in her gaze there was something of a woman who looks out across a well-loved garden, looks at it and leaves it, closing the gate behind her.

'And is it really like you said?' the boy asked. 'All those rooms and an attic and cellar with a bear and stables and will the chickens still be there?' Now a little anxiousness crossed his face, even doubt; he didn't really believe it. But she said, 'Oh yes, it'll all be still there. Nothing changes in Ireland.' She laughed at him and was caught up in his excitement.

'Are you cold, Jimmy?' she asked, but knew it was she who had shivered, but only a little.

'No, I like it, I like the sea,' he said.

'It looks so cold today,' she said, looking at the bleak grey waters, but knowing their colour could change in sunlight, knowing that even this sea was capable of impersonations.

That morning, early, as she had stood in her garden and watched her daughters and Jimmy go back to their beds, she had felt as she used to feel as a young girl, walking across the old Horse Park on her parents' estate in Ireland, passing the beech trees near the field where the fat cattle pushed one another gently, their breath warm and misty in the early morning. It was the same feeling of peace. It was then that she knew just what to do.

It was six in the morning. She stood in his garden for the last time. Her breath was smoky and a slight mist hovered close to the ground as she walked up and down, up and down, looking at the apple tree, holding it with her eyes, looking from it to the house and back again. Then she made her decision and walked quickly down to the garden shed.

Coming back to the tree, she touched its trunk the way she had always touched Humphrey's body – tenderly, possessively. She kept her hand there, pressed against the bark. She felt weak with pain, with grief, and then with a wild erupting rage. She wanted to strike at the tree, to beat her fists against it, to hammer it with blows. She wanted to kill it.

She bent down and looked at the chain-saw that she had carried from the shed. She started it. It hiccoughed and then died out. She checked the safety switch and started it again. It roared and then settled into a steady, heavy purr. She braced her body, she balanced the saw against her thigh, reeling a little from the weight of it. It was unwieldy, reluctant, she felt, and it seemed to pull away from her. She held it fast with both hands, with all her strength, and moved into position.

She had done this before. She remembered lopping branches with Humphrey, he had shown her how to do it the year he had hurt his back. She braced herself and moved forward. The blade bit deeply into the tree trunk and the sound of the saw deepened as though it went far underground. Bark and dust flew at her, a small shard hit her below her eye. She held it firmer, pushing it deeper into the trunk. The tree shuddered in an agony of its own, it seemed to her to be screaming. She bit through her bottom lip, and held on, her body vibrating.

As it began to fall – oh, so slowly at first, like an acrobat poising his body for a dive – she looked up at the great green shuddering tree, her head thrown back in triumph. And anyone watching her wield that chain-saw with her jubilant, barbaric smile could not doubt that she had risen mightily by the execution of this act.

It fell exactly. With a creaking majesty, a nobility that dignified both her action and its own death. It seemed to know what it had stood for and for what it had fallen.

The glass of the conservatory shattered with an outraged shrilling, the piano began to play an insane melody as apples and branches plucked at its notes. Humphrey's exquisite white piano was cut in half as if by a monstrous karate chop. Wedged between its mangled wires and splintered wood, lay the thick trunk of the tree, slowly subsiding. The weight of it had sundered the front leg of the piano so that it lay toppled to one side. The scent of crushed apples filled the air like incense at a funeral.

Then she began to laugh. And as the morning sun lit up her hair and seemed to set it on fire, she laughed louder and louder. Like a lunatic. Quite beside herself.